THE MONASTERY MURDERS

A NEWLY CRIMSONED RELIQUARY

DONNA FLETCHER CROW

GREENBRIER BOOK COMPANY, NEW BERN, NC

For Janet Benrey
Agent, Editor, Friend
Without whom
The Monastery Murders
Would not exist

Praise for The Monastery Murders

A Very Private Grave

Like a P.D. James novel *A Very Private Grave* occupies a learned territory. Also a beautifully described corner of England, that of the Northumbrian coast where St. Cuthbert's Christianity retains its powerful presence. Where myth and holiness, wild nature and tourism, art and prayer run in parallel, and capture the imagination still. All this with a cinematic skill.

A thrilling amateur investigation follows in which the northern landscape and modern liturgical goings on play a large part. The centuries between us and the world of Lindisfarne and Whitby collapse and we are in the timeless zone of greed and goodness. — Ronald Blythe, *The Word from Wormingford*

With a bludgeoned body in Chapter 1, and a pair of intrepid amateur sleuths, *A Very Private Grave* qualifies as a traditional mystery. But this is no mere formulaic whodunit: it is a Knickerbocker Glory of a thriller. At its centre is a sweeping, page-turning quest – in the steps of St Cuthbert – through the atmospherically-depicted North of England, served up with dollops of Church history and lashings of romance. In this novel, Donna Fletcher Crow has created her own niche within the genre of clerical mysteries. — Kate Charles, *Deep Waters*

A Darkly Hidden Truth

In *A Darkly Hidden Truth*, Donna Fletcher Crow creates a world in which the events of past centuries echo down present-day hallways— I came away from the book feeling as though I'd been someplace both ancient and new. Donna Fletcher Crow gives us, in three extremely persuasive dimensions, the world that Dan Brown merely sketches. — Timothy Hallinan, *The Queen of Patpong,* Edgar nominated Best Novel, 2011

With *A Darkly Hidden Truth* Crow establishes herself as the leading practitioner of modern mystery entwined with historical fiction. The historical sections are much superior to *The Da Vinci Code* because she doesn't merely recite the facts; she makes the events come alive by telling them through the eyes of participants. The contemporary story is skillfully character-driven, suspended between the deliberate and reflective life of religious orders in the U.K. and Felicity's "Damn the torpedoes, full steam ahead" American impetuousness.

Her descriptions of the English characters read like an updated and edgy version of Barbara Pym. *A Darkly Hidden Truth* weaves ancient puzzles and modern murder with a savvy but sometimes unwary protagonist into a seamless story. You won't need a bookmark - you'll read it in a single sitting despite other plans. — Mike Orenduff, 2011 Lefty Award Winner, *The Pot Thief Who Studied Einstein*

An Unholy Communion

An Unholy Communion is a terrific mix of history, the church, and very dark deeds with the hugely likeable Felicity as heroine and an excellent hero in Anthony. If you haven't come across the series yet, give it a try as the books are great reads. — Dolores Gordon-Smith, *The Jack Haldean Mysteries*

This book was truly a great mystery and had me guessing throughout the entire book. It was full of twists and turns and I learned a great deal of new information about the occult and spiritual warfare as well. The author most definitely did a lot of research and, although this book is a work of fiction, has included much fact so that it is not only a fun read but also a learning experience. — Alicia, through My I's

Erie feelings, strange happenings, premonitions and unexpected occurrences mark the many events depicted within this well researched, documented and crafted novel. When all of the clues, the pieces and the final reveal come together you will not believe who is behind everything. — Fran Lewis's Book Reviews

Ingeniously plotted by a master of contemporary suspense, *An Unholy Communion* weaves Great Britain's holy places and history with an intricate mystery that will keep readers guessing to the very end. An exciting book that will keep you engrossed in the characters as well as life in England. A wonderful series. — Victor, Vic's Media Room

Acknowledgments

First, thank you to my lovely daughter Elizabeth Kenyon, who studied classics at Keble College and shared her memories of crawling through the rafters of the chapel to muffle the bells for All Soul's. Thank you also to The Reverend Doctor Peter Groves, Parish Priest at St. Mary Mag's, for the help with my research and putting me in touch with Simon Bond and the Oxford University Society of Change Ringers. Kirsty, Helen, Mark, Stephan and Rozy. I loved my bell-ringing lesson. Also thank you to The Reverend Jenn Strawbridge, Keble College Chaplain, and to The Sisters of the Love of God at The Convent of the Incarnation, Fairacres, for their warm welcome, especially Sister Avis Mary for her tour of the Press and quotations from "The Fairacres Chronicle."

Timeline

650-727 Frideswide

1500 St. Frideswide adopted patron of Oxford University

1535 St. John Fisher and St. Thomas More beheaded

1556 Cranmer, Latimer and Ridley burnt at stake

1586 Margaret Clitherow martyred

1729 John and Charles Wesley start "the Holy Club" at Oxford

1833-1845 Oxford Movement

Escape

C. *The year of our Lord 667*
The royal dun of King Didan, Oxenaforda

"No, Father! You gave your word." *Frideswide faced her father, her eyes blazing, and spots of bright pink staining her cheeks.*

King Didan inclined his head ever so slightly. "You must accept it daughter. As a royal princess — a Saxon princess under the high king of Mercia," his slight emphasis made their position more than clear, "you must understand that we owe our client position to King Wulfhere. And the king wishes you to marry Algar of Leicester. Let that be the end of it."

Frideswide raised her head, knowing full well the effect of the light from the central fire on her waist-length blond hair, held in place by a slim gold band around her forehead. "I need not remind you, Father, that there is One who is higher than the King of Mercia, and I am vowed to Him. I will not marry." The gold discs of her necklace clinked together as she strode from the hall, the train of her embroidered tunic scattering the floor rushes behind her.

"I will be obeyed in this!" Didan bellowed, but his daughter did not look back as she lifted the heavy leather doorflap and entered her bower.

Her serving ladies crossed the small chamber to greet her, their faces showing clearly that they had heard every word of the confrontation. "My lady..." The younger of them began.

"Good Ailith." Frideswide held her hand out to her. "Go to the

1

cookhouse and fill a satchel with cheese and bannocks." She then turned to the woman who had been her nurse and companion ever since her mother, Queen Safrida, had died shortly after Frideswide's birth. "Milburga, pack my warmest cloaks. I must flee."

Ailith started to protest, but Milburga stood firm. "Aye. I'll pack a cloak for each of us. And fetch our fur-lined boots."

"You needn't – " Frideswide began, but Milburga's look of stalwart love, and Ailith's answering nod, stopped her. "I should be glad of your company."

Their flight, however, was not to be that night. Knowing well his headstrong daughter, King Didan had set a guard by her door. And the next morning Frideswide was wakened by the shout of new arrivals at the palisade gate. "Open in the name of King Algar of Leicester!"

"Plait my hair with gold cords," Frideswide directed Ailith. "I will not be taken, but neither will I shame my father's house."

As soon as the princess was clad in her ochre outer tunic clasped with a belt of bronze discs, she turned again to her ladies. "Now, having done all to stand, we shall stand. Let prayer be our shield and the God to whom I am pledged will be my protection." She seated herself on a bearskin draped stool at the foot of her bedplace, clasped her hands and her women bowed their heads.

"The Lord is my rock, and my fortress, and my deliverer; my God, my strength, in whom I will trust; my buckler, and the horn of my salvation, and my high tower.

"I will call upon the Lord, who is worthy to be praised: so shall I be saved from mine enemies..."

The words had not left her mouth before the pounding came on the post of her doorflap.

Chin held high and shoulders level, Frideswide strode to the center of the hall. But there she stopped. She would go no further. She faced King Algar's splendidly clad envoys, whose gold chains and brooches glinted from their scarlet tunics. Frideswide's voice rang clearly the length of the hall as she addressed her royal father on his high seat at the far end. "You may tell his majesty King Algar I am conscious of the honour he would do me, but I am pledged to another. From earliest childhood I have vowed to dedicate my life as a holy nun. I do not renounce my vows."

Frideswide stood unflinching as Algar's men drew their swords and lunged forward to take her by force.

The rough hand of Algar's man was so close to her arm that she could almost feel his fingers biting into her skin. Suddenly he stopped. "I can't see! I'm blind!" The man covered his face and fell to his knees.

The man behind him reached to draw his sword but crashed to the floor as he tripped over his kneeling comrade. The wolfhounds lying before the central hearth leapt to their feet and began barking at the uproar.

"Guards!" King Didan summoned his men. "Clear the hall," he ordered his steward. "See them to their horses. Get them back to Algar if you have to lead them all the way to Leicester!"

But the first of the emissaries spoke, "Forgive us. We were wrong to attempt to seize by force one consecrated to God."

"Forgive us Princess. We have wronged you and your God," the others repeated.

No sooner had they spoken than their sight was restored. The chastened men stumbled from the hall.

In all that time Frideswide had not moved.

And so life continued at the court of King Didan, but Frideswide did not relax her vigilant prayers, nor her constant pleading with her father that he build her a monastery where she could be enclosed to fulfill her perpetual vow.

Less than two weeks passed before the word came which she had been expecting. Frideswide had set her own watch and had bade her ladies to keep their satchels packed, for she knew Algar the Mighty of Leicester would not take so easily the refusal of a maiden. He cared little enough for her, she was certain, but his honour would not be slighted.

"Algar and his retinue camp at Wolvercote, my lady. They will cross the ford by midmorning."

"Thank you, Durwyn." Frideswide smiled at the loyal groom who had slipped to her bower as soon as the king and his guards retired from the hall.

"Ailith, Milburga, bring the packs." And with that Frideswide fled the royal dun as calmly as if she were going for a stroll by the riverbank with her ladies.

Days ago she had directed Durwyn to prepare the small boat and hide it in the rushes beside the dark, smooth waters of the river Thames. Now the three women took their seats. Their attendant pushed the craft away from the riverbank and dipped the oars into the water. The boat slid silently upstream.

Hours later the early morning sun illuminated the huddled buildings of Bampton. Frideswide had determined that she would take refuge in this village built on the ruins of a former Roman town that had stood strong so many times when caught in clashes between Wessex and the powerful Mercia. Here she would find shelter among these faithful people.

Days that seemed like years dragged by as Frideswide waited and prayed. "O God, be merciful unto me: for my soul trusteth in thee: yea, in the shadow of thy wings will I make my refuge, until these calamities be overpast."

Would Algar be able to track her flight? Would he call his troops to ravage her father's dun? Had she put the good people of Bampton in danger by taking refuge with them? "Thou art my hiding place; thou shalt preserve me from trouble; thou shalt compass me about with songs of deliverance." She would not fret. She would wait.

Frideswide's heart skipped a beat when the village children ran to her shouting that a boat approached. "A fine, prowed boat that must be from the king," the oldest boy reported, his eyes wide.

Frideswide walked to the river unattended. Whatever the news, she would face it alone. And yet not alone, because the One to whom she had vowed her life was with her.

The faithful Durwyn sat in the prow of the boat. A broad smile split his face telling her she had nothing to fear. The towheaded youth sprang to the riverbank with a shouted greeting as his words tumbled over each other and tangled with birdsong and river splashings. "Oh, my lady, a great miracle! You would not believe — Algar came with a mighty troop — all armed, my lady."

Frideswide paled. It was as she had feared.

"The guards protested, but he stormed right into your bower."

"Mud he had on his boots, my princess," another attendant joined in.

"You said a miracle?" Frideswide demanded.

"Blinded." The messengers spoke at the same time. "Algar was blinded, just like his guards before."

"But he did not repent."

"Bellowed, he did. I heard him — "

4

"He would have done you violence, my lady, if he could have laid hands on you," Durwyn reasserted his position as chief messenger. "Never have I seen such rage."

"And then he fell down dead."

The end was so sudden it was almost an anticlimax until Frideswide realized what they were telling her. Algar was no more. God had struck down her enemy. She was free.

Durwyn gave her a shy smile. "Your father the king says he will build your monastery, my lady."

Frideswide could not speak for joy. At last she turned to her ladies. "Let us go home."

One

"Now don't get into mischief." Antony kissed Felicity on her forehead, then lingered a moment on her lips.

She broke away with a chuckle. "Me? I'm spending a few days in a convent, then joining your seminar. What could possibly be less mischief-making?"

Antony's forehead furrowed as he folded her into his arms. "I can't imagine. But it seems you always manage to find a way."

"Not true," Felicity started to protest, but her words were muffled in his hug.

"Never mind," he said as he released her. "Go get your translating done for the good sisters. I'll be there with my students before you know it."

He watched as Felicity tossed her long blond plait over her shoulder then picked up her small bag as the train drew up to the open platform that served as the Kirkthorpe Station. She turned back for one last quick kiss. "I'll miss you."

"You'd better." He started to wave her away, then paused. "It's only a few days. I'll be there for All Soul's." He knew the assurance was more for himself than for her.

"Don't worry, silly," she mouthed through the glass as the door slid shut between them.

6

But his furrowed brow spoke his anxiety.

He watched her go, his heart in his throat. How much his life had changed since that glorious, maddening woman had stormed into his life. His days would feel hollow until they were together again, but at least it would give him a chance to catch up on his work. He needed to spend some serious, quiet time in study. His desk was piled high with essays in need of marking, he had stale lecture notes that needed redoing for next term, final preparations to make for next week's seminar with the somewhat inflated title of "God in Oxford."

With a final wave in the direction of the train already disappearing down the tracks, Antony turned to walk back up the hill toward the Community of the Transfiguration. He was still running through his mental to do list when his mobile rang. He answered without noticing who was calling him.

He felt his whole body chill at the sound of female sobs. "Felicity?" He almost yelled. What could have happened so soon? If there had been a train wreck surely he would have heard it.

"Forgive me. Such a lack of decorum." A loud sniff interrupted the apology.

He pulled the phone from his ear and looked at the screen. Not Felicity. A much older woman. The voice sounded familiar but the number displayed meant nothing to him. "Who is this?"

Now the voice was brisk with control, command even. "Antony, I shouldn't have expected even you to have forgotten." *Forgotten to walk the dog, forgotten to put out the trash, forgotten to eat your Brussels sprouts...?*

"Aunt Beryl. Forgive me. I—it's been a long time." Long time? How many years? How did she even have his number? It must have been on some document. "Is something wrong?"

"It's Edward. The ambulance just left."

"Ambulance?"

"He was in the garden. Deadheading the roses. I took him his tea. He was..." The voice wavered dangerously.

Dead? Don't let her say dead.

"In a heap," she finished with tight control.

"Aunt Beryl, is there anyone there with you? Anyone you

can ring? What about Mrs. Dwyer next door?"

"She died three years ago." Voice sharp. Criticism clear.

"The vicar at St. Dunstan's?" That should be safe enough. Beryl was meticulous in her religious duty. As she was in all duty.

"Yes. He's on his way. I must put the kettle on for him."

No, let him make the tea for you, Antony wanted to protest, but knew activity would be therapeutic. "Yes. That's good. You do that."

"I must go now. I just thought you should know."

"Yes, yes. Thank you for ringing. Do let me know—" But the connection was dead.

Antony stood looking at the blank phone in his hand. He was amazed how shaken he felt. He thought he had put Blackpool and his antiseptic childhood behind him. But now it all came rushing back: cold baths in cold rooms, overcooked nutrition, reading approved books by a single lamp.

Little wonder his sister had cut all ties as soon as she was out of school. Gwena. Would Beryl have rung her? Should he try? How would he find her number? Where was she? The Internet might tell him if she was in a current production.

Shaking his head he turned back up the hill toward the Community and College of the Transfiguration with a considerably slowed step.

All the way across Yorkshire, Antony's words rang in Felicity's ears and his funny, lopsided, slightly anxious smile produced a mirror image on her own lips. She found herself counting, for probably the millionth time, the months on her fingers. Middle of October to January sixth—twelve weeks. Twelve weeks! And she would be Mrs. Antony Sherwood. Hmm, would that be Mrs. Father Antony? Mrs. Reverend Antony Sherwood? No, that sounded silly. But however it sounded, it certainly felt right. She hugged herself at the thought of being Antony's wife. Just twelve weeks, she repeated.

And here she was headed away from him. No matter how enticing the assignment ahead of her was, she knew she'd left her heart in Kirkthorpe. 'Silly,' she chided herself. You'll see him in just over a week.

Even with such hesitations, however, Felicity became aware of a mounting excitement when she changed trains at Huddersfield. Only one more stop and she would be in Oxford in less than four hours. Assuming all went according to schedule, of course.

Goodness, she hadn't been back to the hallowed halls of her alma mater for more than three years. Yet in a way it seemed longer than that. In a sense it had been a lifetime. She smiled as visions of her undergraduate days studying Classics at Keble College flitted through her mind. It would be strange to be there without her friends who had returned to their homes or scattered to new adventures, yet those days would always be with her. And then her time teaching school in London, feeling more and more claustrophobic and bored until she took the incredible plunge of enrolling in a theological college run by monks in a monastery in Yorkshire...

She shook her head. It all still had moments of such unreality that she expected to wake up and find herself back home in Idaho with her quiet father, her overbearing mother, and her energetic brothers. Instead of pinching herself, however, she chose to buy a cup of steaming tea from the young attendant as the trolley came rattling down the aisle toward her. "And a Kit Kat bar," she added, pulling out her wallet.

When she had been served she broke off one finger of chocolate and allowed herself to savor a few crispy bites before digging in her backpack and pulling out the letter from Mother Monica. Time to get to work. Or at least to get herself up to speed on the work she would be doing.

The Sisters of the Love of God, who were renown for their scholarly publishing on various topics of prayer, spirituality and the lives of saints, had been presented an early Latin manuscript of the life of Oxford's patron saint and wanted to bring out a Life of St. Frideswide for the thirteen hundredth anniversary of the founding of her monastery from which the City of Oxford grew.

Felicity looked back at the letter in her hand. Yes, that was right, thirteen hundred years. Give or take a few. But, indeed Frideswide's priory, where kings were known to have held several councils of state, had been established long before the city's first written mention in the *Anglo-Saxon Chronicle* in the year 912. Felicity shook her head wondering if the document she would be given to translate might actually be that old.

Whatever its age, Felicity still couldn't believe the honor that she had been chosen to help with the translation. Although the learned sisters all had training in Latin and routinely conducted parts of their liturgy in that ancient language, they had requested the College of the Transfiguration to loan them a classical scholar to work alongside Sister Gertrude with the translation. Felicity liked to think that she was well qualified for the job in her own right, but she knew the fact that her church history lecturer, who happened also to be her future husband, had given her such a high recommendation hadn't hindered her selection.

And she was determined to live up to that recommendation. She turned to the potted, if sketchy, information she had been able to find on St. Frideswide to read for background information, trying to flesh out her reading with the vivid images she knew Antony would have used if he had been recounting the story himself.

The exercise kept her engrossed until the very proper recorded female voice rang through her carriage announcing their arrival at Oxford. Felicity grabbed her bag and was the first to jump off the train the minute it came to a halt. A sense of homecoming washed over her as she strode through the station and queued for a bus to take her to the city center. Security? Peace? Stepping back into more carefree days? She quizzed herself to define her feelings. Lost youth? She grinned. It couldn't be all that lost—she wasn't yet thirty.

Although she could have taken a bus all the way down Iffley Road to the convent in Fairacres, she had chosen to arrive early in order to give herself time to renew her acquaintance with the city. Just walking the bustling streets again, passing the ancient buildings, being part of the mix of students, tourists and residents that filled the city was so energizing. Such a contrast to the quiet times she had spent in her more recent studies tucked away in a monastery on a green hillside.

Well, quiet except for those three excursions chasing and being chased by murderers. With a determined shake of her head she put the darker side of those events out of her mind, choosing to retain only the learning she had acquired through those alarms and hugging to herself the wonderful relationship she and Antony had developed by sharing the harrowing events.

At the corner of Cornmarket and High Street she paused at Carfax Tower, which marked the center of Oxford. Carfax was the Roman designation for crossroads, and surely this was the busiest intersection in the city. She glanced up at the clock on the tower that was all that remained of St. Martin's, which had once been the official church of the city for civic events. Ah, just a few minutes until noon. She would wait and hear the Quarter Boys strike the hour before she went on. The two Romanesque figures stood with their hammers at the ready below the motto *Fortes est Veritas:* The Truth is Strong.

Across the street the covered market brought back memories of her delight in finding bargains there in her undergraduate days. Maybe she would just have a quick look-in. She turned to cross the street, when the blue, scarlet and gold figures began striking the hour. She counted to six before the sound of bells drowned out everything else, as all across Oxford, from seemingly every tower, a glorious cacophony called everyone to stop and look upward.

Felicity stood still in the middle of the pavement and raised her face to the blue sky above the tower. The bells had been one of the things she had missed most about Oxford. The monastery had a single bell, rung to call worshipers to prayer, nothing like the glorious change-ringing from Oxford's numerous towers that sang out over the city for every Sunday, holiday and civic occasion.

Somehow, though, this sounded different from the wonderful change-ringing peals that always made Felicity think of a waterfall of crystal drops. This was no sprightly silver shower that lifted the spirits, but a measured peal sounding like an ominous warning, with only half of each stroke ringing brightly, the backstroke a muffled echo.

Then began a stately, single toll of the deep-toned tenor bell. Almost subconsciously Felicity counted as the tolls came, with perhaps ten seconds between each ring: two slow tolls, then a longer pause, the pattern repeated three times. When the final echo of the last muted knell faded, Felicity again turned her steps along the High Street.

How odd that her return to Oxford should be met with a muffled toll. She hadn't heard muffled bells since she left. Although she had graduated thinking she would be a Latin teacher, it was really her time with the student chapel program which she attended because Bruno, one of her best friends, was involved, that had most influenced the path she was now on. Even then—before she discovered that she really believed—when she just thought things like muffling bells for All Soul's Day and filling the chapel with hundreds of tiny candles for the carol service, were cool things to do—before she understood or cared about the meaning behind the symbolism—she was being formed in the path she was now following.

But that was in the past. And it was two weeks yet till All Soul's Day. So what had it meant, this deadened ring emanating from Oxford's towers?

Two

"The feast of St. Frideswide," Sister Dorcas, the guest sister, explained some time later when Felicity arrived at the Convent of the Incarnation. "Isn't it wonderful! There is to be a patronal festival for the whole city tonight at Christ Church. Reverend Mother served on the planning committee and has given permission for us to attend, you see." The blue eyes of this small, blond nun sparkled in anticipation of the unusual treat.

Felicity blinked as the brown-habited sister led the way to the guest quarters. How amazing. Apparently she had arrived on the feast day of the very saint whose hagiography she had come to Oxford to translate. And the whole city was turning out in celebration. "I don't recall anything like that when I was here." True, her interest in religious matters had been late-blooming. It was unlikely she would have attended such a service in her student days, even if she had been aware of it. But surely such an unusual tolling would have caught her attention.

"No, this is new. Well, hardly new, but newly reinstated. First time since the sixteenth century as far as anyone knows. I believe the Oxford Medieval Society or some such is sponsoring it. They got the culture team from the Oxford City Council to put their efforts behind it. Since this stands to be an historic event Mother Monica felt there should be a special relic at the mass, so we're supplying it. It's such an honour."

Sister Dorcas's quick words, and even quicker step, had carried them through the convent, across the garden, past the hedge, and brought them to the door of a small white cottage with a clematis climbing the wall by the door, before Felicity could ask for further explanation of the confusing information. "Ah, here we are." Sister Dorcas took a large key from the deep pocket hidden under her scapular. "St. Columba's." She entered the cottage and crossed the small lounge to show Felicity the bedroom, bathroom and kitchen, pausing to point out the fresh loaf of granary bread on the counter, the milk in the minuscule refrigerator and the tea in the canister next to the kettle. "There, I hope that's everything to make you comfortable. Do let me or any of the sisters know if there's anything else you need. Our main meal is at midday for which you're most welcome to join us. Silent, of course. The other meals you'll have here, you see — if that's all right."

Felicity assured her everything was perfect. "Vespers are at six. That will leave plenty of time for those who want to attend the service tonight. We are a contemplative order, you understand, but since this is a special occasion and we'll be taking our special guest, so to speak, several of us will attend. You'll be most welcome, of course."

That last confirmed Felicity's suspicion that she wasn't the special guest Dorcas referred to. "Thank you. I'd very much like to." This should be excellent background for the manuscript she would be translating. "I wonder, do you know? When will I meet Mother Monica? I'd like to get started on my work right away."

"Oh, yes, soon, I'm sure. Mother has been attending a meeting of heads of religious communities in Canterbury, but she'll be back in time to lead Vespers, I'm sure." Felicity wondered why Dorcas's forehead wrinkled with deep lines even as she spoke with such assurance.

Then the nun's serene look returned so quickly Felicity wondered if she had imagined the furrowed brow. "But, of course, you can get started as soon as you like. Sister Gertrude is in the Press. I can take you there now if you're quite certain you wouldn't rather have a cup of tea and settle in first."

Felicity assured her she was quite ready to make a start, so she followed the brown habit and black veil back outside and along the garden path to the small brick building with a sign declaring it to be the Fairacres Press. Sister Dorcas introduced Felicity to Sister Gertrude, the editor, then scurried away, leaving her in the care of the plump, energetic nun with brown hair peeking around the edge of her veil. "I'm so glad to have your help. I'm afraid I'm all the staff I have here and, as you can see," her sweeping gesture encompassed three rooms with every work surface piled with projects in various stages of completion. "It can be rather overwhelming at times."

"I'm delighted to be here," Felicity replied. "Mother Monica's letter was a little vague as to what I'm to do. Helping with the translation of a manuscript to do with St. Frideswide, I understand. I suppose it's a hagiography?"

Gertrude bit her lip. "To tell you the truth, I haven't looked at it yet myself. I just got the autumn issue of the 'Convent Chronicle' off the press Monday." She placed a green-jacketed journal in Felicity's hands. "You might enjoy having a look at this. We try to give a picture of our lives here, along with articles on prayer, insights from spiritual writers such as George Herbert and Julian of Norwich, book reviews—well, you can see for yourself."

She walked to a small desk in the corner of the room, likewise covered with stacks of papers and books—tidy stacks, but nevertheless stacks—and took a key out of the top drawer before leading back toward the front door. She unlocked a door and walked into a small room filled with bookshelves and racks of pamphlets and cards. "This is our book room. Everything in here is for sale. We open the room when we have groups in on retreat. Do feel free to browse all you want. You're welcome to read anything in here. If you should want to buy anything there's a box there." She pointed. "But don't feel obliged."

The items offered a wide range of spiritual works through the centuries. Felicity knew Antony could happily spend the day—or many days—browsing and reading and buying in here. Just thinking of his delight made her heart crimp. She had only been away from him a few hours and she missed him terribly already. But that wasn't what she had come for. "It looks wonderful, Sister Gertrude, but I really think I would rather get to work. If I could have a look at the manuscript?"

"Oh, I am sorry. Didn't I say? I'm afraid it's locked in Reverend Mother's office. You can certainly start first thing tomorrow, though. Terce and Mass are at 9:05. Shall we meet here right after that?"

Felicity agreed and thanked Sister Gertrude, but opted for a walk in the garden rather than spending time in the book room. Sister Gertrude gave her a small map of the grounds which turned out to be extensive, including a park and what looked like acres of vegetable plots and an orchard in the back, but for now she would stick to the path bordered by hedges which were formed into frequent bays offering benches for meditation. The path turned to circle an enormous weeping willow, its autumn gold branches draping onto the grass. In the far corner, almost covered by vegetation, she glimpsed a small summerhouse.

Felicity stepped off the path to explore. She peered through one of the tiny windows. It was smudged with dirt but she could see a wicker settee and chair, their yellowed flowered cushions layered with dust. What a pity it had been abandoned. It must have once been a pleasant place for retreatants to read or meditate.

It seemed that every bend in the path revealed a new surprise. Around a brick garden wall she discovered a labyrinth cut into the grass. With a smile, Felicity stepped into the mouth of the circular design. She entered deliberately, trying to clear her mind of conflicting thoughts. *Just relax and take each step through each twist and turn,* she told herself. For all her determination to approach the exercise slowly, however, Felicity's long legs and naturally quick motions sped her forward.

Becoming aware of her speed, she stopped and took a deep breath before moving on, determined to go more slowly, more thoughtfully. Unlike any other she had walked, this labyrinth was designed in three sections. Representing the three stages of life, perhaps? Felicity smiled, she was just entering the second one—adulthood. She hoped she had put her impulsive, headstrong childishness behind her. She did try. And every time one of her rash actions led her into trouble she determined to try harder.

Still, her mind followed her measured tread, it seemed that so far all she had learned was how little she knew. What did the path ahead hold? A labyrinth was not a maze. One couldn't really get lost. *Just put one foot in front of the other and keep following in faith*, she reminded herself.

She paced around the long stretch circling the outside to old age. Again she felt herself hurrying and she reminded herself to slow down. *Think. Listen. To hurry it would be to miss the point.*

In the center was the tree of life. And a small bench. She sat and let her mind take her back just a few months earlier to when she had been considering becoming a nun herself. She recalled the peace, serenity, beauty she had found in the convents she had visited. And then she thought of Antony. And remembered her terror at thinking she had lost him. Remembered the joy of reunion. She knew her smile was smug. She would like to congratulate herself on choosing Antony over the veil, but truly, there had been no choice. This maddeningly perfect man was her whole world and that was all there was to it.

As if in reply to the very thought her pocket began emitting a small chirping sound. She pulled out her mobile and glanced at the screen, although she didn't really need to. She knew. "Hello, Antony. How did you know I was just thinking about you?"

"Probably because I was thinking of you." He paused. "I just wanted to check that everything's all right." Why did his attempt at lightness sound forced? Felicity wondered.

She answered as reassuringly as she could, telling him about her accommodation at the convent and about their plans to attend the festival for the patron saint of the city of Oxford that evening. His replies showed his interest, yet he sounded distracted. "Antony, what's wrong?" She finally asked.

"Probably nothing. Aunt Beryl rang."

Felicity had to think for a moment. Antony spoke of his family so seldom. But then she remembered, that dark, rainy night sitting in a bus kiosk waiting to get to Holy Island when he told her about the boating accident that had left himself and his sister Gwendolyn orphaned and about Aunt Beryl and Uncle Edward, the childless relatives in Blackpool who "did their duty supplying all the necessities: healthy food, lots of books, excellent schools." Felicity shivered again, as she had at the first telling, thinking of such an unfeeling childhood. Still, it had produced a strong man who was deeply caring behind his protective defenses.

"Yes. And...?" She probed.

"Uncle Edward had a heart attack. He's in hospital."

"Oh, I'm so sorry. I'll ask the sisters here to pray."

"Yes, do. Thanks."

"How serious is it? What do the doctors say? Is Beryl all right? Do you need to go to Blackpool?" She didn't do it as a technique, but Felicity knew that nothing could make Antony smile as quickly as her habit of pouring out a rush of questions.

Now she heard the easing in his voice. "Felicity, I do miss you. It's too soon to know the prognosis. But I think I'm almost more worried about Beryl."

"Is she ill, too?"

"It's just that—well, first of all, for her to ring me—for her to reach out to anyone at all—it's unheard of."

"She must be really worried."

"Yes, and then," he sounded puzzled as if he hardly knew how to express it. "She was crying."

"Perfectly normal in the circumstances, I should think."

"Not for Beryl. It's the first time in my life I've ever heard her cry. Not when my parents drowned. Never."

"Antony, I think you should go to her."

He sighed. "Yes. I do, too. But I needed to hear you say it. Thanks. It couldn't be a worse time to leave, just before I'm supposed to bring this group to Oxford, but..."

"You'll feel better when you see your aunt and uncle. I'm sure." She wondered how long it had been since Antony had seen his surrogate parents. Surely they had attended his graduation? Deaconing? Priesting? How far did duty to supply the necessities extend? "Antony, go right away. I don't want anything to delay your coming to Oxford." She would have liked to say more, but there was really only one thing to add. "I love you."

The bell for vespers had gone while Felicity was still in the labyrinth. It was too late to attend the brief service now, so she walked back to St. Cuthbert's cottage and opened a tin of soup for her supper. That, with a thick slice of well-buttered granary bread, would do her very well. She would be glad when she had the document to focus on. That would help her miss Antony less and make the time go faster.

She had just washed her last dish and left it to drain in the drying rack when there was a small tap at her door. "Sister Dorcas, come in." She switched on the light in the dim room. She still hadn't become accustomed to it getting dark so early.

The small nun stepped across the threshold, but stood dithering just inside the door. "Thank you. I—I'm not sure... I'm so worried. Reverend Mother hasn't returned. I can't imagine what could have delayed her. You see, she left me in charge, so I must go ahead... Most of the others have chosen to stay here and pray, but someone needs to—" She indicated the rectangle case she was carrying. Felicity thought it looked like an oversize, upended shoe box.

"Would you care to go with me? To the patronal feast?"

Felicity could tell it was as much a plea as an invitation. She agreed readily with sincere pleasure.

Sister Dorcas's smile showed her relief. "Oh, good. Frank, our gardener, will drive us. It didn't seem right to take St. Margaret on a public conveyance. I wonder, are you ready now? I don't mean to rush you, but it's just that we should be there in plenty of time for the arrangements."

Felicity understood very little of what Dorcas was saying, but there was no reason she couldn't leave immediately. She slipped a jacket on over her woolly sweater and picked up the key to her cottage.

When they got to the driveway, Frank was helping two sisters into his aging blue estate car, light from the interior making a pool of brightness against the hedge bordering the drive. Dorcas introduced Felicity to the frail Sister Anna, stooped with age as if a lifetime of prayer had formed her in a perpetual solemn bow, and young Sister Bertholde whose wide smile split her dark-skinned face, revealing startlingly white teeth.

Felicity offered to hold Sister Dorcas's case while she settled herself in the back seat. Dorcas hesitated, then relinquished it, presenting it to Felicity with both hands. As soon as Dorcas was seated, she reached out to retrieve it, holding it firmly on her lap. Felicity's curiosity was growing.

Before she could form a question, however, Dorcas nodded toward the object on her lap and said in a hushed voice, "Saint Margaret Clitherow."

Felicity had the feeling the nun was making a formal introduction and Felicity had to repress the impulse to respond, *How do you do?* Instead she said "Margaret Clitherow?"

She got the impression Dorcas might have been less surprised if she had asked who Queen Elizabeth was, but she answered with equanimity. "'The pearl of York,' she's called. She was put to death for allowing mass to be said in her home and for sheltering priests. She refused to plead because she didn't want her children to have to testify. That would have subjected them to torture, you see. So she was crushed by stones—as was done to those who refused to plead."

Felicity shivered at the horror of the image the stark words conjured. If Antony had been telling the story she would have the full background, and yet, this was almost more powerful for the simplicity of its telling. A young woman, a loving mother, devout in her faith, put to a cruel death for being true to her beliefs.

After a moment, though, Dorcas chose to add detail. "The two sergeants who should have killed her couldn't bring themselves to do it, so they hired four desperate beggars to do the job. She was stripped and had a handkerchief tied across her face, then laid out upon a sharp rock the size of a man's fist, a door was put on top of her and slowly loaded with an immense weight of rocks and stones. The small sharp rock would break her back when the heavy rocks were laid on top of her, you see.

"She died in fifteen minutes. After her death her hand was

removed. That's how we have this precious relic." The nun all but hugged the case on her lap. "After the execution, Queen Elizabeth wrote to the citizens of York to say she was horrified that a woman should be so treated. Due to her sex, Margaret should not have been executed, you see."

The final remarks were lost on Felicity. She was still staring at the case, questions flooding her mind. She recalled all she had learned about St. Cuthbert in those desperate days of trying to save his treasure from plunder. Had a similar treasure built up at a shrine of Margaret Clitherow? Surely not, if she was a late reformation martyr. The days of pilgrims bringing rich gifts would have been long past. She focused on Dorcas's word: "Relic?"

"Yes. As I said, the hand of St. Margaret Clitherow. It's amazingly well preserved—barely shriveled at all. Another evidence of her sanctity, of course. You see—" Felicity noted that Sister Dorcas had a habit of saying 'you see' about things she particularly did not see. "Reverend Mother felt that as this festival was to be so special for the whole city, hopefully to become an annual event, we should have a special relic. As there aren't any of St. Frideswide, she thought St. Margaret— both of them having been such devout English women, willing to face death for their faith... So Reverend Mother applied to the Bar Convent in York—she and their Reverend Mother are very good friends from their interfaith meetings, you see.

"Well, Mother Mary Immaculata agreed to loan us their most precious treasure. It's a great honour. It will be on the altar throughout the service, but it will only be uncovered at the end, for those who wish to remain behind."

Felicity might have received a more satisfying explanation if their driver hadn't interrupted at that moment. "Here we are then. Sorry, sisters. I can't park here. Afraid you'll have to be right quick-like if you don't mind too much."

Quick would hardly have described Sister Anna's exit from the car, but Sister Bertholde with her seemingly perennial good nature, helped her aged friend out and Frank was able to move the estate car on along St. Aldate's with a minimum of hooting from impatient drivers held up behind him. Felicity followed Sister Dorcas who held her precious charge out in both hands as if carrying it in a liturgical procession. They entered the arched gateway under Tom Tower and followed the path across the great green quad, circling around the lily pond with its fountain splashing crystal drops below the statue of winged Mercury, and on across to Christ Church Cathedral, lights from all the surrounding buildings making the quad glow in the evening dark.

Even with their attempts to hurry, the golden stones of the building were already reverberating to the tones of the great organ as they approached the cathedral and the crowd of people all converging on the entrance slowed their progress even more. Once inside, however, Felicity was surprised that Dorcas didn't make her way toward the high altar gleaming white and gold far ahead of them. Instead she turned to the side aisle to a relatively quiet corner. In the center of the space was a stone structure like a sarcophagus, topped with six pillars supporting an ornate, arched covering of carved stone.

"St. Frideswide's Chapel," Dorcas explained. "Well, officially, it's the Latin Chapel, but I like to think of it as hers." She nodded toward the central structure. "That's her shrine. That is, a reconstruction, of course. It once contained her relics, but all that went at the Reformation. They found the bits of stone and put it back together, you see, right over the place where her monastery stood. So you're standing right where Oxford began.

"At least, as near as they can tell." She turned to an intricate stained glass window that would glow jewel-like in the daytime, but was hard to make out now. "The window's by Edward Burne-Jones. It tells the life of St. Frideswide."

Dorcas turned toward the opposite wall where a small altar was covered with the prescribed pure white fair linen. She set the reliquary in the center, made a small reverence and, picking up matches and a taper from a shelf, set about lighting the candle on each end of the altar. With a final genuflection and crossing herself she walked back to the rapidly filling cathedral nave to the seats Sister Bertholde was holding for them. On Dorcas's instruction Bertholde had been careful to get seats that placed them within view of the Latin

Chapel. Although the small side altar holding the relic was out of sight, Frideswide's shrine in the center was clearly visible.

Felicity followed the proceedings, completely bemused. If only Antony were here to explain it all to her. Her plunge into this high church world had seemed so easy for her, in spite of its suddenness. So natural. As she once explained to Antony, her family had been devout CEO Christians — Christmas and Easter only — but the point was, she had loved it. She had always felt an intense drawing to the beauty, the richness, the numinous — the sense of heaven touching earth — such worship evoked. And long before she became a true believer she always found solace, joy and strength in the Eucharist. So there was no question when she — rashly, yes — went off to study theology at a high church college.

But she had no idea there would be so much to learn — far beyond the curriculum of Bible studies, pastoral care and church history. And just when she thought she had the basics under her belt something entirely new blindsided her. She felt completely at home now, however, when the organ pealed forth the opening bars of the processional hymn and the congregation stood to sing "Love Divine, All Loves Excelling" by one of Christ Church's favorite sons, Charles Wesley.

And the theme continued in the Old Testament reading from the Song of Songs, "Love is strong as death, passion fierce as the grave. Its flashes are flashes of fire, a raging flame. Many waters cannot quench love, neither can floods drown it." Felicity realized the reading was chosen to make the hearers think of Frideswide and her passionate choice of God's love over that of a powerful earthly Lord, but Felicity couldn't keep her mind from straying to her own earthly love and noting that that would be a wonderful passage to have read at their wedding.

The response for the Psalm, however, brought her back to Oxford's patron saint as she repeated with those around her, "God's light shines in the darkness for the upright; their righteousness stands fast forever." She was certainly glad she had spent her time on the train that morning reading up on Frideswide, so she could appreciate this verse for a woman whose righteousness still shone through the centuries after she stood so firmly for the right that her opponents were blinded.

As did the collect, "Almighty God, by whose grace thy servant Frideswide, kindled with the fire of your love, became a burning and a shining light in the Church and in this city, inflame us with the same spirit of discipline and love that we may ever walk before you as children of light..."

Felicity's joy in singing the recessional "*For all the saints, who from their labor rest...*" was intensified by the thought that the next time she sang this—on All Saints' Day—Antony would be by her side. But she wasn't allowed to revel in the thought for long. As they came to the end of the second stanza:

> *Thou wast their Rock, their Fortress and their Might;*
> *Thou, Lord, their Captain in the well fought fight;*
> *Thou, in the darkness drear, their one true Light...*

Dorcas slipped from her seat and Felicity moved with her to the chapel they had left earlier. In a moment the small space would be full of the devout and the curious beholding the relic of another holy woman whose steadfast devotion echoed through the ages. Some would stare. Some would pray. Felicity, who had spent weeks of terror and exhilaration searching for the uncorrupted body of St. Cuthbert, wasn't sure what her reaction would be.

Sister Dorcas bowed at the altar, unsnapped the clips on the case covering the reliquary and lifted it off. Felicity gasped at the stunning beauty of the vessel: almost two feet high over-all, a glass dome stood on a silver pedestal. Ornate silver gilt scrollwork encased the glass, allowing the faithful glimpses of the hand inside. Felicity started to cross herself, then stopped mid-motion, her hand frozen in the air.

She stepped closer, ignoring the shuffle of footsteps on the stone floor as the first votaries entered the chapel. She bent so close to the dome her breath clouded the glass. The chapel was dimly lit and the candles flickered, sending shadows across the glass. Still, she was certain.

She snatched the cover from Sister Dorcas's hands and

thrust it back over the dome. "Sister." Her voice was raspy with the effort of controlling the scream she felt rising in her throat. "Say a prayer and send the people away."

Dorcas stared at her openmouthed.

"Do it!" Felicity repeated. "That's no relic, no matter how well preserved. That hand is fresh."

Three

"Oh, if only Reverend Mother were here to tell us what to do." Dorcas, sitting in a chair just outside the cordoned-off chapel, twisted her scapular into a ball in her lap.

Felicity reached over and squeezed her hand. "You're doing fine. Your prayer was beautiful. I couldn't have been nearly so calm in asking everyone to leave." Felicity was always amazed at the authority a nun's habit conveyed. Fortunately those who had gathered in the chapel, although surprised and perhaps disappointed at the abrupt end of their devotions, had left as requested. Felicity summoned the dean, who promptly rang the police, and by the time the representatives of the Oxford Central division of the Thames Valley Police arrived the chapel was empty.

Sister Dorcas had sent sisters Anna and Bertholde back to the convent in the care of the attentive Frank, then taken up a firm vigil before the reliquary she had guarded with such devotion all evening. When the efficient Inspector Zelma Fosse insisted that Dorcas leave the chapel, she took a post just beyond the police tape so she could still maintain visual contact with the dome that had once again been uncovered, this time by the uniformed officer who introduced himself as Sergeant Dick Thompson.

"I don't understand," the distraught Dorcas said for the third time, in response to Sergeant Thompson's questioning.

"It was delivered to us this morning by special courier. Just as Reverend Mother had arranged, you see. She knew it would arrive before she returned from her conference, so I took delivery and took it straight to our chapel. It sat on our altar all day. It never left my hands all evening." She glanced at Felicity. "Except for a moment when I got in the car." She took a deep breath that wavered dangerously on the verge of a sob, but regained control.

"I brought it straight to the chapel. Felicity—our guest, Miss Howard—was with me." She looked at Felicity and Felicity nodded reassuringly. "I tried to do it all just as I knew Reverend Mother would have done if she hadn't been delayed."

"And you didn't take the cover off at any time until after the service?" Constable Evans asked.

"No! I wouldn't." Sister Dorcas seemed horrified at the idea. "It's a very sacred relic. Not something you just look at for idle curiosity."

"I wasn't suggesting curiosity. I meant to ensure that the delivery was correct."

"What else could it be?" She asked, then drew in her breath sharply as she realized the implications of her own question. The switch had been made at some time. "The courier was absolutely reliable. Bonded, I believe they call them. The company works for the Ashmolean. That's how we secured their services—a friend of Mother Monica's is a curator there. He knew the Roman Museum in York was loaning the Ashmolean some objects. They're doing something about Roman Britain when their current exhibition closes. They brought the relic to us with that delivery as a favor."

"Right." Police Constable Ryan Evans, who was assisting the sergeant, nodded his red, curly hair. "We'll check all that out. And make certain the sisters in York sent the correct—er, package."

He looked back through his notes. "You said this, um, Mother Monica was delayed? Has anyone heard from her?"

Dorcas explained about the meeting of heads of religious houses from which their superior was expected to have returned by mid-afternoon. "It's possible she's back by now. I do hope so. Or she may have rung," she added hopefully.

Inspector Fosse suggested Constable Evans take the ladies back to the convent but Dorcas was horrified. "No! I'm responsible for this. I can't leave. I—"

"Don't worry, your property will be in good care." Had Inspector Zelma Fosse's life gone a different direction she would have made an excellent Mother Superior herself. "I'll give you a receipt and it will be returned to you. You understand there are tests we need to run."

Dorcas nodded. "Fingerprints and such?"

"Exactly." The Inspector put a hand under Dorcas's elbow and moved her gently, but firmly down the aisle.

Felicity couldn't have been more relieved. She was wild to get back to the privacy of her cottage and call Antony.

Constable Evans insisted on walking each one of his charges to her door. As soon as the sister on porter duty locked the door of the dorter behind Dorcas, Felicity turned toward her cottage and began questioning her escort. "What's going on? Do you have any idea what this means?"

Evans shook his head. "It's a weird one. Student prank, maybe. They do get up to some strange larks."

Felicity would like to take comfort in his words. But a severed hand sounded far beyond the bounds of a university jape. "Were there any protests to the patronal festival? Did the committee receive any hate mail? Do you think—?"

Evans held up his hand. "Early days yet, Miss. But we'll get to the bottom of it, don't you worry." He waited patiently while Felicity fumbled for the key to her door. "Will you be all right alone in there?"

She appreciated his concern, but assured him she would. She just hoped the alacrity with which she shut and rebolted her door didn't appear rude but her focus was all on reaching the phone she had left by her bedside. She wasn't sure what time it was. It felt like the middle of the night, but even if Antony was sound asleep she needed him.

She looked at the small screen. Ah, Antony had tried to ring her at eleven o'clock. Just over half an hour ago. She pushed the key to return his call. Even cloudy with sleep his resonate tones brought calm to her a moment later. "Oh,

28

Antony, the most unbelievable thing! Sister Dorcas had this relic — a — a hand," even as she said it, she shuddered. "I mean, it was supposed to be ancient — some martyred woman — Margaret somebody — when she took the cover off…" She took a deep breath as the horror of the realization washed over her again. "Antony, it was real. I mean, it was fresh."

"You had the hand of St. Margaret Clitherow there in Oxford?"

"Oh, you know her?" Then she realized. Of course he knew her, he was a church historian. "Yes, sorry. She was on loan from her convent. I mean, the convent where — "

"Bar Convent in York, yes, I know. But what happened to the relic? Where is the hand?" Now all trace of sleep was gone from his voice as his level of urgency rose with each question.

"I don't know. Sister Dorcas was distraught about the relic, but, really, I was more worried about what was going on now. Antony, it was a living hand. I mean, it had been, until recently." Her own urgency matched his.

"Yes, I understand. That's horrible. I'm just trying to get a full picture. You said the police are fully involved?" Then his voice took an even more intense note of alarm. "Felicity! You aren't thinking of taking up investigating, are you? Don't even — "

"No, no. Honestly, I'll have my hands full with the job I came to do. No, what I really called for — well, besides the fact that I want to hear your voice — is that I don't understand this whole thing about relics.

"I mean, I get it how someone like Margaret Clitherow was a really holy woman and that makes her a good role model. She stood firm for what she believed and didn't even try to defend herself in order to protect her children. She must have been an amazing mother. So I can understand wanting to keep something to remember her by — although, cutting off her hand even after she was dead sounds a bit grizzly… No, what I'm trying to say is that bones and things — it sounds like witch doctors." She held her breath. She hoped she hadn't offended him. She certainly couldn't have said that to the devout Sister Dorcas.

"Felicity, I love you." Nothing else he could possibly have

said could have warmed her so. She hugged the phone, savoring the moment. She didn't even want to break the feeling by saying *I love you, too.*

But with his next words, he was back to the teaching mode that was so characteristic to him. "I fully understand that the whole thing can seem eccentric at best today, but relics were a driving force in the middle ages, especially as they served as magnets for pilgrims. Of course, today many are attracted to reliquaries simply as objects of art, but to the medieval mind the ornate caskets were symbols of the inner sacred splendor."

"Um, yes. But was there anything to it? I mean, it was all just superstition, wasn't it?"

"Have you got a pencil there?"

She dug in her bag and produced her notebook and pen before telling him to go ahead. "Right then, II Kings 13:20-21, II Kings 2:9-14 and Acts 19:11-12. Got that?"

"Yeah."

"Okay, when we're through here, look them up. What you'll see basically is that a reverence was given to the actual body or clothing of these very holy people—Elijah, Elisha, and St. Paul—who were indeed God's chosen instruments. And miracles were connected with these 'relics'.

"The really key thing to understand is that it's no magical power existing in the objects, but just as God's work was done through the lives of these holy men, so did His work continue after their deaths. Just as people were drawn closer to God through their lives, so did they, even through their remains, inspire others to draw closer to God."

Felicity thought for a moment. "So it's all really prayer."

"Precisely. God responding to the prayers of the faithful."

"Who are sometimes drawn to pray with more courage when they're inspired by the acts of holy people or in contact with their relics?" Felicity spoke haltingly, as she thought her way through the ideas. A small frown wrinkled her forehead as she struggled to express a concept she saw so dimly.

"That's excellent for starters. This is a huge subject and I'd love to talk about it more..." Felicity was sure he stifled a yawn.

"I know. It's the middle of the night. But thank you so

much. That really helps me." She started to say good-bye, then thought, "Oh, I'm sorry. I jumped right in. What did you call me about earlier?"

"I just wanted you to know I took your advice about coming to Beryl and Edward."

"So you're in Blackpool? How is your uncle?"

"Stable, as far as I can tell. I'll go see him tomorrow. I must say Aunt Beryl was almost pathetically pleased to see me. I had no idea, really."

In spite of the fact that yawns from both ends of the line became more frequent and harder to suppress, they talked on for some time until Felicity could no longer hide the fact that she was falling asleep. She saw it was well after midnight when she rang off so she abandoned all intention of attending Matins at two a.m. And in spite of her best intentions, failed to rise for Lauds at six o'clock.

She finally woke with sunshine filtering around her curtains and the sound of muffled bells echoing through her sleep. It took her several moments to realize she was not hearing a funeral tolling as she had dreamt, but rather her alarm clock. It was almost nine o'clock and she was nearly late to Terce, the brief office preceding morning mass. Hurrying, she made her way across the wide manicured lawn, past the community house, and around to the visitors' door at the side of the chapel. A prayer book and service sheet awaited her on one of the chairs in the small visitors' chapel to the side of the altar.

The altar was a magnificent pedimented structure of red onyx draped with a fair linen. A single red votive candle flickered beside an icon of Christ below a tall gold crucifix. Felicity waited in the silence until a soft shuffle of sandal-shod feet on the wooden floor of the main chapel told her the sisters were entering from a door at the far end. Still hidden from her sight, their light voices chanted the office as the morning sunshine made the yellow and cream barrel ceiling of the chapel glow.

In the silences between the psalms and prayers she could hear a gentle cooing of doves from the orchard, distant traffic on the Iffley Road and the muted chiming of a clock from somewhere deep in the convent. A scuff of sandals on the wooden floor and whisper of habits signaled that the office was ended.

Felicity turned toward the door, thinking she would have a quick breakfast, then hopefully be able to set about her translating work. She had taken just one step, however, when she realized that only one sister had moved in the room beyond. Sister Dorcas stood before the altar to address the community. A glance at the side chapel told Felicity she was included.

Even from a distance of several feet Felicity could see that the small nun hadn't slept well. Her face was lined and dark smudges circled her blue eyes. And yet she seemed to have taken on a new determination as she spoke with a firm voice. "My sisters, I do not wish to alarm you unduly, but I believe you need to know that this morning I rang Father Desmond at the friary in Canterbury. He said Mother Monica did not attend the meeting. No one has any idea where she is."

Four

A hushed intake of breath disturbed the air in the sisters' chapel beyond. "Father Desmond said Mother Superior rang on Monday to say she had been delayed." Sister Dorcas paused as if to give herself time to steady her voice. "Apparently that is the last anyone has heard of her."

This time the announcement elicited a faint murmur. "It is possible that Mother was called away by a family emergency or another duty. I shall, of course, report this to the authorities. In the meantime I ask you to attend to all your essential duties, but for any time that you are able we shall hold a perpetual prayer vigil. Pray for the safe return of Mother Monica. Pray for the work of the authorities that they may aid the victim of last night's alarm, that they may safely recover the relic of St. Margaret, and," only the slightest pause indicated the depth of her plea, "pray for me, my sisters."

Felicity was pleased, and rather surprised, to hear the steadiness and authority in Dorcas's voice. This was far from the frightened, dithering woman of last night. It seemed that facing the emergency, and undoubtedly a night spent in prayer, had brought to the fore the reserve of strength that Mother Superior must have known was there when she named Dorcas her deputy.

Dorcas turned to reverence the altar, then came to the side chapel. Felicity wondered if she would be asked to leave.

Given the unsettling news for the community, it would be understandable, but Felicity would be sorely disappointed not to be able to accomplish the task she had come for.

The sister's first words were reassuring. "I hope you will be able to stay on in spite of the turmoil. I fear Sister Gertrude may be distracted, as we all are, but I believe knowing that the work is progressing would be a comfort to her, you see."

Felicity realized she had been holding her breath. She let it out in a soft rush. "Yes. Thank you, Sister. I would like to continue. Well, to start, really. I haven't seen the document yet."

"I must call the Inspector with my distressing news. I will do that from Mother's office. Would you like to come with me now?"

Felicity suspected it was as much a request as an invitation. Sister Dorcas was showing remarkable resiliency and leadership, but dealing with the police would undoubtedly be outside her expertise. Dorcas confirmed Felicity's thoughts as they moved toward the door. "I hope you don't mind my mentioning it, but I have heard that you have some skill—that is, you have had experience in similar emergencies."

Felicity shook her head. "I'm not sure skill is the right word, but I have had contact with the police on more than one occasion. I'll be glad to help in any way I can."

A simple nod of the veiled head told Felicity her answer was appreciated. "I pray this will turn out to be nothing, but I appreciate your assistance. I will ask Sister Gertrude to join us, but would prefer not to distract any of the others from their duties and their prayers, you see. Prayer is always our most important work."

In order to avoid disturbing the sisters who had begun the vigil in their chapel, Dorcas took Felicity back outside through the bright, crisp October morning to reenter the convent. She drew a ring of keys from her pocket and they entered a well-ordered office at the end of a long corridor. Dorcas went to the desk and indicated Felicity should take the chair opposite. Thames Valley Police answered on the second ring and put Dorcas through to Inspector Fosse. Dorcas explained her concern about the Mother Superior, then her forehead furrowed. "Yes. Yes, of course. But do you think that's necessary?"

Apparently the Inspector did because the nun gave ready agreement to whatever she was requesting. Then Dorcas's face lit in a smile. "Oh, that's excellent. Thank you. Yes, any time this morning will be convenient."

"They found St. Margaret. The relic, that is," she said as soon as she had rung off.

"Wonderful! Where was it?"

"A schoolboy found it in a pile of leaves along the canal in Jericho. Apparently the vandal had meant to burn it, but the leaves were too damp. The boy thought it was 'wicked'. His mother found it in his room this morning and rang the police. It appears to be quite unharmed. Sergeant Thompson will return it to us as soon as they can release it. Although they may need to keep the reliquary somewhat longer. I've already informed mother Mary Immaculata at the Bar Convent. Of course she's most distressed..."

Sister Dorcas continued to talk about the need to reconsecrate the reliquary but Felicity's mind moved on to consider the implications of this discovery. "So that means the relic reached Oxford. The switch must have been made before the reliquary was delivered to you." She paused. "Or, I suppose it could have been done at Christ Church — during the service. What an audacious thing to do, though. He — or she — could have been spotted at any moment."

Distress returned to Dorcas's face. "Yes, I hardly took my eyes off the chapel for a moment. But during the elevation, when the bells ring, one is required to look... Everyone would have been focusing on the high altar. I suppose if anyone had been questioned they could just have said they were helping with the arrangements, or something."

Felicity thought about that. "In that case they would have needed to be wearing a cassock to look official. And they would have known the details of the service." She thought, then shook her head. "No, I think it must have been done earlier."

"I suppose the police will look into all of that. You know,

question the courier and all. But the really wonderful thing is that St. Margaret's hand wasn't defiled or destroyed. Of course, we're terribly distressed for the victim..." she bit her lip.

"I understand." Felicity touched her arm impulsively. "It is lovely to have a cause for thanksgiving in the midst of all the worry."

Dorcas gave a small smile, then took a deep breath as if warning that there was more distressing news to impart. She plunged on. "The police have asked for a hairbrush or something of Mother Superior's. They want to test it. 'For purposes of elimination' the officer said, but it's a very worrying thought."

Felicity agreed. It had been her first thought and she was far more worried than she wanted to let on to Sister Dorcas. "I'm sure the police are just being careful. 'No stone unturned,' you know."

Then she wondered, "That sounds like DNA testing. Can't they just see if her fingerprints match the, er—other one?"

Dorcas shook her head. "It seems the ones they got from the hand were, um, indistinct."

Felicity raised her eyebrows. "The tips had been filed or something? How odd. I wonder why?" She paused. "Obviously to conceal the identity, but still, why?"

But before she could speculate further Sister Gertrude joined them, her quick, determined step bringing a sense of energy into the room. Felicity smiled at her, then asked, "Do you know where the Frideswide document is, Sister?"

Gertrude shook her head. "Not precisely, just that Mother was keeping it here until we were ready to begin work on it."

Felicity stood aside while the nuns searched their superior's office. In their careful, systematic way both women began looking through the shelves and drawers of the tidy, but very full office before Sister Dorcas, using keys she discovered in Mother Monica's top drawer, found what they were searching for in a locked drawer in the file cabinet. Gertrude opened the slim archival box. A pair of white cotton gloves on top of the sheets of vellum issued a clear instruction as to how the pages were to be handled.

Felicity was a classicist, not an archivist. Still, her study of ancient manuscripts had taught her something about working on vellum. She knew the importance of what her initial examination would reveal. The condition of the sheets could make all the difference to her work. Even to the possibility of proceeding. Skins are very reactive to moisture. If the document had been improperly stored near water or in an area of high humidity it could be distorted, stiff or translucent. In other words, nearly impossible to work with.

At a nod from Sister Gertrude Felicity put the gloves on and lifted the top sheet to examine it more closely. As she expected, close inspection revealed veins and hair follicle holes in the calfskin. Fortunately, the ancient scribe who had prepared the pages had worked carefully. The hair side of the skin was burnished smooth with only minimal indentations and scrape marks from the processing knife. She offered a silent *thank you* that the sheets were relatively flat. Skins had a tendency to curl and many ancient documents were rolled for storage. She recalled the painstaking process the archivist at St. David's Cathedral had explained to them when Antony restored a document to their archives.

Now she examined the writing itself. To her relief the brown ink, though faded in spots, was not illegible. The script was even and at first glance it appeared to be reasonably readable Latin. Her scribe had written in a fair hand. The long sigh that escaped when she started to speak made Felicity realize she had been holding her breath. "Yes, this should be fine. Where do you want me to work?"

"Will the desk in your cottage be adequate, do you think?" Dorcas asked. "I believe it has a locking drawer as well."

Felicity was delighted with the suggestion. She hadn't been sure the sister would allow her to take these valuable documents out of the convent building, but she would be much more comfortable working in her own room on her own time schedule. "Thank you, that would be perfect." She took off the gloves and replaced the lid on the box. "How did this come to you?"

"It's on loan from the Sisters of the Holy Paraclete."

Felicity nodded. She had stayed at their house in Whitby

when she and Antony were searching for St. Cuthbert's treasure. She shivered, remembering what that search had cost their superior Sister Elspeth. She squeezed her eyes shut in an attempt to blot out the memory. Surely such a price hadn't been demanded of Mother Monica. She forced herself to respond to Gertrude. "Yes, I stayed with them in Whitby last February. Their archives are remarkable."

Sister Gertrude agreed. "Yes, but they also have a smaller house at Leicester, built on the grounds of a medieval monastery that passed into private hands at the reformation. They were recently doing some repair work and this came to light. Knowing how important St. Frideswide is to Oxford they kindly offered to let Fairacres Press publish the translation."

Felicity clutched the box to her and hurried to her room before the sisters might decide it was too valuable to entrust to her. Back in her cozy cottage she arranged everything on her desk: an angelpoise lamp, several sheets of blank paper, three well sharpened pencils... Then she realized she hadn't eaten breakfast.

After a quick bowl of cereal and two slices of the granary loaf Felicity was at last able to settle into work. In spite of her assurances to Sister Gertrude, Felicity soon realized that she had taken on a considerable challenge. After working at a few lines she began to suspect that this was late Medieval Latin, perhaps twelfth century. And she speculated from the syntax that the author had been a native Anglo-Saxon speaker, which strongly influenced his word choice and sentence structure. For Felicity, trained in classical Latin and becoming accustomed through frequent use to ecclesiastical Latin, this made working on these vulgar phrases slow going.

By the time the bell rang for the midday meal she had completed less than half of the first page. So far it seemed to her this was a fairly standard account of the life of St. Frideswide, either drawn on the writer's research or perhaps simply copied from an earlier hagiography. She put the sheet back in the box, placed the gloves on top and locked the entire project securely in her bottom desk drawer. She needed a break.

The midday meal was eaten in silence at long tables lining each side of the refectory. The room was filled with light from the tall windows that looked out on the gardens. Felicity found a seat between two brown-robed sisters who offered her shy smiles, then lowered their eyes. Across the table Felicity noticed a young woman about her own age in a white novice's veil. Their eyes met and they smiled. One sister stood at a lectern in the corner and read from a book about hermits and solitaries. The meal was simple and nourishing, the vegetables fresh from the garden. Felicity found the experience soothing after the alarms of the night before but when the meal ended she knew she couldn't go back to her room. She must get some fresh air.

She considered simply taking a walk in the garden, but her restlessness, combined with nostalgia for her student days in this lovely city, drew her further afield. Surely she could justify a visit to the Ashmolean. After all, the world famous museum of art and archeology had played an unwitting part in the mystery surrounding the Margaret Clitherow relic and perhaps they would have something of relevance to St. Frideswide. It might even help her with her translating. Once she started on a train of thought Felicity could usually persuade herself to any convenient conclusion.

Although, truth to tell, there was no reason for her feelings of guilt as she left the convent and walked to the bus stop on the Iffley Road. She was under no severe time constraints and even though the work was going slower than she had first expected, there was no reason she shouldn't be able to finish it in a timely fashion.

She had thoroughly convinced herself by the time she got off in the centre of Oxford and walked up the street toward the enormous classical, pale yellow building. Just as she was about to turn to mount the wide flight of stairs leading to the museum a pair of bright pink playbills on a creamy colored building across the street caught her eye. Ah, the Oxford Playhouse was performing G. B. Shaw's "Misalliance." Felicity had loved Shaw's plays ever since she played Eliza Doolittle in a high school production of "Pygmalion," but she had never seen this seldom-produced play. Perhaps one evening she would slip off from the convent.

Her heart rose as she bounded up the stairs and proceeded to the colonnaded porch under the ornate pediment. This was exactly what she needed to reinvigorate her work. Get away from the grizzly events of the night before and the claustrophobic feeling of the convent. She took a deep, free breath.

She wasn't sure what exhibits she would visit. She had spent many hours here in her undergraduate days and always found it fascinating. Her favorite had always been the Alfred Jewel, the cloisonné enamel of a human figure covered by rock crystal, set in a gold frame, thought to have belonged to Alfred the Great. Perhaps she would revisit it, then just wander around.

She was still thinking of some of her favorite finds from earlier days when she noted the long banners hanging on either side of the main door. A red one on her left announced the coming of the "Romans in Britain" exhibition to open in mid-November. On her right elegant gold letters on a black cloth read: "Treasures of Heaven." Felicity couldn't believe her luck. This was the last day to view the current exhibit featuring Saints, Relics and Devotion in Medieval Europe. All thought of revisiting old haunts fled from her mind as she strode forward. She had told herself she might see something useful to her work here, but she had no idea it would be so spot on point.

She made the suggested three pound donation and picked up a floor plan to take her to the special exhibitions area on the third floor. She paid the additional admission and was given an electronic self-guide. She stepped forward and came stock still before a golden bust of a man with curly hair and wide-open eyes. The strange statue was alarming and mesmerizing at the same time. The figure obviously represented a priest because he wore a chasuble dotted with depressions which had once been encrusted with gemstones and his hands were extended in an act of blessing. Lowering her gaze to the words on the glass at the bottom of the case, she read that the statue was a reliquary thought to have held a vial of St. Baudime's blood in the twelfth century. The saint himself was believed to have been sent from Rome in the third century to Christianize Gaul.

The amazing statue had had a hazardous existence. Its precious and semiprecious stones had been removed during the French Revolution, which made the reliquary a rare survivor of the revolution. Then in the early twentieth century it was stolen by an art thief and recovered by the police from its hiding place in a wine cellar.

Still amazed by the irony that she had come here in an attempt to play hooky and wound up in the last few hours that this exhibit of reliquaries would be open, she put the recorded guide to her ear and switched it on. "'Treasures of Heaven' begins in the fourth century when the Emperor Constantine legalized Christian worship." The guide led first into the display of Roman sarcophagi, caskets with peaked roofs that looked like small houses. "In creating reliquaries, early Christians followed Roman funerary practices," the recording explained. The narrator's voice was clear and engaging, making her think of the many similar lectures she had listened to from Antony.

Just the thought made her smile—how amazed he would have been to see her doing this a few months ago. When their first adventure took them to Lindisfarne it had taken all her willpower not to roll her eyes and grit her teeth when her companion would launch into yet another lengthy explanation of the life of some long-ago saint. Now she rolled her eyes at herself, thinking how much she had changed—or rather, how recent experiences had revealed the real person inside her. And how much she had come to appreciate the lectures and the lecturer. And how much she missed him. It was an ache that started in her chest and rose to her throat, threatening to choke her.

But Antony wasn't here and this disembodied recorded voice was. She needed to pay attention in hopes she might learn something that would help solve the mystery she had encountered. "The difference, however, is that these enameled caskets contained only fragments, rather than entire bodies." Before she could wonder why early Christians had departed from the standard burial practice, her lecturer went on, "The answer may be that often only fragments were left of those who were tortured and then martyred for refusing to renounce their faith. Their remains would be secretly gathered up by the faithful. Any remnant, however small, was regarded as holy." Felicity shivered. She wasn't sure she wanted to know this. And yet, it was a powerful statement of the faith of the early believers who had so willingly suffered rather than renounce their Lord. And perhaps something of an explanation of why Margaret Clitherow's friends had kept her hand.

There were several cross-shaped reliquaries, made to conceal slivers of wood reputed to be from the true cross on which Jesus was crucified, but Felicity was far more fascinated by the body-part reliquaries. The elaborately jeweled caskets in the form of an arm or a foot or a head made her think again of the hand she had encountered last night. She shivered at the thought and started to turn away, but was drawn back to the exhibition by the sheer gorgeousness of the vessels on display.

She turned again to her electronic guide. "Their beauty was homage to the saint and a material manifestation of his or her spiritual magnificence. Medieval reliquaries are usually made of luxurious materials such as gold, silver and rock crystal, inset with cameos and precious stones. Gold, which does not tarnish, was a particularly favorite material because it signified incorruptibility."

Again, Felicity was back following the trail of St. Cuthbert's uncorrupted body, and missing her companion. She pushed the button for the recorded lecture to continue. "Our exhibit ends with the Reformation in the fifteenth century, by which time Martin Luther asserted that the veneration of saints through their relics had become counterproductive by drawing people away from the divine, rather than bringing them closer." Yes, Felicity recalled Antony's words last night that the purpose of relics was to lead one to prayer. If they ceased to do that they would become merely eccentric collectibles. She was so sorry this exhibit would be closed before Antony and his students arrived. She would have loved to experience it with him.

She switched off the recording. She would just wander around and let whatever in the exhibit caught her attention speak to her. "Jewels with soul" her narrator had called them. After observing various well-lit cases with their "soul jewels" displayed against red velvet drapes, she found herself drawn to an elegant blackened silver foot with an etched gold cap where the ankle began. A heavily embossed gold rectangle ornamented the *dorsalis pedis*. Top of the foot, Felicity translated. In Medieval times when the vessel held a relic a small "trap door" in the rectangle opened to display the foot inside.

Felicity bent closer to read the information: Thirteenth century reliquary foot of St. Blaise, physician and bishop in what is now modern Turkey; healed both bodies and souls until martyred in the year 316...

And then she looked closer. At first it was hard to see as the lights reflecting off the shiny metal darkened the shadows. But then she observed that, indeed, the cap sealing the reliquary at the ankle was slightly askew as if it had been pried up and hastily replaced.

And the crimson velvet cloth the foot sat on held a few darker red flecks.

Holding her breath, with her hand tight over her mouth, Felicity walked to the side of the display case to see better from that angle. But she didn't really need to. She already knew.

She turned to the nearest museum guard. "I think you should call the police."

Five

Word of the new discovery had already reached the convent by the time Felicity returned after her careful questioning by Sergeant Thompson. She found the entire community at prayer in the chapel. Sister Dorcas looked up at the sound of Felicity's step on the wooden floor and moved outside with her where they could talk without disturbing the others.

The police had informed Dorcas that there had been another incident, but she wanted to hear the details first hand even though Felicity could tell that the nun found it distressing. "And, of course, they don't know... well—don't know anything yet."

"Just that there is a madman loose in Oxford." Dorcas shuddered and crossed herself as a prayer for defense against evil.

"And I don't suppose you've heard...?"

Dorcas shook her head. "Nothing from Mother Superior. The police contacted her family. They have heard nothing. There has been no family emergency. Well, other than this, of course."

"Does she have a mobile?"

"Yes, for emergencies. I've rung it several times since she first failed to return." Dorcas shook her head and returned to her prayers. There was nothing else to do.

Felicity fled to the security of her tiny cottage. She felt desperate to talk to Antony. To seek his comfort and wisdom, but mostly just to hear his voice. In his usual thoughtful way he was quiet for a moment after she had poured out all of the events of the day.

"Yes, it goes without saying that the person behind this is mad. But that's not an explanation. It's as if he's sending some kind of a message."

"That's what puzzles me," Felicity replied. "It's so public. Whatever his reason for dismembering his victim—or victims…"

"The use of the reliquaries seems like a special warning."

"Yes, but to whom? What can he hope to gain by such—" Felicity felt at a loss for words. "By creating such an abomination?"

Antony was silent for so long she thought the connection might have been broken. When he spoke she could picture the furrows in his broad brow. "The obvious answer is that his— and we're assuming it's a he—"

"Yes!" Felicity's reply came out in a burst of fervor. "No woman would commit such a horror." Surely not.

"Right, his goal has to be to shock."

"He certainly achieved that. But for what purpose?"

"I wish we knew. To frighten someone? To discredit someone? To get someone's attention?"

"But why choose to defile religious articles?"

"To mock? To weaken faith? To prove a point?" Again Antony's pause was long.

Felicity ached to have him beside her right now. To feel the security of his arms around her. She wouldn't say it, though. If she did he might get on the next train and come down to Oxford—as she yearned for him to do. But he needed to be with the aunt and uncle who had been like parents to him and his orphaned sister since they were young children. "How's your uncle?"

"I'm afraid he had a bit of a setback today. Aunt Beryl and I are just home from the hospital. I need to fix her something to eat."

"You're cooking?" Felicity hadn't even realized he could

cook since they always ate in hall at college.

"Bit of a role reversal, isn't it? Aunt Beryl never failed to have a hot meal on the table all those years she was raising Gwen and me. Now I don't think she's fixed herself anything but tea and toast since Edward went in hospital. She's doing much better now."

Felicity knew she had been right not to ask him to come to Oxford early. Antony extracted another promise from her not to get involved in any investigating and she assured him there was nothing she had less intention of doing.

As soon as the connection was cut Felicity felt a chill of abandonment. She went through the four rooms of her cottage, checking that the door was locked and bolted, every window latched and curtained, and every light turned on. Then she made herself a bowl of vegetable soup from a tin and settled down to work.

Her workaholic mother hadn't been much of a guiding force in Felicity's growing up years, leaving the formation of Felicity and her two older brothers to their father while her mother pursued her phenomenally successful legal career, but one thing Cynthia Howard had taught her daughter was that hard work could cure anything. Depression, worry, loneliness — all of which Felicity was battling at the moment — could be kept at bay, by simply focusing on the task in front of her. But now she had a new enemy — fear. Would work be sufficient to block those blood-soaked images from her mind?

Before she took the document from the desk she picked up the current edition of "Convent Chronicle", the quarterly publication Sister Gertrude edited. Hoping for inspiration she turned to an article on the craft of translating. She found herself caught by the writer's words, "juggling a love for two languages simultaneously in order to enable others to share something I have found worthwhile, and enabling those words to be published has added a creative and satisfying dimension to my life."

Yes, she thought. She had undertaken this task simply with an eye to help the sisters — and to fulfill a course requirement for herself, it must be admitted. She had not thought of it as something she would find fulfilling herself.

And certainly, she had not given any thought to how important it would become to her to do a good job for Sister Gertrude, for Dorcas and for all the sisters in this place. And for the Mother Monica she was yet to meet.

As she unlocked her bottom drawer and drew on the white cotton gloves she couldn't shake the feeling that more than a simple job of translating was riding on her efforts.

Six

The cramp in Felicity's neck woke her. She raised her head from her desk and looked around. Was that a sliver of morning light peeking under the closed drapery? Her determination to make real progress on the Frideswide document, plus the fact that she feared the images her recent encounters might produce in her dreams, had combined to make her force herself to stay at her task most of the night. But she hadn't intended to sleep here as well.

She snapped off her desk lamp and opened the curtain, then drew back, blinking. Not a gentle morning light, but full midday sun streamed in her window. How long had she slept? The bell ringing for the midday office answered her question.

Felicity turned back to her desk, praying she hadn't rumpled the manuscript in her sleep. She breathed a sigh of relief when she saw it lying unharmed. It had been her penciled notes that cushioned her head. With her gloves still on she placed everything back in the box and locked the drawer. She took time to splash water on her face and pull on a fresh turtleneck shirt, but didn't bother to replait her long braid before joining the sisters in the chapel. She could tell from the tone of the intercessions that there apparently had been no new developments in the investigation. No information on whose foot and hand had been in the reliquaries. And no word from Mother Monica.

After lunch she knew she couldn't possibly return to her desk without some fresh air and exercise first. A good jog around the convent grounds in the bright October afternoon would be just the thing. Felicity didn't feel it would be appropriate to do an energetic jog around the sister's garden designed for prayer and meditation, but she recalled that the map in her room indicated extensive open fields beyond the tall hedges and graceful willows.

The orchard smelled of ripe pears and apples on the warm autumn air and golden leaves crunched under her feet as she made her way to the back of the grounds. Through a gap in the enclosing shrubbery she emerged into a wide, rough meadow dotted with bushes and crisscrossed with footpaths. Perfect. She shook her hair back and lifted her face to the sun then did a few bending and stretching exercises before setting out at a gentle lope along one of the paths. She had to rein in her desire to race the length of the expanse. It had been many days since she had gone for a good run and longer than that since she had done a full workout of the ballet exercises she normally was so careful about keeping up with. She didn't want to overextend herself and wind up with sore muscles.

Besides, the day was so beautiful she didn't want to rush the experience. Autumn had always been one of her favorite seasons at home in Idaho: the crisp mornings with frost on the grass followed by golden afternoons with the sun filtering through amber leaves all under startlingly clear blue skies. And she had found it to be an equally lovely time in England, blessedly free of the rain-soaked days that could get to be a bit much for this desert-bred girl.

Her thoughts moved in easy rhythm to the steady movement of her legs as she sped on around the field, passing occasional joggers and dog-walkers. Several gardeners toiled at their plots in the allotment which stood to one side of the open field. Felicity wondered at this glorious open space so near to the heart of Oxford. Did it belong to the convent? Perhaps it was only on their visitor's map for those who wanted to stretch their legs further afield. This would be quite an enormous property for a handful of nuns. But then, their order had perhaps been much larger when it was founded more than a hundred years ago as a community of women who wanted to live lives dedicated wholly to prayer.

That brought her mind back to the life of St. Frideswide and the translating she had done last night. Although Felicity had read much of the story before, she had been struck anew at the devotion of the Saxon princess and her determination to live a life of prayer. Frideswide had been clear in her call at a young age. Clear enough and forceful enough that she was able to persuade her father, King Didan, to found a double monastery—for both men and women—and appoint her abbess. And yet, in spite of her consecrated life, King Algar of Leicester had been so insistent that she marry him that he was willing to risk his eyesight and his life to bring it about. Felicity had checked a map earlier to be sure and her impression was correct. Leicester was more than sixty miles north of Oxford. A long distance courtship for those days, surely. She had been too sleepy last night to wonder what fueled Algar's passion. She had merely translated the words as recorded. But now she wanted to know more.

Now Felicity's long, loping strides carried her back toward her cottage and the document in her locked drawer. The fresh air and exercise had done their work. She was ready to delve further into the life of this Saxon woman. Hours later she looked up, rubbed her eyes and indulged in a good stretch. And now she understood Algar's insistence on marrying Frideswide. She smiled. So, whatever the princess's charms, apparently they had not been the Mercian King's major inducement.

The lands Frideswide's father ruled lay between the kingdoms of Mercia and Wessex. This frontier position made Didan's lands the scene of frequent battles between the Mercians and the West-Saxons. And marriage to the princess of those lands would secure a battle treaty for the wily Algar. Felicity smiled. No wonder Frideswide found the marriage proposal repugnant. She could hardly have been flattered even if she hadn't considered herself already wed to the King of Heaven.

Felicity was dubious as to how much the document she

was translating would add to the scholarship of the period, but it was certainly adding to her own knowledge. And it had added a sufficient amount for this day. She looked at the vellum sheets still in the box. Ten left. That would be perfect. If she could complete two a day she would have her work finished before Antony arrived and she would be able to concentrate on him—even though he would need to focus on his students and his lectures on the Oxford Movement, she reminded herself.

She locked her work away and indulged in a lengthy shower to make up for the fact that she had slept in her clothes last night. Dressed in her favorite long skirt with her waist-length blond hair fanned over her shoulders to dry she picked up her coat and set out toward the bus stop to indulge in the treat she had promised herself when she saw the placard at the Playhouse yesterday.

The brightly lit, brilliant red interior—walls, carpet and seats—of the Oxford Playhouse welcomed Felicity in from the dark night. As soon as she was seated in one of the plush seats she turned to her program notes. Ah, Shaw's exploration of what drives people to be attracted to one another. This should make for a lively evening. The curtain rose to reveal the conservatory of the Tarleton family's large country house, the back wall of the set dominated by a floor-to-ceiling bookcase. Felicity was immediately drawn into following the witty dialogue.

The first act came to a, literally, crashing end when an airplane fell from the sky and burst through the roof of the set, one wing piercing the ceiling with its propeller whirling around like the blades of a ceiling fan. After her initial startle Felicity laughed and applauded with the audience, then wandered out into the lobby, pondering Shaw's ideas on marriage and the family which the Tarletons had debated. How she wished Antony were here to discuss it all with her.

The second act picked up minutes after the crash with the propeller of the plane still turning in an empty room, the family having all rushed outside at the crash. Felicity jerked to attention when a striking figure in aviator's gear climbed through the high, round window next to the bookcase and, using the shelves as a ladder, descended with a leap to center stage. The actress, clad in high leather boots, a long aviator's coat and a helmet over her blond hair, riveted the audience with her daring descent and striking appearance. Felicity sat forward. What was familiar about her? Perhaps the cheekbones? Or something around her eyes? When she spoke Felicity recognized a certain ring in her voice. This must be someone she had seen on television.

Felicity tipped her program forward to catch the dim spill of light from the stage. Lina Szczepanowska was played by Gwendolyn Sherwood. Felicity blinked to be sure she was reading the name correctly. Was it possible that this was Antony's sister? She sat back, observing the stunning actress. Of course, that was the familiarity she had picked up on. She had known that Antony had a sister. An actress-sister. But after that cold rainy night, huddled in a shelter awaiting a bus to Holy Island—which never came—he had almost never spoken of her again.

Felicity, though, had never forgotten his words: *Gwendolyn and I were orphaned when I was ten. Gwena was fourteen. Our parents were sailing off the coast of Cornwall.*

An aunt and uncle in Blackpool took us in — Beryl and Edward, my father's older brother and his wife. They didn't have any children of their own and really didn't know what to do with us.

And that would have been the end of his information had she not pressed him. She could still see his dark form silhouetted by the dim, grey light beyond the door of the kiosk as he stood with his back to her. Self-revelation had never come easily to Antony and this first confidence had been a major step forward in their relationship. She remembered commenting that his childhood sounded sterile. His reply was almost offhanded: *Well, there wasn't much emotion, if that's what you mean. I had my books. Gwena had her friends. Mostly men friends, to be honest. She's on her third or fourth partner — I've lost track. But that's rather par for the course in the theatre world, I guess.* He hadn't sounded disapproving, just resigned.

She recalled that he had said that Gwendolyn's specialty was farce, so she must have moved on a bit in her career to be doing more classical drama now. And very good she was at it, too, Felicity thought as Lina strode across the stage, the long skirt of her ivory Aviator's coat swishing behind her. This Polish acrobat and aviator character was just the energetic, liberated "New Woman" Shaw admired. As did everyone on stage and in the audience.

As the plot developed through the many marriage proposals, Felicity smiled at Lina's lengthy speech rejecting marriage in favor of independence, thinking how those words could so easily have been her own less than a year ago. Truly amazing how different—and how happy she was now.

When Lina grabbed the bright, but cowardly, Bentley, to take him off in her aeroplane, the curtain came down to rousing applause, no one clapping harder than Felicity. Then she jumped to her feet and, making her apologies, squeezed past the others in her row and headed toward the exit. She had no idea how to get to the stage door, but she knew she had to connect with Antony's sister. Since the playhouse stood right next to the Randolph Hotel she turned the opposite direction, hoping for a break in the solid wall of buildings lining Beaumont Street. Ah, yes, along the left side of the street was a little passage marked Friar's Entry. Another left turning lead past a car park. Beyond that a dim light hung over the stage door of the Playhouse.

Her first knock brought a small, bald man wearing a peaked cap with a theatre emblem on it. He peered at her through gold-rimmed spectacles. Felicity tried to explain, then stopped the breathless rush of words that wanted to tumble out. "Never mind." She dug in her copious shoulder bag for pen and paper. "Gwendolyn Sherwood. She doesn't know me, but I'm engaged to her brother. Could you take her a note?"

Wordlessly, the guard held out his hand. She scribbled a few lines and gave it to him with a two pound coin, hoping that would be a sufficient tip to ensure delivery. Felicity smiled uneasily at the others who gathered beyond the stage door in small groups, laughing and chatting. What would Gwendolyn think when she read the note? Would she have any interest in meeting this woman she probably had no idea existed? Would Gwena have plans that Felicity was interrupting? She pulled her jacket tighter around herself, wishing she had worn a warmer coat.

"This way, Miss." The guard opened the door just enough to allow her to pass. He glared at the others waiting outside, then closed the door with a solid thud. Felicity followed down a long corridor, dodging stagehands and others involved in the production. It brought back happy memories of her days as a serious ballet student, thinking she was preparing for a life on stage. Before she grew to be over five foot ten inches and fell in love with Latin, that was. Still, the memories of working her way year by year through the Nutcracker roles from mouse to candy cane to Clara and finally the Sugar Plum Fairy herself brought a smile to her lips.

Her guide knocked at a door marked Gwendolyn Sherwood and opened it for Felicity. The actress turned from her dressing table and stood, hands on hips, surveying Felicity. "Thank you for—" Felicity started.

But her future sister-in-law cut her off with an accusation. "Well, so you're actually going to marry my monkish brother?"

Gwendolyn was smaller than she appeared on stage. Clad now in tight jeans and an oversized jumper she looked as though she could still be a teenager, although Felicity knew she was considerably older than herself. The short, blond bob framing her heavily lined eyes gave her a gamin look. "I, um—" Felicity wasn't certain how to respond. Finally she blurted out a fervent, "Yes!"

Gwena tossed back her head and laughed. "Ha! Good for you. And I must say, you look surprisingly normal."

Felicity wasn't often thrown off her stride, but Antony's sister was certainly an experience. It would be hard to imagine two siblings more different from one another. "I loved your performance," she decided to try a different tack.

"Thank you. This is a fun role. A bit of typecasting, I suppose. Antony has probably told you I'm thoroughly liberated. Although I can't claim to pilot a plane like Lina."

"Antony said you did Farce..." She wasn't sure where to

go with that.

"Ah, so you were surprised to see me in something literary?" That was true, but Felicity didn't want to say so. "Actually some of our best plays are farce: 'Comedy of Errors,' 'Importance of Being Earnest'. Even such a talky play as this one is close to the genre with its deliberate absurdity of the plane crash."

"Yes, and your entrance down the book case gave a touch of physical humor."

Gwena seemed to regard her with new respect. "Yes, you're right. But I'm sure you didn't come to discuss British drama." She turned and picked up her bag. "I'm parched. I'm meeting a friend at the pub just behind the theatre. Want to come along?"

Felicity would have said yes even if she hadn't wanted to. After all, she could hardly confirm Gwendolyn's worst suspicions about her by saying she wanted to go back to a convent and read a twelfth century Latin document. Put like that, Felicity could hardly believe it herself.

"So," a short time later Gwena leaned across a table at the Gloucester Arms. It had taken several minutes to thread their way through the students and after-theatre crowd around the bar to this relatively quiet corner. Several people had recognized Gwena and applauded or called "Good show!" as they passed, but the friend Gwena was expecting to meet didn't materialize.

Gwena took a long drink of her pint and started again. "So, you're serious, aren't you? You and Antony?"

"Absolutely. You hadn't heard then?"

Gwena shrugged. "We don't keep in touch much. Different worlds, you know. Actually, I'm rather surprised he told you about me. I don't think he approves."

"Really? I got the idea he was rather proud of you."

"Humph." Gwena shrugged, but Felicity thought she saw a glimmer of pleasure in her companion's eyes.

Felicity took that as encouragement to continue, so she told Gwena about her uncle's heart attack and that Antony would be coming to Oxford in a few days with students on a study trip.

Again, the actress shrugged, seemingly unwilling to commit herself on family matters. "And what are you doing here?"

Felicity laughed and admitted to her own work on an ancient manuscript in a convent. "Sorry. I know that probably confirms everything you must be thinking about what an oddball I am. I would never have believed it of myself a year ago. Actually, I used to be quite normal." She paused, thinking she should say more. "But I'm happier now." Funny, she hadn't really thought about that before. She felt a wide smile split her face as the truth of her own statement dawned on her like the sun coming out.

She was thinking how she could explain that to her new acquaintance when she realized all of her companion's attention had turned to the man approaching their table with quick, energetic strides that could result in disaster should anyone carrying drinks be in his way. He was tall and thin with angular cheekbones, spiked hair and snapping black eyes. "Derrick!" Gwena rolled the double 'r' as if she were spelling the name.

He slid into the booth beside Gwena with a rapid motion and gave her a quick kiss. "Sorry I'm late. Thought we'd never finish at the mole. Allyn is an impossible perfectionist

Felicity blinked, trying to figure out what he was talking about, but before she could inquire he turned to her as if he hadn't seen her sitting there before. "Ah, and you are?" He gave her a cheeky grin that made her catch her breath.

Gwendolyn made the introductions, simply referring to Felicity as a friend and omitting that they would soon be sisters-in-law. "Derrick's in antiques. A recognized authority," she added with a note of pride in her voice. Then she turned back to him. "So how is the new exhibit coming?"

"Slow, but we'll get there. If I can convince Allyn to quit fussing."

As they continued to talk it became clear that 'the mole' was Derrick's term for the Ashmolean and that he was consulting with someone there on a new exhibit they were arranging. But Felicity was feeling increasingly like a gooseberry, she stood up. "Well, it's been lovely to meet you.

Both of you," she added quickly. "But I really must be going." They both made the appropriate responses. "I really enjoyed the show." She wanted to give Gwendolyn every opportunity to suggest another meeting or to send a message to Antony, but nothing was forthcoming so she made as graceful an exit as possible.

Felicity debated with herself all the way back on the bus. Should she tell Antony about her evening — about meeting his sister? He hadn't indicated there was an actual estrangement, but it was clear there was little warmth on Gwena's side. And she had shown no interest at all in their uncle's health. Would such news just add more to Antony's worries at the moment?

When she got back to her room she discovered that the issue was moot — at least for tonight. There were two missed calls from Antony and in the end he had sent her a text saying that it had been a long day and he was going to bed. Not even the final "luv A" did much to warm the chill inside her.

Seven

Felicity's ringing phone woke her the next morning. "Antony! I'm so glad you rang! It was awful not getting to talk to you at all yesterday. I hope your uncle is better. And you'll never believe who I met last night!" Oops, now she recalled her decision of the night before not to burden Antony with more family problems.

At least her outpouring made Antony chuckle. "Tell me anyway. I'm good at believing impossible things before breakfast."

So she did. In minute detail. Starting with the play. She wanted Antony to understand how it had all come about, just as if he had been there with her. "And then in the second act this absolutely startling figure came in through a high window and climbed down the bookcase and—"

"Wait a minute, what play were you seeing?"

"'Misalliance,' I told you."

"Gwendolyn. You met Gwena."

"How did you know?"

"Aunt Beryl follows her. She takes great pride in Gwen's career."

"Really?" That didn't sound like the aunt Felicity pictured in her mind.

"I know, I'm amazed, too. She told me she had always been so proud of both of us. I think she even toyed with using the 'L' word. She did go as far as saying she regretted not being softer with us as children, but that she was so terrified of not raising us properly. Now I realize what an enormous undertaking it must have been for her and Edward to be suddenly landed with the sole care of two young children."

"Antony, when you get here I think you really should try to see your sister. Tell her what Beryl said."

"Do you think she'd care?"

"I don't know. But she should know anyway. Oh, and I met her—boyfriend, partner, whatever he is. Derrick Mowbray. An antiques dealer—at least I think so. Does something with antiques. He was helping set up some exhibit—at the Ashmolean if I translated correctly. He reminded me of David Tennant's Dr. Who. Oh, you probably didn't see that," she added before he could ask. "Well, tall and thin and lots of nervous energy." She didn't bother telling him about the snapping eyes and the cheeky grin. "So how's Edward?" She wasn't quite sure why she wanted to get off the topic of Gwena's rather overwhelming friend.

"Stable again. On a new medication. I'm hoping to find someone to help Beryl with the caregiving when he comes home. I really need to get things sorted out here so I can get back to the college. Father Thomas has been more than generous about covering my lectures, but I need to get things organized before we come to Oxford on Wednesday."

Felicity wanted to prolong the conversation, just to stay connected with Antony. But she had delivered all her news—in considerable detail—and they both needed to get busy. "Love you, bye. Bye" was a very poor substitute for the embrace she would like to be sharing. "Bye," she said again, drawing out the last syllable.

Then he was gone and it was time to get back to work. The first page she set herself to translate went quickly. Well, as quickly as such work ever went. She did find one discrepancy which she simply couldn't sort out. Did Frideswide take refuge in Bampton as the account first said—she looked back at the original to be certain she had that correct—or was it Binsey as it said now? She read over the account of how pilgrims came to the holy well, which had sprung up in answer to Frideswide's prayers when the nuns there complained of having to fetch water from the distant Thames.

Felicity had long ago discovered that when she hit a brick wall, the only sensible thing to do was to walk away. Removing herself from a stressful situation would most times result in finding a resolution when she returned. So she put down her pencil and cleared off her desk. After all, she could just translate what it said. Some other scholar could sort out which version was correct. No need for her to worry over the answer.

Unfortunately, this time, attending the midday meal with the sisters hardly amounted to removing herself from a stressful situation. Even though the refectory was as quiet and as filled with late autumn sunshine as before, with simply the voice of the reading sister providing background for the gentle clink of cutlery, the stress caused by the continued mystery of Mother Monica's disappearance vibrated in the air. There was no need to ask whether the police had results on their DNA tests yet. Felicity was beginning to feel that even the catastrophic news of a match would bring relief by ending the uncertainty.

Back in her room Felicity decided simply to leave the Bampton/Binsey discrepancy unsolved for the moment and move on. She was rewarded by discovering that the concluding paragraph of this section of the document was written in present tense. This indicated to her that the account of Frideswide's bones being disinterred and laid with great ceremony in a reliquary by the prior of the Augustinian Priory, which had developed on the grounds of Frideswide's original monastery, was a contemporary account. This must have been the event that gave rise to the writing of this hagiography. And since it was known that this had taken place in 1180, the document could be dated with some precision. Surely this would add authenticity to the publication the Press planned to issue.

With renewed energy Felicity translated the final paragraphs recounting, in true hagiographic style, the stories of pilgrims flocking to the shrine, praying for and receiving miracles. That accomplishment put Felicity just over halfway through finishing her task. She pulled off her gloves and locked everything carefully away with a great feeling of satisfaction. She couldn't wait to tell Sister Gertrude. Surely she would welcome some scrap of good news to offset the convent's worries. And perhaps the scholarly nun could help her solve the discrepancy.

With a considerably lighter step than she had felt for some time Felicity strode along the path across the convent grounds, smelling the autumnal tang in the air and enjoying the crunch of leaves under her feet. Bronze and purple chrysanthemums bloomed in the beds on either side of the steps leading up to the door of the Press. Frank had bordered them with a tidy row of white stones that made them stand out from the scattered leaves. There was no answer to her knock, so Felicity tried the handle and found the door unlocked. If Gertrude were working in the back room she might not have heard her. Of course, if the sister were at prayers in the chapel she would simply have to delay the conference.

Coming in out of the bright afternoon sunshine Felicity blinked. Somehow the large workroom seemed fuller of clutter than before. And considerably less orderly. "Sister Gertrude," she called. She heard a scuffle, followed by a mutter in the back office, as if someone had dropped a file.

She hurried forward to help the nun pick up her papers, then stopped with a soft cry. It wasn't fallen papers, but Sister Gertrude herself. The nun was lying in a tumble of brown habit, scapular and veil.

"Sister Gertrude." Felicity knelt and reached to cradle the nun's head.

Felicity barely sensed the swift movement behind her until a searing pain shot through her head. She heard herself groan as she pitched forward across Gertrude's fallen body. Then the world went black.

Eight

At first, Felicity thought the tolling bells were muffled. Had someone died? She started to sit up, but the pain that stabbed through her head, forced her back on the pillow. Then she realized that the muffle was not on the bells but from the bandage on her head.

A thin nun, with skin as brown as her habit, slipped into her room. "You're awake. Excellent. Can you sip some water?" she asked in her soft Afro-Caribbean voice as she supported Felicity's head and held a straw to her lips.

The water was cool and fresh. Felicity hadn't realized her throat had been burning.

"Not too much."

The nun withdrew the straw and let her lie back. "We'll see how you get on with that. If it stays down you can have more."

The continued ringing of bells told Felicity that it was Sunday morning. Now things were starting to come back to her. She had gone into the Press Saturday evening... She touched her bandage gingerly. "What happened?"

"You were hit in the head. There was an intruder."

"Am I in hospital?"

"No, just in our infirmary. Dr. Patel who tends our infirm sisters said you just need rest. "I am Sister Magdalena, the infirmerer."

"Sister Gertrude?" Now she remembered seeing her lying on the floor.

Sister Magdalena pointed and Felicity turned her head with some caution. She had not even been aware of the bed beside her own.

Gertrude opened her eyes and managed a weak smile. "Who would think a convent could be such an exciting place? We're supposed to be a refuge from violence."

Felicity was relieved to hear the nun making a feeble joke. She must not have been injured too badly. "Do you have any idea what happened?"

Sister Gertrude started to shake her head, then stopped abruptly with a small moan. "Ooh, the doctor warned against quick movements. I see what he meant." She touched the bandage on the side of her head gingerly. "I went to the Press yesterday afternoon, thinking I'd get caught up on some correspondence. We get orders for our books from all over the world, you know. I heard noises in my office. When I went to investigate... Well, that's the last I remember."

"What do you think the intruder was looking for? Do you keep money in your office?"

"Not much. A few of the orders still come with enclosed cheques, but most people order online and pay by credit card now. There's never enough there to bother bashing someone over the head for."

"Anything else of value?"

"Everything in there is of scholarly value to us, but I can't imagine it having any monetary worth. I suppose the manuscript you're working on would be of the most interest. But only to a museum or specialized collector."

"Well, I'm finding it interesting," Felicity said, but I certainly haven't discovered anything another scholar would steal for. If that's what they were after I suppose it's fortunate it's in my cottage."

When the words were out she paused to consider whether that was truly fortunate, or whether she would now be in danger, but Sister Magdalena put an end to further speculation by giving her patients sips of cool water and insisting on quiet.

In spite of the pain in her head Felicity forced herself to think through the situation. She would dearly love to ring Antony and discuss everything with him, but she knew the unlikelihood of Sister Magdalena agreeing to let her use her mobile. She would have to try to puzzle it out for herself.

The intruder must have been looking for the manuscript. Her manuscript. But why would anyone possibly want to steal that? Had some startling fact in what she had translated just gone right over her head? Had she misinterpreted something? What might she have gotten wrong that could have provided a vital clue? But, hard as she thought, she could think of nothing. Even by academic standards it would hardly make a bestseller.

Could it have anything to do with the mockery of relics, if that was what it was? It seemed that the only connection was that the first one was found in Saint Frideswide's Chapel. And yet if it wasn't connected — wasn't that just too much of a coincidence? Lightening striking twice or rather, three times — in the same place?

And then there was still Mother Monica's continued absence...

She struggled against the drowsiness that threatened to overcome her. No. She needed to think. She would go back to that first night. Margaret Clitherow's hand replaced in the reliquary by... She shuddered. And had it been done while Felicity herself was no more than a few feet from the entrance to the chapel? Almost before her very eyes? Had she seen something as yet unrecognized as a clue to the desecration?

In her semiconscious state she forced her mind to watch the events of the evening again: Their driver Frank had at no time touched the reliquary. Nor had the frail Sister Anna, nor the cheery Sister Bertholde. Felicity herself had accompanied Dorcas to the chapel and no one else had entered while they were there. When they took their seats in the nave the chapel had still been in Felicity's line of sight. Not the altar with the relic, but certainly the entrance to the chapel. Had she seen anyone enter?

She played back through the service in her mind. Singing *Love Divine, All Loves Excelling*, then, after the opening prayers, the Old Testament reading—something from Isaiah, followed by the Psalm sung by the choir. She distinctly recalled looking into the chapel because the refrain "happy are they who trust in him" had seemed so appropriate for St. Frideswide.

The service had been the standard *Book of Common Prayer* Eucharist with which she had become so accustomed, that she could follow it without reference to the prayer book, with only the addition of prayers for "us to follow Frideswide's example of courage and faith." So she had allowed herself to look around, letting her eyes follow the soaring pale stone arches up to the intricate fan vaulted ceiling. No, she couldn't swear that no one could have slipped into and out of the chapel during one of her moments of abstraction.

But had even her subconscious mind registered any activity in the chapel? Had she seen anyone near the entrance—even from the corner of her eye? The cathedral had been full. White-robed servers had moved about as was usual. Perhaps during the Gospel procession? That must have been the moment. When everyone had been turned to the center aisle for the reading of the Gospel. It had been from Luke— about laying up treasure in heaven, not on earth.

If a tall, stealthy, white-robed figure had slipped into the chapel then she wouldn't have seen him. Felicity opened her eyes. Why did she say tall? *Had* she seen a figure enter the chapel? The figment was too ephemeral to grasp. Her eyes closed.

Besides, they had no evidence that it hadn't all occurred hours earlier before the reliquary was even delivered to the convent.

Pain in her head and emptiness in her heart washed over Felicity. She wanted Antony. She who had always been so independent and could manage anything on her own knew this was too much for her. A tear rolled from the corner of her eye and dampened her bandage.

Whoa, she called herself up. No way was she going to give into this. That bump on the head must have been worse than she thought to make her so maudlin. Painful as it was to move, she turned toward Gertrude. After all, she wasn't the only one who was undoubtedly aching and depressed. "Sister

Gertrude, tell me about yourself."

Gertrude's ready answer indicated that she welcomed the distraction. "I grew up on a farm in Lancashire. The eldest of a large family—seven of us. They called us the Von Trapps because we liked to sing. Ironic, I guess, since Maria started out to be a nun.

"But all I ever really wanted to do was read. And write. There was never much quiet in our house, but I could always find somewhere out in the fields. I loved the cows, too." She paused with a small smile of remembrance. "Especially one. Daphne. She would come to me when I read under a tree in the pasture. Sometimes I read aloud to her."

Six brother and sisters. Did she miss them, Felicity wondered. "Do you ever see your family now?" Living in such a large family must have been good preparation for living in a house of nuns.

"Eleanor, the sister just younger than me, visits occasionally, but they all have busy lives. I go home once a year. My parents are getting on but they're still on the farm."

"Go home?" Felicity was surprised.

"Yes, we have holidays. We're not strictly enclosed."

Felicity would have liked to ask more, but drowsiness was taking over.

She had no idea how much later it was when a movement in the room startled her awake. Her eyes flew open to see a large, rough, hand reaching for her. She opened her mouth to scream, but only a gasp came out.

"Ah, I'm so sorry. I didn't mean to waken you. You were sleeping so soundly I meant only to give you a blessing and slip out."

Felicity raised her gaze from the hand still hovering above her head to see a tanned, lined face above a clerical collar. The coarse hand withdrew, leaving her shaken.

"Sister Magdalena said you need rest." In spite of the roughness of his features the voice was strong and pleasant with an accent Felicity couldn't quite identify. "I'm Father

Benjamin, but please call me Ben. I said Eucharist for the sisters and thought I'd stop by and offer home communion, so to speak, to our invalids."

Felicity continued to stare. Was this true? Had the hand been merely making the sign of the cross over her? Surely it was so. He would hardly have strangled her with Sister Gertrude in the next bed. "You're the sister's chaplain?" Hadn't Sister Dorcas said it was a Father Alcuin?

"Only filling in today."

Did she trust this man enough to accept his ministry? She ran her eye up the length of his black cassock. He appeared to be tall, like her transitory image. Somehow, though, the white-robed figure she had conjured up had seemed thinner. But was that only because she had imagined it all?

"Father Ben is newly come to Pusey House." Sister Magdalena appeared at his shoulder.

"Just as a temporary assistant to their chaplain. I try to give a hand where I can."

Felicity smiled. Yes, that seemed to add up. She recalled Dorcas mentioning that Father Alcuin was chaplain at Pusey House. "Where are you from?"

"The Bahamas," he replied. Ah, that explained the accent and the tan. And perhaps the work-hardened hands? Perhaps missionary priests were called on to do field work, too? Felicity relaxed.

Father Benjamin slipped a stole over his black cassock and turned to pick up the pyx in which he carried the communion host. Felicity tried to sit up, but the effort made her head swim, so she received the body and blood of Christ lying down. It gave her an uneasy feeling—as if she were receiving last rites.

Nine

In spite of Felicity's impatience to be up and about, Sister Magdalena decreed another day of rest for her even though Gertrude had been allowed to return to work on Monday afternoon when the police requested her assistance in showing them exactly what had been disturbed by the intruder in the Press. Felicity hoped they would find something useful like fingerprints or a muddy footprint, but she gravely doubted the possibility. At least the police were taking the whole matter seriously.

Felicity wasn't certain whether her lightheaded feeling on leaving the infirmary was due to an after effect of her coshing, or the simple relief of having the bandage removed. She held her breath as she unlocked her cottage, praying there would be no sign of an intruder. She let her breath out in a slow stream at the sight of everything apparently exactly where she had left it Saturday evening. She did double check her locked drawer and shot a fervent *Thank you!* heavenward to see the manuscript still safely in its box.

And her mobile sitting on her desk. With a dead battery. She plugged it into her charger and headed to the shower. She felt almost wild to wash her hair — as if her assailant had left contamination. She winced when she whirled the luxurious mass of bubbles over the back of her head with too much vigor, but just letting the clear, warm water run over her head was heavenly.

She emerged a short time later glowing and invigorated. And ravenous. She went to her kitchen to find the heel of her granary loaf moldy, her milk off, and the tins of soup unappealing.

In spite of her desire to get back to her work, she decided to treat herself to lunch in town. She would go to her favorite coffee house where she and fellow students had spent many a happy hour debating the issues of the day, just as scholars had done on that site since it opened in the fourteenth century.

It was a lovely day, the sun sparkling with that unusual clarity that seemed to happen in England most often in late autumn, and Felicity felt a bounce returning to her step as she strode up the High. What joy to be alive and in Oxford. She walked down a small lane by the side of St. Mary the Virgin, crossed Radcliffe Square, then entered the Old Congregation House which claimed to be the University's oldest building. Felicity was greeted with the strains of a medieval melody played by a trio of musicians in the far corner. The lively tune echoed from the deeply vaulted ceiling as she crossed the room filled with people chatting, laughing and eating at small, round tables. She chose a table near one of the ornately mullioned windows that offered a stunning view of the wonderful, domed Radcliffe Camera where she had occasionally read in her student days.

Happy to be free of the invalid diet Sister Magdalena had insisted on, Felicity chose comfort food—a tuna mayonnaise jacket potato. Filling, cheap and nutritious. That and a cup of tea would do her nicely. Creature comforts provided for, now she longed for the lively companionship she had always enjoyed here in former days and had to stop herself looking around for long-ago classmates. Sadly, her mobile was still in her room charging, so she couldn't ring Antony as she longed to, either.

Instead, she turned her attention to the musicians in medieval garb playing recorder, crumhorn and drum. The clear notes helped fill the space Felicity would like to have filled by a companion. One very special companion.

She pushed the sides of her potato apart to let the steam escape before she attempted a bite and sat back in her chair to enjoy the music. When the piece came to an end the crumhorn player stepped forward. "M'lords and m'ladies, this being a most auspicious day in the history of our fair land, the day of Brave King Henry's triumph over the evil French," here the audience hissed, "at the Battle of Agincourt," Felicity joined in the ensuing cheers, "we are happy to bring you, from the Oxford Playhouse, Terry Fry, a.k.a. King Harry."

From the far side of the octagonal room an actor strode forward clad in a red and blue Plantagenet surcoat. "I thank you, brave fellows all." He bowed and swept the room with his arm. "We join in revels as others could have done on this very spot to celebrate Brave Harry's victory, for this very building in which you are enjoying your libations, was more than a century old when Harry so inspired his troops." Felicity gazed around her with a frisson of wonder as King Henry strode through the room proclaiming:

> *This day is called the feast of Crispian:*
> *He that outlives this day, and comes safe home,*
> *Will stand a tip-toe when the day is named,*
> *And rouse him at the name of Crispian...*

All chatting, eating and drinking stopped as everyone was drawn into the moment:

> *And Crispin Crispian shall ne'er go by,*
> *From this day to the ending of the world,*
> *But we in it shall be remember'd;...*

Felicity noticed several in the room mouthing the lines with Harry:

> *We few, we happy few,*
> *We band of brothers;...*

And now Felicity joined in repeating the words in her head:

And gentlemen in England now a-bed
Shall think themselves accursed they were not
here,
And hold their manhoods cheap whiles any speaks
That fought with us upon Saint Crispin's day.

Felicity applauded with the general cheering and thought
it a test of her recovery that the ringing noise in the vaulted
room didn't make her head hurt. She was just about to return
to her jacket potato when the young woman at a table across
from her turned around. Their eyes met with a startle of
recognition. Felicity was the first to smile and raise her hand in
a small wave.

Much to her surprise Gwendolyn picked up her coffee cup
and came over to her table. "Shall I join you? I came along
with Terry, but he has plenty of adoring public to keep his ego
stoked for the moment. Actors." She shook her head.

"But he was brilliant. What fun to celebrate St. Crispin's
day."

Gwen laughed. "More like St. Harry's day. Who was
Crispin, anyway?"

Felicity blinked. "Goodness, I have no idea. Must have
been an early Christian that died for his faith. Antony would
know." Just saying that made her miss him.

"I'm sure he would. Head chock full of useless
information. Some things never change."

"He was so pleased when I told him we'd met. Did I
mention that he's coming to Oxford tomorrow? Maybe we
could all get together?"

Gwena looked doubtful, but didn't refuse. "After you left
the pub the other night Derrick realized you must be the
woman who spotted that bloody awful foot at the Ashmolean.
What a beastly thing."

"Yes, it was, rather. Especially after..." Felicity didn't go
any further. No need to rehash all the appalling events of the
week.

"You must be incredibly observant to have noticed.
Although, I must say, I got the impression Allyn would have
been happier if you hadn't. It's made an awful fuss for the

museum."

"Allyn?" Felicity thought she had heard that name before.

"Allyn Luffington, the administrator that Derrick consults for sometimes. Very high up in archeological circles, I understand. Anyway, your 'find' has set them back days on preparing the Roman exhibit."

"Oh, dear."

"Police crawling all over the place. Plus they had to close the 'Treasures of Heaven' exhibit early. Well, only a few hours, but still — the director was not amused."

Felicity wondered if she should apologize.

Gwena took a final sip of her coffee and pushed the cup away. "Don't worry, they'll open on time. They always do. Allyn's a bit of an old woman if you ask me. Thinks the world owes him a living because his mind is on higher things. Still, the extra consulting fees are nice for Derrick. I'm on my way over there now. Want to come along?" She started to rise. "Oh, maybe you'd rather not go back?"

"It isn't that, although from what you say I might not be terribly welcome. I really should get back to work. I, er — didn't feel too well over the weekend, so I didn't get much accomplished." She stood and walked to the door with Gwena. "Would you like to give me your mobile number? I know Antony would love to see you. Maybe we could arrange something."

She thought her companion hesitated, but she dug in her bag and handed Felicity a small card. "Fine. Of course, I'm at the theatre every night." And with that she was off.

Felicity hated the frustrating wait for a bus to come along. She couldn't get back quickly enough to Fairacres — and to her mobile.

And then the interminable wait while the phone rang. And finally, the joy of hearing his voice. "Felicity! I've been mad with worry. Why didn't you ring? I tried and tried to leave a message but your phone wouldn't pick up. And those nuns never answer their phone. What's going on?"

She didn't know whether to laugh or cry. It was so wonderful to hear his voice she was too choked to speak.

"Felicity?" The tenderness in his voice that had been

accusing made all her pent-up emotion come out with a sob.

"Oh, Antony, it's been so awful. We still don't know anything about Mother Monica and someone tried to steal my manuscript—at least I think that's what they were doing—and I found Sister Gertrude on the floor and then they hit me over the head and Sister Magdalena insisted I rest and my phone lost its charge and, and… I…I miss you!"

Antony's laughter came out in a rush as if he had been holding his breath. "Well, that's all right, then." But it quickly changed to concern. "Hit you over the head? Felicity—what's going on?"

"I don't know. We think someone tried to steal the manuscript I'm translating. But there doesn't seem to be anything very important in it. But it must have something to do with those dreadful—things," she couldn't bring herself to say body parts, "in the reliquaries."

"Yes, but are you all right?"

"Yes, I'm fine. And so is Sister Gertrude. We're just all so awfully worried. The sisters are praying around the clock."

"Yes, a vigil. I'll ring the brothers at Kirkthorpe and ask for their prayers too. I'll be going back there this evening…"

"How's your uncle?" she interrupted.

"Stable again and Aunt Beryl seems to be back to her old self bossing everyone around, so I feel comfortable leaving. Anyway, I'll be driving the group down to Oxford tomorrow morning in the community's mini bus. Any chance you could get away and join us for lunch at Keble?"

"Yes! Absolutely!" She all but bounced with excitement at the prospect. "Oh, Antony, hurry! No, I mean, drive carefully, but—"

Again his warm, tenor laughter came across the way. "My darling, you have had a bad time. Of course I'll be careful. And you keep your door locked."

Felicity got a grip on herself and asked him about the tutorial group he was bringing with him. "How many?"

"Five."

"Who are they? Do I know them?"

"Marc and Brian," he began. They were fellow ordinands, she knew them well.

"Clare and Gareth are on the Northern Ordination Course."

She thought she might have seen them on occasion, but didn't really know them. NOC students only came to the community occasionally.

"And Sheila, a Companion of the Community," he concluded.

"Companion?"

"Like an oblate. They live normal lives in the world, but obey a rule and offer special support and prayer for the Community."

"Right. Sounds like an interesting mix." They chatted a bit longer — as long as Felicity felt she could reasonably keep him on the phone, then reluctantly said good-bye and disconnected, feeling a sudden emptiness in the room when she did.

Right, girl. To work, she ordered herself and turned to her desk — after double checking to ensure that her door was locked as Antony had ordered.

Sometime later she dropped her pencil, pulled off her gloves and pushed back from her desk with a sigh. Goodness, this part of the manuscript was an entirely different sort of instrument from the quite easily translated, somewhat flowery biography, the first part had been. Felicity had always preferred to work with documents that told a story and therefore had their own sense of logic. It made working out obscure meanings much easier if one had a vivid context in which to work. But this was quite another matter.

It might have an internal logic, but certainly no picturesque storyline. It was clear that it was a legal document. It seemed to be partly a will, part royal charter and part land survey. She had the sense that it would be much better off in the hands of a legal expert — which she made no pretense to being. But even if it were to be taken to a lawyer for interpretation, surely he or she would want to work from English. Felicity thought the best she could do would be to attempt a very literal, almost word-for-word transcription and then seek advice for interpreting subtle meanings.

What the production of such mind-numbing legalese

would mean to the Sisters' plans for publication would be another matter. That wasn't really her problem. It might be interesting, however, to include facsimile reproductions of the pages. Including a close up of the pattern stamped into the blob of black wax hanging from a ribbon affixed to the last page. Felicity reached out and touched the small round lump, turning it over to observe the smooth underside, then drew back guiltily, remembering that she wasn't wearing her gloves.

She took a break for a cup of tea and a few bending and stretching exercises, then dutifully returned to her task. The closely written lines of brown ink on the yellowed vellum continually threatened to swim before her eyes. It became clear that she was working on a charter granting land. How much land was twenty-five hectares, anyway?

And it was clear that the grant was to a religious house because it was in exchange for perpetual prayers for the soul of the grantor, for all his dead relatives and descendants in perpetuity, and for his burial. Just where this land was, was unclear to Felicity, but perhaps that would be explained on the next page. How she wished she had taken that seminar on Medieval Legal Latin that she had foregone in her undergraduate days.

Felicity was just gathering her willpower to force herself back to work when there was a rap at her door. She startled and instinctively moved to hide her papers when she heard Sister Dorcas's voice through the door. "Felicity, are you there?" Followed by another soft rap.

"Yes, Sister, just a minute." Still, she took the precaution of locking the document back in her drawer before opening the door. She wasn't certain whether that was sensible or paranoid, but she did it all the same.

One look at the nun's red-rimmed blue eyes and the grey hollows in her usually pink cheeks made Felicity want to take the small woman into her arms, but instead she merely stepped back, holding the door wide. "Come in. What is it?"

"The police were here. The DNA..."

"It matched Mother Monica's," Felicity finished with certainty. She had been expecting it. It was the only thing that made sense. She had even wished for a speedy answer. But the cessation of hope was a terrible blow. Both women sank into chairs. "I'm so sorry." It seemed all she could say.

After a moment of silence she asked, "Is there anything I can do? Did she have any family?"

Dorcas nodded. "She had an older sister. Lucille, I believe. She lives..." She made a helpless gesture. "Somewhere north. Loughborough, perhaps." She was quiet for a moment. "I must inform her. Of course, she knew Monica was missing. We rang her as soon as we knew something was wrong— hoping Mother was with her..." Her voice trailed off.

"Let me give you a cup of tea first." Felicity rose with the relief of finding something concrete to do.

But when Dorcas departed a short time later to perform her sad duty, Felicity was left with the echoing emptiness of her cottage. Alone with the finality of death.

Ten

Felicity awoke the next morning feeling the heavy weight of depression in her chest. She had never even met Monica and yet she missed her. Grieved for her, even. The beauty and orderliness of the convent, the discipline and devotion of the sisters, the wide esteem of the community and their far-flung ministry, all spoke of the competence of this woman who had directed it for so many years. And the evident grief of the sisters told her that the loss was more than institutional. The Sisters of the Love of God had lost more than an excellent administrator. They had lost a beloved mother.

But all that made it even harder to understand. Why would anybody do anything so horrible? And why do it to a nun who had lived in an enclosed order since the 1980's?

Felicity could only hope that her body might be discovered soon. The nuns would spend the day in prayer retreat, but the requiem mass would be delayed. Even the partial remains that were now held in the mortuary—Felicity shuddered at the thought—couldn't be released until the crime was solved.

And then an even worse thought occurred to Felicity. She could only hope Monica was dead. The idea of her being held somewhere and tortured was too gruesome to contemplate. And there had been no ransom note or anything of that sort, so surely this wasn't a kidnapping.

One thing was clear to Felicity, though, she couldn't

possibly stay in her room alone. She looked at her clock. Just after ten. No sense in trying to ring Antony. He would be on the road.

Driving to Oxford. To her. She smiled and hugged herself at the thought. She had given him the sad news last night and felt the comfort of his prayers for Monica's soul across the miles. His prayers would be with her today. And in less than three hours he would be with her in person.

But there was the rest of the morning to be gotten through. She only knew one other person in Oxford. She hoped it wasn't too early to be ringing an actress who had had a performance the night before, but she needed to talk to someone. The sense of the sisters gathered in their communion of grief, so near and yet so separate, made her feel more alone than ever. Dorcas had assured Felicity that she was perfectly welcome to remain in her cottage—as a matter of fact, they very much hoped she would be able to finish her project—but did she think she would be able to fix her own dinners, too?

After three rings Felicity wondered whether or not she should disconnect her call, when a rather sleepy voice answered. "Oh, Gwena, I am sorry. I was afraid I was ringing too early. It's just that I've had some rather terrible news and I'm feeling—" what word should she put on it? She decided on: "Isolated."

"Ah, you poor old thing." Felicity was surprised at the note of sympathy in Gwena's voice. She wouldn't have been surprised if the woman had hung up on her.

It might have been better if Gwen had told her off because the commiseration from a voice that sounded oddly like Antony's made her long for his arms even more. But then she realized she didn't want sympathy. She wanted action. "No, actually, I'm all right. I was just thinking what I need is a good jog. Would you be interested in joining me for a lap around Christ Church Meadow?"

Gwendolyn's silence made Felicity realize what a stupid suggestion that probably was. But then, to her surprise, Gwena agreed. "Ohhh, I'm such a slug, but I've been saying I needed to exercise more. All right, I'll meet you at the entrance to the Broad Walk in half an hour."

Just time for Felicity to pull on her red and grey jogging suit and running shoes and catch a bus.

She arrived before Gwena, so chose a grassy spot beside the walk to do her stretches. She was on her second set of lunges when she noticed a tall man in a blue tracksuit leaning against a low wall. Had he been watching her? She started to turn away when he smiled at her. For some reason that made her even more uncomfortable. She turned away, then realized that she hadn't pulled her flowing blond tresses back since emerging from the shower that morning. With the golden sun shining on the tangled mess she supposed she shouldn't be surprised if someone stared. She turned away, fishing in her pocket for a scrunchy. By the time Gwena arrived she had tidied her hair the best she could and had finished her warm-ups. And the man had moved on.

"Sorry it took me so long," Gwena greeted her. "Looks like you're all ready to go. Don't let me make you wait I'm sure you'll lap me, anyway."

"No, no, go ahead and warm up. I'm not a great runner at all." Besides, companionship was her primary objective this morning.

Actually, Gwena was in much better condition than she made out, and had no trouble at all keeping up with Felicity's easy jog, in spite of having shorter legs. "Sorry you've had bad news," Gwena said as they turned into the tree-lined path along the Cherwell.

Felicity tossed her head back in a gesture that always reminded her to keep her courage up, then slowed her pace slightly and told her companion about Mother Monica.

"How absolutely dreadful. Do you think it has anything to do with the incident at the Ashmolean? Oh, of course it does. You mean that was her foot? A nun's?" Before Felicity could answer she added, "I wonder if Derrick knows about that? I hope it won't delay his work more." Then her hand flew to her mouth. "Oh, sorry — that sounded crass."

"No, it's okay. That's one of the beastly things about murder — the ripples. It's just awful for everyone."

"How is your work going?"

Gwena's question spurred Felicity to tell her about getting

hit over the head and spending the weekend in the infirmary. "I'm making progress on the translation, but it's slow. I suppose I should be working right now, only I couldn't bear staying in that locked room by myself. We have to be so careful now, because we think the intruder... Anyway, he might have been looking for the manuscript I'm working on."

"Is it important?"

"Wouldn't have thought so. Although the part I'm working on now appears to be a legal document. But ancient. So I can't see how anyone but academics would be interested."

She might have said more, but at that moment they met a jogger coming from the other end of the meadow. Felicity probably wouldn't have looked at him if Gwena hadn't raised her hand in greeting. Felicity jerked her head around to look back. It *was* him. It was the man who had leered at her earlier. "You know him?"

"That's Allyn. The man Derrick works for occasionally."

Felicity increased her speed to put even more distance between the man and herself. They continued on with no more talking. They were approaching the boatyard on Folly Bridge when Felicity felt her mobile vibrate. She pulled it out of her pocket and dropped to her slowest pace. "Antony! Are you here? Guess who I'm jogging with."

When she rang off she turned to Gwena. "I didn't plan this very well. I'm supposed to meet Antony for lunch and here I am all sweaty. It will take ages to go back to Fairacres on a bus."

"You can shower at my flat and I can loan you a clean shirt. My trousers would be too short for you, but yours should be fine."

"That's great, thanks. And Antony said he hoped you'd come along for lunch."

At first she thought Gwena was going to refuse, but after a lengthy pause she agreed. "Are you sure you wouldn't rather have lunch alone together?"

"We'll hardly be alone. He's eating in hall with his seminar students."

Felicity thought Gwena seemed relieved that it wasn't to be an intimate threesome with the brother she hadn't seen for so long.

When they arrived at the porter's lodge of Keble College, both women fresh from their showers and ravenous for lunch, Felicity was pleased at how animated and relaxed the other woman seemed. "This must be like coming home for you," Gwena said, looking at the intricately patterned red brick buildings. "You studied here, didn't you?"

Felicity nodded. "It was great. Life-changing, really. I never considered going back to America after that. Well, never very seriously for very long, anyway." There had been moments of blinding frustration when she wondered what in the world she thought she was doing on this side of the all-too-wide pond. And yet, this little island held everything in life for her. Especially since she'd met Antony. Felicity gave their names to the porter and was given the meal tickets Antony said would be there for them.

They walked through the arched passage and emerged at the edge of a wide green quad surrounded by Victorian Gothic buildings. "Sheesh, you must have felt like you were at Hogwarts."

Felicity laughed. "I read somewhere the buildings were intended to make a statement of high Anglican principles. It was a bit Alice in Wonderlandy for me, but going to Kirkthorpe was really falling down the rabbit hole."

They followed the walk beside the vibrant green grass, the exact color of the jacket Gwena wore, toward the college hall in the far corner of the quad and, in company with several others, went up the wide staircase to the first floor. Gwena took one look at the length of the dining hall filled with rows of long tables and benches leading to the arched stained glass window at the far end. "Impressive." She raised her eyebrows.

"One of the guiding principles of the founders—" Felicity explained, "was for the whole college to eat together in fellowship and economy. I think Keble is the only one of the colleges that still has formal hall every night of the week."

"True to their founders' principles, hm?"

Felicity was about to add that they remained true to their founder's high church ideals as well, but then she caught sight of the head of dark hair above a wide ivory brow that she had been looking for. Impervious to the looks from those around her, she cut a line through the others waiting to enter, and flung herself into Antony's arms.

He hugged her, then pushed her away with a wide smile. "I'm happy to see you, too." Then he sobered and put a gentle hand to the back of her head. "Are you sure you're all right?"

"Fine yes." She indicated her casual attire. "Even went jogging this morning, and I managed to talk Gwena into accepting your invitation." She beckoned across the anteroom for Gwendolyn to join them.

Antony's face was a study of hesitant pleasure. After a moment he opened his arms almost as wide for his sister as he had for his fiancé.

Gwendolyn returned the hug just a bit gingerly, then looked at him, shaking her head. "Just the same Squib." She sounded pleased at the discovery. "I wasn't sure how happy you'd be to see me."

"Why ever not?" Before she could list any of the things that had separated them over the years, he hurried on, "besides the fact that you're my only sister, my time with Aunt Beryl and Uncle Edward have rather underscored the importance of family ties to me. I think I owe you an apology for not getting in touch more often." He held his hands out to both women and they entered the hall to take seats on a long bench across from his waiting students.

In spite of her assurances of her well-being, Felicity found the hubbub of the busy room a bit much. She longed to talk to Antony about Mother Monica, but the general activity of the hall and the business of introductions and getting acquainted, made serious conversation impossible. Felicity greeted her fellow ordinands, Marc and Brian, thinking as she often did when she saw them together at college, what a contrast they made, the lanky, loose-limbed Marc, his brown hair cut so short he looked almost bald, and the stocky, out-going Brian with his almost white-blond hair.

When Antony introduced Clare and Gareth, Felicity reached across the table to shake hands. "I'm so pleased to meet you, Clare." She looked at the woman's vibrant red hair, falling in waves to her shoulders. "I've seen you at the college, but I don't think we've met before."

"Yes, on NOC. We only get to Kirkthorpe once every half-term. I would love to be there more often, but this way I can continue teaching RE."

Religious Education, Felicity translated. Not a course offered in American public schools, that was for sure. "Where are you from?" She asked.

Clare replied that she was from Hull. Felicity turned to Gareth. "And you're on the Northern Ordination Course, too, aren't you? Where are you from?"

"Newcastle," Gareth, whom she judged to be in his mid-forties, replied, then explained that he was an accountant, but had been a licensed reader in his parish church for years and now felt he wanted to move into the full-time ministry.

Antony presented the last of his charges, the plump, cheerful grey-haired Sheila who said she had recently retired from nursing and now wanted to be a hospital chaplain. Felicity recalled that Antony had said Sheila was a Companion of the Transfiguration and would have liked to ask her more about it, but at that moment the servers entered to set plates of gammon, chips and peas in front of the diners.

After pudding—treacle tart for Antony, a fresh pear for Felicity—Antony invited both of his companions to come along to his first lecture. Felicity wouldn't have considered missing it, but Gwena looked doubtful. Antony smiled. "Don't worry, Sis. It's a history lesson, appropriate even for a secular tourist. Not a sermon."

"So what's the topic?" Her question was accompanied with a small smile that indicated assent to his invitation.

"The seminar is on the Oxford Movement, but today I'm starting with the story of the martyrs." She rolled her eyes at him, but he was quick to point out that she could hardly suggest a more appropriate topic for the venue. "And, it'll be on location, so to speak."

"Martyr's Memorial?" Felicity asked.

"Got it in one." Antony gave her hand a squeeze that made even her toes tingle. Goodness, what a basket case she was. They had only been apart a week.

As it turned out, they started around the corner from the

memorial in the middle of the Broad, across from the gate of Balliol College, where a brass plaque embedded in stone marked the site of Cranmer's execution. Antony encouraged their small group to gather around, although Sheila, the senior member of the group, who walked with a cane, seemed uneasy about standing in the middle of the street until Antony pointed out that it was a pedestrian precinct. "It's quiet enough now," Antony began, then looked up with a smile at a pair of passing cyclists, their short black gowns flowing behind them.

"But on 21st March in 1556 it was filled with the cries of an angry mob, with eye-stinging smoke, and with the stench of burnt flesh." In spite of the grisly subject, Felicity felt herself relax at the pleasure of once more entering into one of Antony's vivid lectures, which she had come to love as much for the information, as for the pleasure of listening to his voice.

Antony took his place, standing squarely on the marked stone. "The flames crackled and leapt at Cranmer's feet," Antony began his narration. "'In all time of our tribulation...in the hour of death...Good Lord, deliver us...'"

"The bundle of faggots nearest the stake caught fire."

"'That it may please thee to forgive our enemies, persecutors, and slanderers, and to turn their hearts; We beseech thee to hear us, good Lord...'"

Antony stretched out his right hand as history recorded that Cranmer had done. "All he had to do was lean forward just a little and it would be in the searing flames.

"'O Lamb of God: that takest away the sins of the world; Grant us thy peace.

O Lamb of God: that takest away the sins of the world; Have mercy upon us...'"

"He had given that prayer to the church. Now Thomas Cranmer could only plead for such deliverance for himself."

Antony looked around the little circle of intent faces and gave a somewhat rueful smile. "Well, that's the way I like to think it might have been. That the author of *The Book of*

Common Prayer might have found solace in his own prayers in those last awful moments. But I've started at the end of the story. Let's go back around the corner and start at the beginning." He led the way back to Magdalen Street, past the church of St. Mary Magdalen, fondly called St. Mary Mag's, and on to stand in clear view of the Victorian Gothic Martyrs Monument.

Standing under the golden autumn trees beside the church, Clare cocked her head to the side, letting her long red hair fall across her shoulder. "It rather looks like the steeple of a cathedral," she remarked to Gareth, her fellow from the Northern Ordination Course.

Felicity turned to grin at her. "Rumor has it that a popular student jape in years past was to tell tourists it was the top of an underground church and send them down those stairs over there." She pointed, then added. "They lead to public toilets." She turned back to Antony. "Sorry. Not very respectful. Of course, it was just a rumor."

Antony smiled, then returned the lecture to its proper tone by pointing out the statues of Cranmer and his fellow martyrs Hugh Latimer and Nicholas Ridley before returning to his lecture. "The story began a quarter of a century before the martyrdom with one of those seeming happenstances that change history. Cranmer was a fellow of Jesus College, Cambridge, when the town was visited by a pestilence in the summer of 1529.

"Cranmer removed to the home of a relative at Waltham Abbey in Essex. At the same time, Henry VIII, in perplexity over the Great Matter of his divorce suit, likewise moved to Waltham. Henry's two chief agents in the divorce matter, both old college friends of Cranmer, accompanied the king and were lodged in the same house with Cranmer. In the course of the long evening conversations that naturally ensued, Cranmer suggested that the most efficient way for Henry to receive the assurance he sought of the invalidity of his first marriage, was to put the matter before the divines of Oxford and Cambridge universities, rather than waiting for the pope to rule."

Antony's ordinand charges, especially Marc and Brian,

were taking careful notes, but Sheila, who would not be required to produce an essay on the subject, took out her camera and snapped several pictures as the story continued:

"Henry was delighted with the scheme and he was delighted with Thomas Cranmer. Henry appointed Cranmer ambassador to Rome, and then to Germany, before making him Archbishop of Canterbury. It is probably a considerable understatement to say that Cranmer was shocked by the appointment. Not the least of his reasons being that while abroad he had married his second wife, his first having died some 15 years earlier in childbirth. Cranmer accepted the appointment with reluctance hoping that Henry would change his mind.

"Henry did not change his mind. Thomas Cranmer was consecrated Archbishop of Canterbury on 30 March 1533. And so Cranmer set about shaping the Church of England—a job which required careful balance because Henry desired as little change as possible, especially in worship forms. Cranmer began by promoting the publication of an English Bible, 'The Great,' which was made compulsory in all parish churches. Then in 1544 the king issued a mandate for prayers to be in English. This was the perfect assignment for Cranmer. He set about translating feast day prayers from the Latin, giving rein to his poetic instincts by taking considerable artistic license with the translations.

"The archbishop was that most unusual of creatures—a man much in the king's favor who never seems to have sought anything for himself and who was willing to plead for those who fell from favor, including Sir Thomas More and Anne Boleyn. Of course, his pleas fell on deaf ears. Henry liked Cranmer, listened to him and protected him, but allowed him no political influence whatsoever. When the end came for Henry, however, the king turned to Cranmer on his deathbed."

Felicity felt Gwena fidgeting beside her. It made her think of those early days in her relationship with Antony, before she came to appreciate the value of his history lessons—both for the sake of understanding what had happened to bring society to where we are now and, often, for the sake of helping to solve the crime they were working on. But, of course, that wouldn't be the case today. Fortunately, she and Antony weren't involved in trying to solve Monica's murder, so she could merely enjoy Antony's account for its own sake. She smiled encouragingly at Gwena as Antony went on to tell about Cranmer's work under Henry's son Edward VI as he revised church services in the tongue of the people and wrote *The Book of Common Prayer*, giving the Church of England the beauty of its liturgy.

"And then it all changed. Edward died in 1553 and Cranmer, much against his will, was dragged into politics. Cranmer was the last of the council to sign the document for the Protestant Lady Jane Grey to succeed to the throne. But he did sign. And thereby signed his own death warrant as surely as he signed Jane's. Her nine days' reign ended on 19 July. On 3 August Mary Tudor entered London in triumph. On 5 September, Cranmer was committed to the Tower. Along with his old friends Nicholas Ridley, Bishop of London, and Hugh Latimer, former Bishop of Worcester." Antony gestured again to the statues standing high above their heads just below the pinnacle of the monument.

"Nicholas Ridley possessed one of the finest academic minds of the English Reformation. He was chaplain to Archbishop Cranmer, then to King Henry and Edward made him Bishop of London.

"Hugh Latimer was perhaps the greatest preacher in the land. As royal chaplain, it had fallen his task to preach the funeral sermon of Jane Seymour, Henry's favorite wife and mother of the future King Edward.

"But all their achievements only counted against them when Mary Tudor ascended to the throne of England, determined to purge her nation of heresy.

"In March of 1554 'the late Archbishop of Canterbury,' as Cranmer was then styled, and Latimer and Ridley were taken from the Tower of London to Oxford 'so that their opinions might be the more thoroughly sifted in disputation with men of learning.' Ironically, twenty-five years earlier Cranmer had suggested just such a panel sit in judgment on the issue of Henry's divorce.

"And so we arrive at Oxford." Antony swept the scene before them with an arc of his arm. "The three were incarcerated in the Bocardo prison, which was just down the street from here— where I shall be continuing my lecture tomorrow. But that's enough for your first day." He grinned at his hearers who had the honesty to nod in agreement as they returned notebooks to rucksacks and began talking among themselves as to how to spend the rest of the afternoon. Brian proposed a spot of punting, which Clare enthusiastically endorsed. But Sheila excused herself to explore bargains in the covered market.

Antony turned to Gwena. "Thank you for coming. I hope that wasn't too eye-glazing for you. It really is so good to see you. Do you want to get a cup of tea or something and catch up?"

Felicity was surprised at Gwen's almost trapped rabbit look. She couldn't understand why the woman would be nervous of spending time with her brother, but Gwen shook her short cap of pale hair. "No, I, er—need to get back to the theatre. It was great to see you. I'll catch you later." She skittered away.

Felicity felt, more than saw, Antony's shoulders slump as his sister was swallowed in a crowd on the pavement. She linked her arm in his. "I'll take you up on that cuppa. The Eagle and Child is practically across the street. Not sure they do tea, though..."

Arm in arm they walked up Magdalen Street toward St. Giles. They were waiting to cross Beaumont Street when Felicity caught sight of a bright head of blond hair above a vivid green jumper sprinting up the steps toward the column-lined porch of the Ashmolean. She stifled the impulse to point out Gwen to the brother she had just lied to, but Felicity felt a sudden cold stab in the pit of her stomach. Did this mean she couldn't trust the woman she had been coming to consider a newfound friend?

Eleven

The next morning Felicity still had no answers to any of her questions, even after the lovely afternoon-into-evening she had spent with Antony at the historic pub. She had told him, in far more detail than she had on the phone, about her shocking discoveries in the reliquaries and all she knew about Monica. They stayed on to order plates of fish and chips and Felicity explored her questions about the document she was translating, but, as good as it was to share it all with Antony, and as comforting as his thoughtful suggestions were, nothing made any more sense to her than it had before.

One thing was certain, though, today she was determined to finish her translating work. And hopefully, in time to meet Antony and his students for his next lecture in the late afternoon. Antony's students were scheduled to spend the morning on research in the Bodleian Library, so she would follow their scholarly example.

She downed a quick breakfast and set to work. At least today she knew she would be facing a tangle of legal technicalities, so she approached it with some mental preparation as she pulled on her gloves and set to work. By midmorning she had sorted out the general outline, determining that the document laid out terms of who, what, when, where and why in rather grandiose Norman Latin along with a sprinkling of Old French, in which she was not the least bit fluent, having had only an introductory class years ago. Still, she managed to slog through it all.

Three hours later she dropped her pencil and gave her wrist three sharp flips to relax her hand. Okay, this was the best she could do. It seemed that in the 8th year of the reign of Stephan of Blois, Radulphus, Baron of Anstey, liege subject to Robert, son of Count Robert, the 2nd earl of Leicester, and Justicar of England, granted 25 hectares of land, bordered by the River Soar on the east, the Fosseway on the west, Leysway to the north and Woodgate to the south, to the Abbey of St. Mary de Pratis, with all rights and appurtancies (was that a real word? she wondered) thereunto in perpetuity according to the aforesaid conditions with reversionary interest should the aforesaid contingencies occur.

About the only word Felicity recognized in all of that was the Earl of Leicester. Frideswide was supposed to have married Algar of Leicester. Was it possible that this Robert, Earl of Leicester, could have been descended from Algar? Well, from Algar's father, or perhaps a brother, since if the story was correct, Algar died unwed. But apparently the land actually belonged to Radulphus who owed allegiance to the earl—or to his son. It was very confusing. Wasn't land often granted to subjects who performed well in battle? Perhaps Radulphus had been rewarded by Robert.

But there were 500 years between Frideswide's story and this land grant. Yet there must be some connection for the manuscripts to have been kept together in the cartulary of the Order of the Holy Paraclete. It was a slim enough connection, but she was certain of the correctness of her translation—as far as it went. And that was the end of her responsibility.

Still, she was curious. She had noticed a history of religious houses in England among the books in the case by the door of her sitting room, so she pulled the volume off the shelf and turned to the index in the back. Ah, here it was—The Abbey of St. Mary de Pratis, commonly called Leicester Abbey. The article showed a picture of the foundations of the abbey that had been excavated in the 1920's and 30's. Apparently the site was now in the center of a park. Sure enough, on the banks of the River Soar. Good, that much checked.

Hmm, the abbey grew to be the wealthiest religious establishment in Leicestershire, being granted numerous royal privileges such as exemption from paying tithes on certain lands. In spite of this, however, the abbey fell into financial difficulties and became debt ridden. That rang a bell. She looked back at her notes to be certain she remembered the wording correctly. Yes. Maintaining solvency was one of the requirements listed for the monastery "continuing in good fettle."

Oh, here was an interesting bit—In 1530 Cardinal Wolsey died at the abbey, whilst travelling south to face trial for treason. Almost unfair, that, she always thought—for Wolsey to die a natural death after all his corrupt machinations, including promoting the execution of Sir Thomas More.

Felicity returned the book to its shelf and turned to her desk, where she carefully replaced the manuscript in its box. She was pleased to have finished the job she set out to do. She was unhappy, however, that she couldn't offer a more definitive explanation of the whys and wherefores of the attached charter. And, most surprising of all, she felt a tiny hollow of loss at leaving the project.

Still, she firmly placed her translation on top of the box and set out to find Sister Gertrude hoping she wouldn't be enclosed in the chapel. To her surprise, she found the sister at her desk in the press. "Sister Gertrude, I didn't really expect to find you here."

The nun removed her glasses and rubbed her eyes. "Sister Dorcas said we should return to our duties and do our best to keep our normal schedule. It may still be some time until matters are—cleared up. Of course we'll maintain our prayers, but work is part of our calling as well."

Felicity nodded. "Very wise." She held out the box. "I've finished."

Gertrude's features brightened. "Oh, excellent!"

Felicity pulled back slightly. "Well, I don't know that it's so excellent. I know you wanted to publish it, but I'm not sure how worthwhile it will be." She told the editor about the rather standard hagiography and the confusing legal document. "I think you should have someone like a legal historian look at the charter. They might be able to make a lot more sense out of it than I could."

Gertrude replaced her glasses and looked over Felicity's carefully written sheets. "Oh, you've done a fine job. It reads very well. I can't thank you enough. Yes, I think having a specialist consult on the legal document would be an excellent idea."

Felicity was relieved to have the responsibility moved to a superior academic. Her own thoughts seemed too silly to voice, and yet—"I did wonder. I don't suppose this land grant could possibly still have any force? I mean today? I wouldn't suggest such a thing, except—"

"Except there must be some reason you and I were both hit over the head?" Gertrude finished for her.

Felicity sighed with relief that this very sensible sister seemed to give credence to her wild imaginings. "Well, there must have been some motive." She was about to get up her courage to suggest Gertrude might want to mention this to the police when Sister Bertholde entered in her serene way.

Felicity hadn't been with her since the night of St. Frideswide's festival and she was struck again at the grace of the Jamaican woman as the folds of her brown habit seemed to fall around her more easily than those of the other nuns. Her eyes lit up when she saw Felicity. "Oh, good. I am happy to find you here. I was to seek you next. Sister Dorcas has asked that you join her." She gestured to them with long, slender fingers. "Mother Monica's sister, a Mrs. Knighton, has arrived. Sister knows all the sisters will want to offer their condolences and since you," she turned to Felicity, "were the first..."

"Yes, absolutely. I would very much like to meet her."

Lucille Knighton stood ramrod straight in the middle of the parlor. Her navy blue suit and coiffured iron grey hair made her look every inch the business executive she was telling Dorcas she had been before retiring to work fulltime for the charity Age Concern. Dorcas introduced the newcomers and Lucille turned to Felicity. "Ah, yes, you found Monica's hand. What a shocker. Awful for you."

Felicity murmured her agreement, amazed at the woman's

straightforwardness. Felicity considered herself a no-nonsense person, but she couldn't have spoken that without hesitation. "I'm so sorry for your loss."

"Yes, thank you. Most kind. Still, nothing to do but get on with it. Not that there's much we can get on with as it is. A hand and a foot. And I gather the police are less than useless."

"Um, can we offer you a cup of tea before we go to her room? The police are finished there, so you are quite free to take any of her things. Not that she had many personal possessions, of course."

"No, you don't go in for that sort of thing do you? Of course, Pooky never did, even as a girl." She pronounced it 'gel' with a hard 'g'. "Otherworldly, I suppose you'd say, although some would say impractical." Felicity got the clear message that Lucille was among that number.

"No, thank you, I won't stop for tea. Things to do, you know. If you could just box it all up for me when you find it convenient. I can't imagine she had anything worth keeping, but I suppose it would be nice if there's some memento I could put aside for her son—just in case he ever surfaces. Which I don't suppose he will. Hasn't been heard from for yonks. And undoubtedly just as well. As useless as his father he was."

Felicity blinked. "Son? Mother Monica had a son?" She noticed that Dorcas looked as surprised as she was. The Mother Superior had a past?

"Oh, yes. One of the more quixotic things she did—worse even than joining a—" Lucille Knighton looked pointedly at the women around her in habits. "Yes, well. I told her that wispy Frenchman she married wouldn't amount to anything. Of course, I was right. Died of pneumonia before the boy was born."

"I'm so glad you've told us," Dorcas said. "We must do everything we can to locate him. What's his name? Perhaps there will be something in the files."

"Leroy, she called him."

"Right. Leroy Simmeon, that would be, then. And do you have any idea where he might be?"

Lucille looked slightly scandalized that she should be expected to know. "Not in England, I should think. Australia, maybe? Something do-gooding. Like his mother. Can't remember what. But that was ages ago." She paused. "Could be dead, I suppose. Who knows?"

"Yes, well, I'll give his name to the police. Perhaps they can do something to find him. He really should be notified."

Lucille waved her hand as if to brush the whole matter away. "I really must be getting on."

Dorcas led her from the room.

Felicity would have liked to consider what this new piece of information might mean. Was it beyond consideration that a long-lost son might have abducted his mother? Well, not possible, of course, if he wasn't even in England. But Lucille was only guessing, wasn't she?

And what about Lucille? She seemed like someone who would be capable of almost anything she considered necessary. But for what motive? Surely the Mother Superior had owned nothing that anyone would kill to inherit. Could she have known something someone would kill to keep from being found out? And if that something had anything to do with the manuscript, did Felicity, without realizing, now know of it? And would the murderer at least think she knew?

Twelve

With the knot in her stomach getting tighter by the moment Felicity fled from the convent and almost ran to the bus stop. It was nearly time for Antony's lecture and she couldn't wait to tell him of this new development. And relax in the security of being with him.

When she arrived at St. Michael's, however, it was clear that there would be no chance for a private conversation until later. Antony's eager students were gathered around him in the narthex of the church. And to her surprise Gwendolyn was also there.

Gwen shrugged and gave a small, rueful smile when Felicity expressed her surprise. "Thought I might as well come along and hear the rest of the story."

Antony gave them both a little wave and a welcoming smile, then stood on the bottom tread of a flight of stairs leading into the tower behind him. "As I mentioned yesterday, this is essentially the site of the Bocardo prison where the martyrs were held. The tower is Saxon, from around the year 1000 and is considered to be Oxford's oldest building. The name of the prison was a pun, bocardo being a term in medieval logic for a syllogism from which it is particularly difficult to escape. The prison was pulled down in 1772 and all that remains today is the door which you'll see on the landing about halfway up the tower." He pointed upward, then moved aside to let the others ascend the stairs for a closer look.

Felicity climbed the tall, square tower. About halfway up she came to a landing and stopped to view a door of thick, dark wooden planks with heavy iron hinges and a formidable lock. Indeed, it looked like the door to a medieval torture chamber. Felicity shivered.

She read from the large brass plaque affixed to top of the door: "This door was at the entrance of a cell in the old city gaol Bocardo, called the Bishops Room, wherein the Bishops Cranmer, Ridley and Latimer were confined..."

Gwena suggested they go on up for a view of the city. Felicity followed, wondering if she should mention having seen Gwen enter the Ashmolean yesterday, but when they got to the top she realized how little she wanted to promote a confrontation, so she turned her attention to the stunning view of spires, pinnacles and turrets. Surely one of the most splendid skylines in the world.

When they descended Antony was marshaling his group to lead them around to the site of the next scene in the story: the Church of St. Mary the Virgin, whose graceful spire Felicity had just been admiring from the top of the tower. Antony had them gather before the baroque wrought iron entrance gates and look up at the statue of the Virgin and child standing high over the arched doorway. "This is the 'Virgin Porch' which was added in 1637 with the support of Archbishop Laud. Erecting a statue of Mary caused a scandal and was one of the charges brought against Laud by his Puritan opponents at his trial. Those of you with very good eyesight may be able to spot the bullet holes in the statue made by Cromwell's troopers. All that belongs to another sad period of history, but I mention it as a reminder that wrongdoing falls on every side."

Felicity smiled, thinking of Antony's devotion to ecumenical causes. These accounts of sectarian violence must be particularly painful to him. She started to say something to that effect to Gwena, then stopped, surprised by the smug look on her friend's face. She had no time to ponder what it meant, though, because Antony was leading them inside the building and across the black and white tile floor into the nave. Pale stone Gothic arches lined each side, leading to a carved stone pulpitum supporting the organ. Antony suggested they take seats in the dark wooden pews.

"St. Mary's Church was where the Marian trials were held." He paused. "Maybe I should make it clear that the term refers to the Queen of England, not the Queen of Heaven. This church served as the center of university ceremony from the twelfth century until the building of the Sheldonian Theatre in the seventeenth century. In medieval times, bells from St. Mary's tower mustered students to the all-too-frequent Town and Gown affrays. Queen Elizabeth I attended lectures here and herself delivered a Latin speech. In 1733, John Wesley preached one of his most famous sermons, and John Henry Newman was vicar here throughout his time of leading the Oxford Movement." Pens scratched as students made notes. Antony smiled. "Don't worry. You'll get more about the Oxford Movement in another lecture. I'll just also mention that C. S. Lewis preached his 'Weight of Glory' sermon before one of the largest congregations ever assembled here."

Gwena, sitting next to Felicity, seemed hardly aware of her brother's recital of historical events, but became oddly alert when he returned to the account of the trial. Felicity couldn't understand her seeming fascination with history of the religion she had so outspokenly rejected.

"On the day the trials began, Oxfordians knew they were in for an historic moment and made the most of it. Thirty-three commissioners assembled from Oxford and Cambridge to sit in judgment on Cranmer and his fellows. Those from Cambridge who had failed to bring their scarlet academic robes with them, were provided for so that the entire body could process in full regalia through Oxford's streets: First here to St. Mary's; then to Christ Church where a Mass of the Holy Ghost was sung with a great burning of candles and incense; once more along The High and on to dinner in hall at Lincoln College; then again to St. Mary's for each prisoner to be called in singly and presented with the three articles proclaiming the doctrine of Real Presence which he was to affirm or deny." Felicity pictured it all in her mind: the splendid pageantry, the sense of triumph for some, the utter despair of others.

"Cranmer was brought in between armed men to face the commissioners seated before the Altar. The former archbishop stood, refusing the seat offered him. He was a venerable figure with the long white beard he had worn since King Henry's death, more than seven years earlier. He leaned upon his staff, ready for the argument in which he delighted. His answers caused so much confusion among his opponents that he was asked to put his opinions in writing for further consideration and disputation.

"Ridley was next. Then Latimer. Poor Latimer, that past winter in the Tower of London his cell had been so cold he notified his jailer that he would likely perish by cold and not, as expected, by fire. He was no warmer in Oxford. Latimer met his disputants wearing a kerchief and three caps on his head."

Antony went on to detail for his listeners the intricacies of the disputations over the doctrine of the Real Presence on which the trial centered, but it was too much for Felicity to follow. She wouldn't have been surprised if Gwena had gone to sleep or walked out in disgust, but when she stole a sideways glance at her companion in the pew, she was surprised to see her smiling with that odd look on her face that she could only describe as an I-told-you-so complacency. Why would Gwena be pleased about this account?

"And so all three were to die."

Felicity could only shake her head. Did anyone care that passionately about matters of faith or theology today? But then, she supposed, in that day people truly believed entrance to heaven was based on a theology exam.

"The three were kept in prison for nearly a year and a half longer." Antony continued. "On the morning of 16 October 1555, the Spanish friar who had frequently visited Cranmer in an attempt to make him recant, entered his cell in Bocardo and led him to the top of the tower of the gatehouse adjoining the jail. The friar bade him look southward toward the open ground where a drainage ditch ran in front of Balliol College. Cranmer saw heaps of faggots and brushwood piled high around an eight-foot iron stake. But he knew they weren't for him. Not yet.

"Ridley went first, carefully dressed in a furred black gown, which he distributed to bystanders along with most of his other clothes. Latimer followed as closely as the slowness of his seventy years allowed, wearing a threadbare gown girded to his frail body with a penny leather belt. Ridley's brother-in-law hung a bag of gunpowder around the neck of each of the condemned men in hopes of cutting short their suffering. They were lashed to the stake by a chain of iron. The faggots at their feet were set ablaze.

"'Be of good comfort, Master Ridley,' Latimer spoke the words that have lived in history. 'We shall this day light such a candle by God's grace in England as, I trust, shall never be put out.'

"Latimer succumbed to the smoke almost instantly and died without much pain. Ridley, however, suffered terrible agonies as the fire first seared the flesh from his body, then burned his legs entirely off without killing him. 'Let the fire come to me, I cannot burn!' he screamed.

"In a frenzy to help, his brother-in-law added more brush to the pile, but it was wet and only damped down the flames. Wind blew away the smoke, which might have brought merciful asphyxiation. The agonized screams carried to Cranmer standing on the roof of his jail. Finally the flames reached the gunpowder.

"With the memory of that scene seared in his mind Cranmer lived for five more months. For a time he was housed quite comfortably at Christ Church and allowed use of the pleasant walks behind the college across the meadow. When his excommunication arrived from Rome he was returned to Bocardo."

Antony paused and held out his hands to his small audience. "What excellent listeners you are." Pens stopped their note-taking, faces turned up to his. "You've earned a break. But don't get too excited, we're just going around to Christ Church, to the site of the last, most humiliating ceremony of all Cranmer was to undergo."

As they left St. Mary's and turned up the High toward

Carfax, Felicity took the chance to fall into step with Antony, cutting out Sheila who appeared to be aiming for that position. In spite of her uneasy concern that she, or at least her work, might be the target of the crimes surrounding them, Felicity chose to start on a happier note. "I finished," she announced.

"The translation? Congratulations." Antony's smile was wide and generous. "Did you learn anything new?"

She told him about the legal document. "Sister Gertrude is going to send it on to some authority on legal history for a clearer interpretation. I don't see how there can be anything in a charter that old, though." They walked on for some time as she thought how to put her niggling worries into words and debated with herself over whether or not she should disturb Antony who would be immediately anxious for her safety.

They were in the arched passage under Tom Tower when she drew breath to speak. At the same moment Clare and Brian claimed Antony's attention with a question about the theological debate. Felicity slowed her step to walk with Gwena as they followed the path past the fountain and on across the wide, green quad of Christ Church.

"Grisly story, isn't it? I'm surprised you've stayed with it," Felicity remarked.

Gwena shrugged. "It just goes to show, doesn't it?"

Felicity was as puzzled by the edge to her voice as by her words. "What? The machinations of history?"

"I suppose that's one way to put it."

Something in her tone made Felicity reluctant to delve further. Besides, Felicity was having her own qualms. She wasn't usually hypersensitive, but entering the cathedral brought back to her all the unpleasantness of her previous visit. She was just about to give herself a stern talking-to when she felt a warm arm embrace her back. "You all right?" She looked up into Antony's concerned brown eyes. And she was fine. How silly of her to worry. What could possibly happen to her here, in what was probably the most civilized city in the world?

Antony led the little group up the long center aisle to seats in the choir and directed their gaze up to the rood-loft just under the rose window above the high altar. "Cranmer was placed up there as if in a showcase, carefully clothed in the layers of vestments of each of his offices: sub-deacon, deacon, priest, bishop and archbishop—alb, stole, scapular, chasuble, cowl, one on top of the other. All, including the archbishop's mitre and pall had been made of rough canvas for the event. A crosier was thrust into in his hand. Then each garment was successively stripped off.

"The degradation ceremony proceeded to strip him of even the most minor orders: acolyte, reader clear down to doorkeeper. A barber shaved his head in order to destroy the tonsure he had worn for forty years, but left the thick, flowing beard. Then the final humiliation. A bishop scraped his fingertips where he had once been blessed and anointed for the serving of Holy Communion. After forty years as a priest Thomas Cranmer walked back to prison a condemned heretic.

"Then began the period of Cranmer's successive recantations." Antony outlined the increasing denials demanded by each document and paused for the note-takers to catch up before he proceeded. "The seventh recantation, which was printed and distributed in London ahead of time, he was to take to his execution and read aloud at the stake. That March day was pouring with rain, which required the proceedings be moved inside—once again, to St. Mary's Church.

"At first all went according to plan. Cranmer asked for the prayers of his listeners, then prayed for himself, 'a wretched caitiff and miserable sinner.' He exhorted all to obey the queen, to treat one another with brotherly love, and to be charitable to the poor. He repeated the Lord's Prayer and affirmed his belief in every word and sentence taught by our Lord Jesus Christ.

"His hearers must have held their breath when he announced, 'And now I come to the great thing which so much troubleth my conscience, more than any thing that ever I did or said in my whole life, and that is the setting abroad of writings contrary to the truth, which now here I renounce and refuse, as things written with my hand contrary to the truth which I thought in my heart...'"

Antony's students smiled as they caught the drift of Cranmer's words and Antony returned their grins. "Yes, I've always wondered at what point Cranmer's audience realized he was not talking about signing the document annulling the marriage of Henry and Katherine or any of his writings forming the Church of England. Cranmer was renouncing all his carefully worded recantations. '...since my degradation I have written many things untrue. And forasmuch as my hand offended, writing contrary to my heart, my hand shall first be punished therefore; for, may I come to the fire, it shall be first burned.'

"Cranmer was pulled from the platform. He raced to his place of execution with such speed that few could keep up with him. There he was chained to the stake and the wood kindled. He reached out and thrust his hand into the leaping flames. 'This hand hath offended.' Very soon he was dead."

Felicity felt a release of tension in herself and in the others as the account came full circle to the execution Antony had begun with a day ago. She couldn't help thinking it must have been a much greater release for Cranmer. People moved and chatted around her, but she sat, replaying in her mind the scenes Antony had described.

She was jolted out of her reverie by Gwena as she approached, Antony in tow. "All right, you two. My treat. Tea at the Randolph."

Felicity gasped. "Are you serious? I had no idea you were so POSH. That's a place we only looked at in my student days."

"Well, high time you went then. I'm only suggesting tea and a scone, mind you."

Felicity, who had skipped lunch, wasn't about to refuse, but she was still puzzled by Gwena's air of triumphalism. It was almost as if she had been trying to make a difficult decision and had come to a conclusion. Perhaps she had an announcement to make. Was going to marry Derrick?

When they were settled in the plush seats of the drawing room of the five-star hotel, however, their bountiful hostess seemed only to have more questions.

"So, what would you say, little brother," she began, sipping the China tea she had ordered, "Was it worth it?"

"The martyrdoms?" Antony split his scone with the tines

of his fork and considered. "There's such an inexorable quality to history. I gave up long ago playing *might have been* with it. It seems clear, though, that Latimer spoke true. The flame lit by their deaths still burns strong today. As does that of Sir Thomas More, Saint John Fisher — really all who have stood strong for their principles on both sides of the ecclesiastical divide in every age.

"Of course, as to Cranmer himself, even from a secular standpoint, *The Book of Common Prayer* is one of the key literary works, alongside Shakespeare, that has molded the beauty and richness of the English language. Its influence wouldn't have survived if its author had abdicated his stand. It could be said that Cranmer's language remains the candle, which by God's grace, shall never be put out.

"When Thomas Cranmer died on that rainy March day, most people, including Cranmer himself, probably, believed the English Reformation was defeated. Had the new forms of worship lasted through a whole generation, the reasoning went — had they been in use long enough to become part of the rhythms of the nation's thought and breathing — they might have endured. But it had been only six years since the prayer book was issued. The burning of the flame was too brief. But the candle did burn. Because Cranmer and the others stood firm at the last."

Gwena rolled her eyes. "All right, Squib, I'll give you beauty of the language — Shakespeare, at least. But it was all so unnecessary."

Antony savored a bite of his scone, piled high with strawberry jam and clotted cream. "Well, I suppose it was the times. We are all children of our time. We can't help it. Even if we try to reject popular culture, to live above mob rule and to do the right thing, we are affected by whatever popular culture we are attempting to reject.

"The hundreds of faithful adherents to both the old and the new faiths who were martyred in those years were victims of the ancient curse, 'May you live in interesting times.'" Antony leaned back in his chair and ticked them off on his fingers: "John Fisher and Thomas More, for whom Cranmer interceded; Anne Askew, whom he avoided; Frith, Lambert, and Joan Bocher, whom he condemned; the Oxford Martyrs and the 300 some, largely common folk, who were burnt by Mary after them; the 250 executed by Elizabeth at the time of the Spanish Armada...down to the last burning of a heretic in 1612 under James I."

Gwena looked scornful. "You're trying to excuse the barbarity by showing how widespread it was?"

"Not at all. I'm merely citing examples of heroism—and, yes, barbarity if you like—on both sides of the divide. The point is, it's not possible for us to understand in this distant day. The concept of tolerance as indulging the practices and opinions of others didn't come into the language until around 1765—two hundred years after Cranmer.

"It was almost a hundred years after Cranmer died before it occurred to anyone that it was possible for a nation to have more than one religion—an idea that struck people as making as much sense as having two kings. William Penn," he nodded at Felicity, the American, "was one of the pioneers of that grand experiment and everyone predicted utter chaos for his Pennsylvania where settlers were allowed freedom to worship God in their own way. After all, where would it stop? Why, there might be a hundred religions—or more!"

Gwena sniffed. "Or preferably none."

"Why do you say that?" Antony asked.

Gwena shrugged. "It seems obvious. Freedom from prejudice and superstition."

"And you really think if there were no religion there would be no bigotry and killing?"

"It would eliminate one source of fanaticism. A very powerful one."

"Ah, fanaticism." Antony's smile made Felicity marvel anew at how relaxed Antony's whole approach to this conversation was. She would have thought he would be intent on convincing his sister, but instead he merely answered her questions as he would have any enquiring student. Gwena was the one with a bee in her bonnet. And Felicity was puzzled by her intensity. She understood that Gwena had rejected any personal faith, but she had no idea she was so— well, evangelistic about it.

"You tempt me to drag out one of my favorite lectures on the *via media,* but I'll spare you. Just let me suggest that the evils of fanaticism aren't confined to religious circles." He refreshed the tea in his cup and added two lumps of sugar with the silver tongs. "As a matter of fact, I would go so far as to suggest that true faith offers the best antidote to prejudice and insularity."

Gwena was about to answer when her frown turned to delight and she waved to a tall man with spiked hair entering the room. He returned her grin and strode over to their table. "Derrick! I didn't realize you were back."

"Just."

"Good stuff?"

"Amazing."

Gwendolyn turned back to indicate her companions. "You remember Felicity—you met at the pub. And this is my brother." She waved a hand in Antony's direction. "This is Derrick. He's been off evaluating an estate in an old castle for a client. Something hush hush because the heirs are squabbling or something."

Antony rose to shake hands. "Sounds like interesting work. Won't you join us?" He indicated the empty place at the table.

Derrick pulled his phone from his pocket to check the time. "Well, I'm meeting a client—an American, as it happens," he smiled at Felicity, "but I'm a few minutes early. I don't want to interrupt, though."

"Not at all," Antony assured him, resuming his seat.

"You must, Derrick," Gwena insisted. "We're hot into your favorite subject."

"Antiquities?" He sounded understandably surprised.

"No, silly. My learned brother here has just delivered the most telling lecture on the atrocities committed in the name of religion, yet he refuses to admit that the world would be better off if all religion were outlawed. You can help me keep up the side."

Derrick sat, eyeing Antony's dog collar with a smile that seemed to be equal parts amusement and sneer. "I can see you would hardly be unbiased on the subject," he said.

"I hope it's more than bias. I'd be the first to admit that historically there has been a great deal of fanaticism in the name of Christianity, although today ninety-nine percent of it would be in another court entirely." He paused to take another sip of tea.

"The thing is that religion promotes fervor. And fervor causes people to go to extremes. It's not the religion that makes them act out in unacceptable ways, it's the fervor. True religion teaches love, charity and peace. And Christianity teaches turning the other cheek as well. Hardly a fanatical practice.

"Just to put things into balance, take a look at the Church's humanitarian record through the ages: charities, schools, hospitals. How many hospitals do you find dedicated to St. Bertrand of Russell? Or St. Richard of Dawkins?"

Derrick acknowledged the hit with a lazy grin. "Well, I see I need to get you along to a SASS meeting."

Felicity turned to Gwena with a quizzical look.

"Secular Atheist Student Society," Gwena supplied, then smiled. "Pure coincidence that the acronym is SASS, of course."

"I'm always ready to listen to other viewpoints," Antony said.

"Allyn Luffington, chap I do some consulting for, is giving a talk next week. I'll let you know." Derrick started to say more, then looked toward the door where a broad shouldered man in a white western-cut shirt stood. "Ah, there's Cody. Come meet him, Gwena. I expect to be doing a lot of business with him." He smiled. "Very lucrative business. Wants to furnish his Texas ranch house in authentic Tudor."

Felicity watched them cross the room, then turned back to Antony, but the sight of the worried look in his eyes drove out all thought of sharing her own concerns with him.

Thirteen

Friday morning Felicity slipped into the tiny side chapel to join the sisters for morning prayers. She had come to pray for the community, for strength and wisdom for Sister Dorcas as she struggled to lead them in this uncertain time, and for protection for them all. Words jumbled in her mind as she struggled to form coherent thoughts. She had been there only a few minutes, however, when the beauty of the rose marble altar, the lingering scent of the incense, the soft murmur of the sisters' chant, the sense of peace in spite of the turmoil just beyond these walls, penetrated her own anxiety and she felt herself relax. This would be her last morning in the convent, but she hoped she could take some of its serenity with her.

When the brief service ended, she stepped into the sanctuary where the nuns worshipped. She didn't want to leave without bidding Dorcas and Gertrude farewell and thanking them once more for their hospitality and the opportunity to work on their publishing project. "Oh, no, it's we who must thank you," Gertrude insisted.

"I do hope my work will turn out to have been useful. I don't suppose you've heard from your legal authority yet?" Felicity didn't wait for an answer. "Here's my mobile number. Please ring me when you learn something. I would love to know what all that meant." She resisted apologizing again for not knowing more of a subject outside of her field.

Felicity and the nuns turned questioningly at the sound of a heavy, masculine tread on the wooden floor. "Oh, Father Ben," Dorcas said, "I need to speak with him." She put her hand on Felicity's arm. "My dear, I wish you Godspeed." At that, she pivoted and abruptly left, cutting off any response Felicity might have had.

Felicity was once again struck by the power the priest exuded. "What did he do in — Barbados, was it?" She asked Gertrude.

"Worked in an orphanage, I think. He's only just come, so I don't know much about him."

"He came to study at Pusey House?"

Gertrude nodded. "People do. From all around the world. But I suspect he might have been a bit homesick. Something he said in a homily gave me that idea."

"Oh, I didn't realize he was from around here."

"I don't know if he was. I just meant, missing England."

Felicity nodded. She would have liked to know more about Father Ben, but she needed to get on. Getting back to Keble would be a bit of a homecoming for her as well as a holiday. She was looking forward to being closer to Antony and away from the stress of Mother Monica's murder. There she could relax and not worry about lurking shadows.

It only took her a few minutes to pack her small bag, strip her bed and check to be sure she had left the kitchen tidy. As she boarded the bus she was already mentally treading the grounds of her alma mater. She saw herself passing the ornate Butterfield buildings to the modern student accommodation in the far corner of the campus. In her mind she entered the glass and concrete Hayward building with a sense of coming home. Almost of revisiting her childhood, although she had hardly been a child when she was a student here — just a few life-changing years ago. And she had learned so much, changed so much more since then. Thanks largely to the lovely man who was waiting for her outside the entrance to the porter's lodge.

She greeted him with a quick kiss. "Hi, hope you hadn't been waiting long."

"Not at all." He grinned and inclined his head toward the imposing neo-Gothic edifice of the Museum of Natural

History across the road. "This seemed like a good spot to muse on yesterday's conversation with Gwen and Derrick."

"It did? Why?" The traffic whizzing down Parks Road made this seem an unlikely spot for meditation on any subject.

"The University Museum. Pusey saw building Keble College across from it as something of a face-off. Godless evolution versus faith." He smiled. "Interesting how some things never change. It's ironic, though, because the museum building was financed with the sale of Bibles."

"Good grief," Felicity replied. "I must have been in and out of this gate thousands of times and I never knew that." She observed the high, peaked roof on the central tower of the museum and double rows of Gothic arched windows with fresh perspective.

Antony smiled. "That's what you get for missing my lecture this morning. It's also interesting that the inside ornamentation of the museum's stonework and iron pillars is intertwining leaves and branches; a conscious effort to combine the Pre-Raphaelite style with the scientific role of the building."

Felicity shook her head. "Of course I've been in to see the Dodo bird, but I'm afraid all that escaped me. I can see I'm needing your talk on the Oxford Movement."

"Well, let's get you settled first." He took the handle of her small rolling suitcase. "Actually, you'll have to wait a bit for that one. Today it's John Keble. And I promise to keep it short because I've booked a punt after that."

Felicity gasped. "Antony, don't tell me you can punt!"

He turned and grinned at her. "You've forgotten that I was at 'the other place'. We had a river there, too."

As a matter-of-fact, she had forgotten that Antony had studied at Cambridge. He talked so little about his past. But now she recalled his mentioning it. And even the fact that he had had a girlfriend there. What was her name? Christa? Christine? Christina, maybe. Had he spent languid afternoons punting the Cam with Christina? Felicity made a face.

She gave herself a little shake. Well, if so, she was grateful to Christina. Now she would benefit from the experience Antony gained then.

Felicity checked in at the lodge and received her room key. She looked at the name on the tag with disappointment. "Hursley House? Not Hayward?"

"Not in term, Miss," the porter replied. "Come back in the long vacation, we offer tourist accommodation then."

"But I'm not..." Felicity began. She did not view herself as a tourist.

Antony grinned and led the way back toward the street. "Sorry I didn't explain. We're in the seminar house. Very convenient. Just across the University Parks."

At least they still took their meals in hall. Felicity renewed her acquaintance with Antony's students at lunch a short time later. The elderly Sheila was enthusiastic about all she was learning. "Of course, you know what an inspiring lecturer Father Antony is. The Community sponsors so many retreats and study courses. I'm very fortunate to be able to take advantage of so many. And this is one of the best."

Felicity smiled encouragingly as her companion went on detailing one of her most recent courses on the English Mystics. Felicity was listening, but she couldn't quite help noting what appeared to be a budding romance between Clare and Brian, who bent their heads together across the table and interspersed their quiet conversation with shy smiles.

After lunch, Antony led his group around two sides of the quad, to the most ornate building in the college—the chapel. Felicity smiled at the poster in the church porch inviting students to "Worship like it was 1066." How clever of their current chaplain to make a virtue of their counter-cultural, high church ways.

She entered the cool, still sanctuary with a sense of nostalgia and regret. It was good to be back and to recall the few times she had attended chapel as a student—most especially the candlelight carol service when the entire space shimmered with the lights of hundreds of tiny candles. And the solemn All Souls' requiem mass with the clergy all wearing black vestments and the special dark orange beeswax candles which gave the chapel the appearance of being decorated for Halloween.

She had only attended because the fellow student who was

her special friend at the moment had been active in the chapel program and had invited her along to climb through the rafters to muffle the bells for All Souls'. Now she regretted not having taken regular advantage of all that was on offer. Thank goodness she had had a second chance at The Community of the Transfiguration.

Felicity walked up the aisle floored with red, ochre and blue tiles, and sat in a pew near the front next to Sheila and Gareth with Clare, Brian and Marc behind them. Felicity looked around the long, narrow room with its highly ornamented brick walls, which the architect Butterfield had designed with special care as part of his mission to "give dignity to brick." Patterned tiles behind the rows of Gothic arches lining the walls offered an endless variety of geometric patterns. Above that, vivid Pre-Raphaelite-style murals depicting Bible stories gleamed from their gold leaf backgrounds. And at the front, above the intricately carved reredos, the enormous stained-glass window glowed like a casket of jewels.

Antony stood in front of the altar rail, gold from the high altar shimmering behind him, but instead of delivering the talk himself, he introduced a young woman in a clerical collar as the current chaplain, and asked her to give some background on the college and chapel. Felicity admired Chaplain Jenn's sleek hairdo and gracious manner. If the "Worship like it was 1066" campaign was her idea, this was a very savvy lady.

"The college was built in 1870 and named in memory of the Victorian clergyman John Keble, who was one of the founders of the Oxford Movement. The ideals on which Keble College was founded, namely a community of students and their tutors centered on common meals, study and worship, and particularly on the sacrament of communion, are still the heart of the life of the chapel program today. That's why the configuration of pews is congregational, all facing the altar, rather facing each other like a monastic choir, as in most college chapels."

She waved a hand to encompass the highly ornamented walls around them. "Our chapel is without doubt the most unique in Oxford." She smiled. "It, and the whole college, was very controversial when it was built, some said it was 'the ugliest building in the world.' Although I must say I've grown to love it. Butterfield's style is never easy. And certainly never bland. It challenges the understanding.

"Butterfield has taught generations of students to use their eyes and judge for themselves, which I invite you to do, as well—taking into consideration the Victorian belief that 'the Gothic is the style in which God wishes to be worshipped'." She smiled. "And, of course, the aims of the Oxford Movement to restore high church principles to the Church of England. The founders believed that church architecture should reflect, as best it could, the glory of God. Therefore, the lavish use of gold leaf, for example—often referred to as Tractarian gold. But I understand you'll be having more on the principles of the Oxford Movement another day." She looked at Antony and he nodded.

"So then, to Keble himself. He had a brilliant academic career at Oxford in the early 1800's, was ordained priest and then served as curate to his father in a country parish in the Cotswolds. There he wrote his collection of poetry *The Christian Year* which became simply the most popular volume of verse in the nineteenth century and led directly to his being appointed Chair of Poetry at Oxford in 1831."

Felicity smiled when Jenn looked at her watch. Apparently Antony had warned her that he had promised a short lecture today. Few of his were ever such a bare bones explanation. Antony must be as anxious as she was to get out on the river. And the sound of shuffling in the pew behind her told her that the others were as well. It was an unusually beautiful afternoon, and with only three days left in October, it was unlikely these golden days would last much longer.

"Keble and others, Especially Edward Pusey and John Henry Newman, were becoming increasingly worried about dangers to the Church of England from liberal movements, and on 14 July, 1833, Keble preached his assize sermon on National Apostasy in St. Mary's Church. This is considered the founding event of the movement. Keble also wrote several of the 'Tracts for the Times' which gave the movement the name

Tractarian.

"In 1836 he retired from academia to become Vicar of Hursley, a small town near Winchester. He remained there as a devoted parish priest until his death at Bournemouth in 1866 where he had gone to recover from an illness. It was said that his beauty of character impressed all who came into contact with him and his advice on spiritual matters, which was always given with great diffidence, was widely sought after." Jenn smiled and took a step back.

"Father Antony, you asked for just a brief overview, but I wonder if any of your students might have questions."

The scratching of pens stopped, followed by a shuffle of papers and notebooks being crammed into rucksacks, indicating that the others were ready to go, but Felicity's earlier reminiscences had brought one question to her mind.

"This might be a little off topic, but since All Souls' is next Wednesday, I'm wondering if you still muffle your bells?"

Jenn looked surprised. "No, we haven't done that in my time here." She furrowed her brow. "Goodness, did they do that? We don't really have a proper bell tower. It must have involved crawling through the rafters. I can't help but think Health and Safety would have something to say about that."

Felicity nodded and thanked her. What a pity. That had been a great adventure and had certainly made the point of the solemnity of the occasion even to one with so little awareness of such things as she had at that time. Her disappointment must have shown because Jenn quickly added, "The Change Ringers Society does ring muffled changes for All Souls', though. At Saint Mary Mag's, I think."

Antony thanked their speaker and dismissed his students with a simple, "Enjoy your afternoon."

Clare and Brian were the first out the door, walking hand-in-hand. And Felicity and Antony weren't far behind them. It was a long walk across Oxford to Magdalen Bridge where they would rent their punt. When they arrived Felicity was happy for the shade of the trees along the riverbank as she settled herself on a cushion facing the prow. Antony looked uncertain as he hefted the long pole.

"Are you okay? Do you want me to have a go?" Felicity

offered. "I was never very good, but I have done a bit of punting."

She was relieved when he didn't take up her offer. "No, no. Just trying to decide. Would you mind turning around?"

Felicity laughed. "Oh, it's the 'punting from the wrong end' thing, isn't it?"

Antony mounted the platform across the bow, even though most others on the river were standing in the upward-sloping prow. "It's more a matter of wrong design." He grinned. "Either way, you punt from the rear — it's the only way to steer. It's just that Cambridge punts are completely flat, so we must stand on the platform." He shrugged. "One of those eccentricities of tradition."

"Ah, whereas Oxford punts offer a choice. I get it." Felicity readjusted her cushion and settled again as Antony, holding the pole vertically against the side of the punt, let it drop through his hands to the riverbed. With a single push they glided smoothly to the center of the river. "At least this way if my technique isn't up to snuff I'll have an excuse. It has been a good few years, you know."

Felicity leaned back and dangled her hand in the cool water. "I'm not in the least worried. Just so you don't dump me. This is pure luxury." Felicity let her mind drift with the light playing on the water as they went under Magdalen Bridge and floated along the Cherwell past the Botanic Gardens, the glass houses beyond the hedges reflecting in the water.

After a few fumbles, mostly due to other boats passing them too closely, Antony seemed to catch his rhythm and the punt glided between the golden, tree-lined banks of the Magdalen School Cricket Field on one side and Christ Church Meadow on the other. Occasionally an autumn leaf drifted down to be ignored by the paddling ducks, and overhead the sky was almost translucently clear with an occasional bright white cloud as accent.

And the sun was warm. "What a shame we didn't think to bring a picnic basket." Felicity noticed several groups sitting along the riverbank or in the meadow, many of them enjoying provisions from well-stocked hampers.

"Ah, Pimms and strawberries?" Antony asked.

"It's been known, but actually, I was thinking more along the lines of tea and chocolate." Felicity started to comment that it had been a considerable time since lunch, when a couple in the punt a bit up the river ahead of them took her attention. "Look, it's Clare and Brian." Clare's fiery hair and Brian's cottony mop, not to mention his trademark purple trainers, were an unmistakable combination.

Antony's students were heading toward the gently sloping bank just beyond a clump of trees overhanging the water. Apparently they had thought to bring a picnic tea. As Brian steered the punt toward the bank Clare reached out to grab one of the graceful willow branches dipping in the water. Her action made the boat slew sideways. They disappeared under the golden boughs, Brian dodging to the left to avoid being hit in the face by a limb.

Felicity started to ask if Antony thought they should try to help them when a female cry tore from the leafy cover. A moment later the punt shot back into the river, Brian poling for all he was worth.

With a few fluid strokes Antony pulled alongside. "What's the matter?" Felicity called.

Clare, her long red hair tangled from the branches and her ruddy cheeks blanched white, pointed. "A—a body!" It came out in a strangled cry.

The commotion attracted the attention of a group in another punt. All three pulled to the bank and the punters clambered to shore. Brian put his arm around the trembling Clare as she tried again to tell what she had seen.

"Are you certain?" Antony asked as he pulled out his mobile.

Clare's emphatic nod was enough to convince Felicity, and a short time later when officers from the Thames Valley Police station, located just across the meadow, arrived at the riverbank with long grappling hooks, it was beyond question.

The police were discreet and did their best to keep the gathering crowd away, but Felicity glimpsed the sodden brown habit and black wimple.

Horrible as it was, it was almost a relief. Now the sisters

could have their Requiem Mass.

Fourteen

"Yes, it is a relief, I suppose." Sister Dorcas remained dry-eyed, but the effort to maintain her calm composure showed in the lines of her face. "It's just that this makes it so final. We knew, of course, but to be honest there was always just this tiny ray of hope that there had been some horrible mistake."

It was late Saturday morning before Felicity and Antony went to Fairacres to offer their condolences to the community. Even in these, the most stressful of circumstances, the convent retained its air of serenity and peace.

Dorcas explained with an almost imperceptible shiver, that she had been the one to identify the body. "Fortunately, she hadn't been in the water long..." Felicity's mind went to questions of how long Monica had been dead, how she had died, where she had been held, but it was unlikely that even the police knew yet, and there was no point in distressing Dorcas. "And, of course, I rang her sister."

Felicity would have liked to know how the brisk Lucille Knighton had received the information, then she chided herself for her unfair cynicism. Surely the sister's grief was real, even if she didn't show it. Perhaps more real for its lack of display.

"When will the requiem be?" Antony asked.

Dorcas shook her head. "We have no idea when the... when she will be released to us. I explained to Inspector Fosse about our usual mass for the dead on All Soul's it would be so appropriate... But it's unlikely things can be settled by then, you know."

Dorcas seemed to give herself a little shake and returned to matters closer to hand. "Father Antony, it's almost the sixth hour. I wonder, would you care to say Sext for us?"

Antony agreed readily, and he and Dorcas went to the chapel to prepare for the midday office.

Gertrude, who had stood quietly just a step behind Dorcas during the earlier exchange, turned to Felicity. "I hope this doesn't seem disrespectful in the face of so much more immediate concerns, but I wonder if you could give me a few minutes in my office? I've been puzzling over the question of where Frideswide fled to for sanctuary."

Felicity, who was well aware that focusing on an academic problem could serve as an escape from pressing turmoil, was glad to follow her. "Oh, yes, the Bampton/Binsey dispute. I wondered about that myself, although our chronicler seems to come down on the side of Binsey."

Gertrude gave her glasses a shove along the bridge of her nose as she turned to Felicity. "Oh, yes. I'm not questioning your translation, but I felt our publication should perhaps offer an endnote explanation on the issue, so I've been looking a bit further afield." She took a ring of keys from her pocket and led the way into the tiny grey brick building that was her special domain.

"I've rather been focusing on side issues while I await our legal expert's analysis. It's more than a bit frustrating, since I'd prefer to get into the meat of the matter."

"So you haven't heard anything yet?" Felicity had been wondering.

Gertrude shook her veiled head. "Early days, I expect. He's a busy man and just doing this as a favor." She opened a drawer in her desk and pulled out a file. "Now, this is what I've been looking at."

"*Oxoniensia*," Felicity read.

"Yes, the journal of the Oxfordshire Historical Society. Now, here, in their 'History of the County of Oxford' they speculate on Bampton's prominence before the eighth century based on it's frequent mention in the accounts of St. Frideswide written four hundred years later, but it's so frustrating because they offer no other arguments."

Felicity considered. "Perhaps that's because there isn't any other evidence. Looking at it logically, it seems that Binsey has the stronger claim." Felicity pulled an Ordnance Survey atlas from near the top of a stack of books on Gertrude's desk and opened it to the appropriate page. "If the story of Frideswide and her maid fleeing by boat are to be believed, Bampton would have been a very long journey." She traced the circuitous route of the thin blue line indicating the River Thames. "And, unless the course of the river has shifted significantly over the centuries, Bampton must be at least two miles from the river. Whereas Binsey would be a matter of— what?" She considered the distance on the map. "Perhaps a couple of hours or less in a small boat, and then a short distance across the meadow?"

Gertrude nodded. "And, of course, Binsey does have the well to offer in evidence, so to speak."

The ringing of a bell made Felicity look up. "Oh—the midday office." Gertrude said with an impatience that led Felicity to think she might have preferred to say, 'Oh bother.'

Felicity moved toward the door. "Yes, you go on. I'll be there in just a moment." Gertrude returned to studying the map.

Felicity hurried along the path across the garden and down the side of the church. She slipped into the tiny visitors' chapel and found her place in the office book in time to join in the responses as Antony, somber in black cassock, bowed before the red onyx altar and began the opening psalm: "I am deeply troubled;"

"Preserve my life, O Lord, according to your word." Felicity never failed to be amazed at how the readings appointed for each day always seemed to speak to her need.

"My life is always in my hand," Antony said.

And the response: "Yet I do not forget your law."

"The wicked have set a trap for me,"

"But I have not strayed from your commandments."

After two more psalms and a brief scripture reading the

office concluded with prayers. "Heavenly Father, send your Holy Spirit into our hearts, to direct us according to your will, to comfort us in all our afflictions…" It might be some time yet until their Mother Superior could be laid to rest with a full requiem mass, but every office was a service for the peace of her soul and the comfort of this community.

Dorcas invited Felicity and Antony to join the community for their midday meal and they were walking toward the refectory when Felicity realized Gertrude had not attended the office. She understood how easy it was to get sidetracked with a research question, and yet she was surprised at the nun's absence. She stopped and turned back toward the Press. Should she go remind Gertrude of the time? Surely she would want her lunch.

Felicity had taken only one step when Antony turned as well. "Do you smell smoke?"

Sister Bertholde was the first to spot the thin grey cloud issuing from the small window. "Fire! The Press!"

Antony pulled his phone from his pocket, but Felicity knew they couldn't wait for the fire department. "Sister Gertrude!" She darted ahead, her long legs carrying her the length of the convent grounds in moments.

She rounded the corner of the building, grabbed the railing and took all three steps in a single bound. Then stopped. The door was locked. Did that mean Sister Gertrude had left the building? But if so, where was she?

Felicity pounded on the door. "Sister Gertrude!" She repeated the cry, twisting the knob and pulling on the door. All futile.

She flew back down the steps and stooped to pluck one of the large white stones from the border of the flowerbed. She hurled it through the window with some idea of letting the smoke out and fresh air in. Then remembered that oxygen fed flames. But it could also keep Gertrude alive—if she hadn't already succumbed to smoke inhalation from the smudge now issuing through the hole Felicity had just broken.

Then she saw it, the window latch. Just below the gap in the broken window. She could easily reach the window ledge and shimmy through once the window was up.

She had her foot on the sill when Antony caught up with her. "No you don't!" He pulled her back with such a jerk that they both landed sprawled on the ground.

Felicity was the first to her feet. "What are you doing? Sister Gertrude is in there! We have to save her!" She turned back toward the window, which she could now hardly see for the black cloud billowing out.

Antony's arms came around her waist like a vice. "It's too dangerous. And you don't even know she's in there."

Felicity twisted in his grip and opened her mouth to argue but the quantity of smoke she inhaled gave her a coughing fit. She was moving backwards with Antony's tugs when she heard the siren.

"Leave it to the professionals," Antony said, his mouth against her ear.

She nodded, choked and sobbed all at once. Then turned in his arms for an embrace. Antony more dragged than carried her out of the way of the firemen approaching the building with axes and hose. "There's a woman in there!" Felicity cried. A nod of a neon helmeted head told her that her message had been received.

She sank to the grass a safe distance away, her head in her hands and Antony's arm around her. Now that she had done all she could do, Felicity began to shake. How close had she come to being locked in a burning building herself? Had Gertrude been attacked just after she left for Sext? It couldn't be an accident, could it? There were no candles, lamps or open fires in the Press. No one smoked. It was a relatively new building. Surely no faulty wiring. No, this had to be another attack by whoever had bludgeoned both her and Gertrude a few days ago.

They had come back to finish the job. And this time it looked as though they had succeeded. Or had they?

If they again came to steal the document, it wasn't there. Gertrude had passed the manuscript and translation on to her academic friend. But it was unlikely the intruder would know that.

Or did he? Did he know where the original was but wanted to eliminate any possible copies? And Gertrude who would have read it? And if that were the case, what about Felicity who had translated every word?

She curled into Antony's arms, refusing to allow herself to think further. The sound of fire hatchets smashing into the door brought gasps from the brown-robed nuns fluttering around them. The determined activity of the firemen blurred before her eyes as they rushed through the door.

Felicity felt that she couldn't breathe until she knew Gertrude was out of that burning building. Where was the ambulance? Surely they had called one. It must be further back in the narrow lane. She could just glimpse the red truck with the neon stripe down its side. But why didn't they bring her out? Even if it was too late, surely they wouldn't leave her inside? Felicity wanted to yell at them. She tried to struggle to her feet.

Then she felt Antony lifting her and she saw the reason. A Fireman in his thick beige uniform with neon bands was walking across the lawn toward her. "Are you certain there was someone in there?" He almost shouted to be heard over the grind of the pump engine and noise of the water surging through the hose.

"She was when I left," Felicity began. "We haven't seen her—"

Dorcas approached. "We've searched the convent." She ended with a shake of her head.

The fireman turned back to the building with a determined stride.

"The garden," Felicity began. If Gertrude had chosen to walk the long way round to Sext, perhaps to gain a moment to clear her thoughts before prayer... Surely she would have heard the commotion, seen the smoke, but even so... Felicity started toward the bottom of the wide green lawn at a near run.

"Felicity, wait!" She heard Antony behind her and slowed her pace.

Together they pushed through the gap in the hedge into the park beyond. "Do you think she came here?" Antony asked. The garden was deserted but the sound of digging came from the far side of the hedge enclosing the vegetable garden. Must be Frank harvesting potatoes for the winter.

"I don't know. It seems unlikely. Still..." She recalled the series of meditation cubicles formed by shrubbery and garden walls. The first bench was unoccupied. As was the second. And the third. In spite of the scene they had left behind, it was surprising how sheltered and almost quiet it seemed in this distant corner of the grounds. The hubbub at the press faded to a distant roar, muffled by the vegetation.

Antony stood to the side of the path, almost hidden by the drooping branches of a weeping willow, surveying the space. "Felicity?" He pointed to the abandoned summer house in the far corner. Felicity had seen it on her first stroll in the garden, but had turned away quickly when she saw the door tied shut, sealed with cobwebs. An oddity in such a well-cared-for space.

Felicity turned to it with a shrug. It was hardly a place Gertrude would have chosen, but she started forward, determined to explore every possibility. Focusing on the shed as she was, Felicity would have been unlikely to notice a small disturbance in the bushes beneath the thick trees, had not a large blackbird in the tree above taken to wing with a screeching caw.

Felicity darted off the path and peered through the undergrowth. It was only a glimpse. A dark figure in a cassock. Maybe. She blinked and he was gone. Surely a he, but she couldn't be certain. Before she could give chase, Antony called her back.

"Felicity! Here!" A grating of rusty hinges told her he was entering the building.

She arrived to see Antony bending over the limp form of Sister Gertrude slumped in a wicker chair. Felicity clapped her hand to her mouth. "Is—"

Antony held the nun's wrist. "There's a pulse."

Gertrude stirred and began muttering. Her slurred words sounded as if she were saying, "Don't know" over and over again. Or maybe it was, "Don't! No!" Or was it, "I won't!"

"She's alive! What's the matter with her?" Felicity bent forward, her hands held out, then jumped back when Gertrude raised a hand to strike at her. "What is it? Is she sick?

Delirious?"

"I don't know, but she needs help." Antony put one of the nun's arms around his shoulder and with his arm around her waist, struggled to hoist her to her feet. Felicity started to take the other arm but Antony stopped her. "No, you run ahead. Get help."

"But what's wrong?" Felicity demanded.

To her surprise, the answer came from Gertrude, "Frideswide refused. She won't marry him. She ran away." Her words became garbled. If Felicity didn't know better she would have thought Sister Gertrude very drunk. "Charter. Yes. Algar's lands." She attempted to nod her head, but bumped Antony's ear.

"Felicity, go!" Antony urged her out the door ahead of himself.

The knowledge that Gertrude was alive gave Felicity wings. She crossed the grounds in moments and grabbed the first fireman she came to. "There! We found her! Help!" She pointed urgently to the figure of Antony and his brown-robed burden just rounding the hedge onto the green lawn.

As two firemen darted toward them Felicity surveyed the scene before her. Firemen were rolling up the hose and collecting equipment, others exited the building. "Is it out?"

Dorcas was already heading across the lawn toward Gertrude but Bertholde turned to Felicity. "Yes, thanks be to God. And you found our sister. Unharmed?"

Felicity was uncertain. "I'm sure she'll be all right. In time."

"Ah. Good. That is good, then. And so will the Press be all right. In time." She shook her head. "Such a mess. But not too much actually burnt, I'm thinking." She tipped her head toward the fireman directing the action. "They said there will be an investigation." Sister Bertholde shook her head. "So much mystery."

Suddenly it was too much for Felicity. A number of sturdy brown wooden benches circled a spreading oak tree in the center of the lawn. Turning her back on the turmoil she headed for the nearest one. She had to think. To make sense of what had happened. Had she left the door unlocked when she went out leaving Gertrude alone? Had Gertrude been pulled out before the fire was set? Or had she escaped from a blaze intended to kill her? Why would anyone want to silence her and destroy her work?

Felicity was still asking those questions, and variants of them sometime later, when she and Antony sat in the convent parlor, searching for answers that wouldn't come. Dorcas came in from her office and sank into a faded chintz-covered chair. "That was the emergency room at the John Radcliffe Hospital. Gertrude will be released tomorrow. They think she was given a barbiturate. Most likely sodium thiopental."

"A truth serum?" Felicity asked. "But why? Wouldn't she have been glad to talk to anyone who wanted to know about her work?"

"I asked the same thing," Dorcas replied. "Apparently the drug is often administered when someone wants to be sure they are being told the truth. It relaxes a person so completely they will answer whatever they are asked." She smiled. "It seems the problem is that they will say anything and usually pour out so much information it's impossible to separate fact from imagination."

"Ironic," Antony mused. "Too much 'truth' can make it useless."

"But she will be all right?" Felicity insisted.

"Yes. Perfectly all right. She is woozy and confused at the moment, but she will sleep it off."

"I wish I could talk to her. I don't understand..." Felicity began.

Dorcas shook her head. "None of us does."

Fifteen

Sunday, Felicity awoke to dismal grey with rain dribbling down her window—which perfectly fit her mood. And to top it off she had a splitting headache. Even looking across the corner of the University Parks, where she could just glimpse the east end of Keble Chapel through the autumn leaves, did little to elevate her spirits. Usually just looking at that gloriously eccentric architecture would bring a smile to her lips, but this morning all she could do was groan as the questions that had kept her awake most of the night started around in her head again.

And then the bells began. Usually one of her favorite sounds in the whole world, but now she clapped her hands over her ears. She looked longingly toward her bed. She could just burrow in the duvet and put the pillow over her head. And stay there for the rest of the day.

And that's exactly what she did. At least she dug deep into her comforter, pulled it and her pillow over her head for about three minutes. But then she realized that not only did the pillow not keep out the dark images whirling through her mind, it didn't even blot out the sound of rain which was now pelting her window with increased vigor. She rolled to face the wall and pulled the pillow tighter, squeezing her eyes shut.

And there, projected on the back of her eyelids was the

scene she had only glimpsed the day before. A black-robed figure disappearing into the bushes, leaving Sister Gertrude drugged in the abandoned shed. She forced her mind to play it again, this time more slowly. Yes, the figure was tall, broadly built. Did she have an impression of dark hair and tan skin? Or was her imagination embellishing?

The harder she strained to look, the less certain she was. And yet, she had the feeling the figure was somehow familiar. Goodness knows she had seen enough men in black cassocks to find a match for anything. And yet, someone more recent. In Oxford.

She sat up and flung off her duvet. She needed to talk to Antony. She reached for her mobile, but before she could push the buttons there was a knock at her door. "Just a minute." She pulled a light dressing gown on over her pajamas and padded barefoot to the door. "Who is it?"

"Antony. Are you ready?"

She slid back the bolt on her door and opened it. "Ready?" He stood before her in clerical splendor, his collar gleaming, his dark hair smooth. Looking perfect as always. She pushed at the strands of long blond hair falling over her face.

He grinned. "I can see you aren't." Then his expression turned to one of concern. "Are you all right?"

"Yes, I'm fine. Just didn't sleep very well. I need to talk to you." She opened the door wider, but he didn't move.

Instead he looked at his watch. "Solemn Eucharist at St. Mary Mag's at 10:30."

She groaned. Oxford's high church Mecca, the living heart of all that his seminar was about. Not the dry history or the theological theory, but the vital worship played out in everyday lives. This was what mattered. "Yes, of course. Time got away from me. Sorry. Go on. I'll be there."

He looked undecided. "Are you certain? I'd wait. It's just..."

"Your students. Of course." She was already shutting the door. "I'll hurry. Go on. Save me a seat."

And she was quick. A three minute shower. Washing her hair would have to wait. She twisted it into a single plait and let it fall down her back. A smear of lipstick, her favorite skirt and poppy red jumper, raincoat and hat, and she was out the door. In spite of the soggy grass, she cut across the park and dashed down Saint Giles. Now the peal of bells that had irritated her so earlier, called her forward.

By the time she reached the Martyrs Memorial the bells had stopped. She slowed and realized the rain had stopped as well. Felicity pulled off her hat as she hurried toward the double doors in the wide Gothic entrance to the church. The sound of organ and congregational singing beckoned her. She increased her speed, then halted abruptly inches from cannoning into a tall, slim man exiting the church at a near jog. "Oh, is the service over?"

"No, no. You're all right. Changes done for now, so I'm off for some fresh air."

Their eyes met for a moment before he loped on up the street. Felicity stood watching him. Strange man. Shaking her head, she turned back to the church and moved forward into the warmth and the light. An usher put a hymnal and prayer book in her hand and, in spite of the full congregation, she located Antony with an empty spot beside him.

Felicity tried to focus on the service, the beauty of the wide chancel, the stained-glass window and golden reredos glowing even on such a cloudy day. She sang the Gloria to its familiar Merbecke setting automatically. But the puzzle at the back of her mind wouldn't stay in the back. Who was that man? Why did he seem familiar? And what did he mean 'changes done'? Then the choir began the anthem, Purcell's "I Was Glad" and she was fully swept up into the service.

It was only when the service had ended, and she and Antony were standing outside surrounded by his students, each sharing their thoughts on the service, and the peal began in the tower above her head, that Felicity realized what the man must have meant. He was a bell ringer. She looked at the service folder which she still carried, yes, here it was, a note thanking the Oxford University Society of Change Ringers who had rung St. Mary's bells since 1886. That man had seemed considerably too old to be a student, but perhaps once a ringer always a ringer. Still, that didn't explain why he seemed familiar.

Antony was ready to ask Felicity about her abstraction as they walked back to Keble for Sunday lunch in hall, when his mobile rang. He pulled to the side of the pavement and waved the others on. "Gwendolyn," he mouthed to Felicity who had chosen to wait with him.

His sister's abrupt demand made him raise his eyebrows. "Debate? What debate?"

"Squib, must you always be impossible? You promised Derrick days ago. The Student Atheist Society. Derrick's boss is speaking."

Antony vaguely remembered agreeing to hear his opinions. "Er—I'm not certain. I'm doing a lecture this afternoon..."

"Great! You'll be in form then. Actually, the SASS is in a bit of a bind. The chap upholding God and all that has come down with Bubonic plague or something. So, I told Derrick I knew you—"

"Gwena! You told him I'd what? What have you got me into?"

Her dramatic shrug was audible over the phone. "I knew you couldn't resist speaking for God. Never let it be said that my little brother let the side down."

He started to protest, but all he could do was groan and give in to an overwhelming urge to run his hand through his hair—a nervous habit he thought he had broken.

"Right!" Gwen's voice held a ring of triumph. She had obviously taken his silence for consent. "Eight o'clock. The Old Library on Michael Street, off Cornmarket. How many students do you have with you? I'll get tickets for them, too."

"Gwena..."

"Oh, yes, the resolution is: This House is Resolved that God does not exist."

"Gwena..." he tried again, but she had rung off. He turned to Felicity shaking his head. "You won't believe this."

When he told her, however, she not only believed it, but thoroughly endorsed the plan. "That's brilliant! *You'll* be brilliant. What an opportunity."

Antony appreciated her support but he was far from convinced. Actually, he was convinced — convinced he'd make a hash of it. He meant it when he told Gwena he was always open to hearing other opinions. And he enjoyed a lively discussion with an honest exchange of ideas. But that was a far remove from a public debate with a polished speaker.

He continued to think as his feet carried him back to college. He took a seat in hall still oblivious to his surroundings and was only vaguely aware of the plate of food set in front of him.

After all, how did one prove the existence of God? His field was church history. He knew the classic approaches: the ontological argument, the first cause argument, the argument from design, and the moral argument. A full university course at the least. Better, a lifetime of study and thinking. How to present that in a limited time to a hostile audience?

Focus on just one, perhaps? But which one? He personally found the teleological — first cause — argument, persuasive. Nothing could create itself. The logic seemed clear. Certainly he believed in a big bang. What else would you call God stepping out into an utter void and calling all into existence? But surely one would need to be a scientist to make headway before the student atheists with this argument. And the same with the argument from design.

The ontological argument? He shuddered at trying to prove the existence of God by logic alone. He was a storyteller, not a mathematician or philosopher.

That left him with the moral argument. Human beings have an instinctive sense of justice, we are offended when we are treated unfairly. Moral laws transcend human law because many human laws are unjust. Therefore, there must be a moral Authority above human authority...

"Antony, you haven't eaten a bite." Felicity cut across his reverie. "Isn't it almost time for your lecture?"

He felt the blood drain from his head. Surely not. He had hours yet to prepare. Then he realized. "Oh, yes. At Lincoln. Yes. Soon." He looked down the table at the group he had brought to Oxford with him. Clare and Brian smiled at him.

Fine for them. This was a holiday, even a bit of a romance, he suspected, an easy way to earn seminar credits. And it was supposed to be something of a break for Antony himself—sharing some of his favorite bits of church history with a few students, spending time with Felicity in graceful surroundings.

And here he was in the middle of a murder and on the line to prove the existence of God. He stifled a groan and forced himself to take a bite of roast beef. Unfortunately, the gravy had congealed and he couldn't swallow it. He was saved from choking by a large swallow of water. A bite of his roast potato was the best he could do.

He chewed slowly, letting his mind revert. *There is an authoritative nature to the moral law. But laws are only as authoritative as one who commands them...*

"So what's at Lincoln?"

It was fortunate Felicity was on topic or Antony might have sat there the rest of the afternoon chewing on a cold potato while he alternately thought and fretted. "Ah, Lincoln. John Wesley's rooms. One bit of Oxford history we skipped over in going from the martyrs to the Tractarians—the Holy Club."

Felicity laughed. "What an awful name."

"Yes, it was intended as a put-down of their being sanctimonious. Rather like 'Methodist' was meant as an insult for being methodical."

Felicity nodded. "Like the Redcoats calling those obnoxious rebels Yankees."

A short time later Antony faced his little group gathered around him in the rather cramped quarters of a room in Chapel Quad of Lincoln College overlooking Turl Street. *Focus on the job at hand,* he admonished himself. *Tonight's problems will be with you soon enough.* He cleared his throat. "This is the room that John Wesley is believed to have occupied when he became a Fellow in 1726. It was renovated by American Methodists at the beginning of the last century."

"Student rooms should be so elegant today." Felicity ran her hand over the exquisite linenfold paneling covering the walls. "And that fireplace is beautiful."

"Love the red carpet," Sheila agreed. "But they're murder to keep clean. Red shows every spot."

"Of course, Wesley would have had a servant to worry about such mundane things." Antony took his place beneath the portrait of John Wesley hanging over the marble fireplace Felicity had admired. He could picture the small, earnest young man sitting in one of the brown leather wing backed chairs at the round table in the centre of the room. At barely five foot two and of slight build, the capacious chair must have nearly swallowed him.

John rubbed his forehead and frowned at the small red notebook open on the table before him. He had begun keeping this record of his days whilst a gownsman at Christ Church College. He flipped back through some of the early pages and, reading the code he wrote in as easily as if it were English, reviewed his undergraduate days: He never stinted his study of classics and logic – subjects which came easily enough to him since he had learned Greek at his mother's knee. But most of all he had enjoyed the 'Oxford Life'. He shook his head as he read accounts of the time he spent frequenting coffee houses, playing cards and making excursions up the river.

He got up to put another coal on his fire, then continued his reminiscence. Winning the Fellowship to Lincoln College had been a fine thing. He liked to believe he would have won it on his own merit, as he had already become known as an exceedingly conscientious Greek tutor, but it had been most convenient that the position was open only to one born in the diocese of Lincoln. And that his father had connections with Dr. Morley, Rector of the College. The examination in Homer and Horace was an easy enough formality for one of his scholarship. And his father had been ecstatic at his election.

A knock at the door interrupted his reverie and his brother Charles came in. "Are you ready, Brother?" He asked in Latin, for the brothers had long ago adopted the habit of conversing in that language.

"Semper paratus." I am always ready, John replied and rose to his feet. He pulled his hat and cloak from a hook by the door and hurried down the staircase.

On the street they met six of their companions. It was only a few steps around the corner and down the High to Saint Mary's, but the mob who had gathered to mock them made it somewhat slow going. "Bible bigots!" A young man in a short black undergraduate gown yelled after them.

That opened the floodgate of jeers and catcalls. "Bible moths!" Another flung at them. "Sacramentarians!" "Methodists!"

John took his brother's arm to speak in his ear so as to be heard, "Should not we all be called by the same name? Surely accusers and accused alike are all simply Christians."

Charles, however, didn't reply. Instead he stepped aside to the edge of the pavement where a young man whose shabby clothing proclaimed him to be a servitor rather than the gentleman commoner the Wesleys and their companions were. The servitor's face spoke clearly his longing to join this group on their unfailing weekly trek to receive Holy Communion.

Since it was forbidden for students of a higher rank to speak to servitors in public, Charles simply beckoned to the fellow to join them. At first he seemed not to notice or to understand. John added his nod as endorsement to his brother's unspoken invitation. Just as they reached the door the ragged student slipped in behind them.

"Who was that scruffy fellow?" John asked Charles when they were returning to John's rooms after the service.

"Chap by the name of George Whitfield. He's a servitor at Pembroke. Seems his father is an innkeeper, so his experience as a bartender makes him well suited as a servant. He has approached me — secretly, of course — for religious counsel. I gave him some books, which I believe he has found helpful. He said he has long observed our group and intently wished to be part of it."

Charles paused and looked at his older brother, as if fearing his disapproval. "I did suggest he might join us one evening. After dark, of course."

John did not forbid the invitation, but George Whitfield didn't appear at any of their nightly meetings the following week. And John himself had other things to think about.

On Monday he went to the stationers in the Broad to purchase some much-needed paper and ink with the few pennies he had in his pocket.

As was the practice of all in their little society, he gave away each year all he had after providing for his own necessities. He smiled as he recalled that in the first year of his endeavor, having thirty pounds he had lived on twenty-eight, and given away two. The next year, receiving sixty pounds, he still lived on twenty-eight and gave away thirty-two. The third year he received ninety pounds and gave away sixty-two. This year having received one hundred and twenty pounds he continued to live on twenty-eight as before, giving to the poor all the rest.

Reflecting on that as he left the stationers he was feeling tempted to self satisfaction when he caught sight of one of the poor girls he and his fellows had been teaching to read since the Bishop of Oxford had given approval to their work.

"Mary," he called to her. She seemed half starved and was shivering with the cold. Have you nothing to cover you but that thin linen gown?"

She looked at him with eyes that seemed far too large for her face. "Sir, this is all I have." Wesley put his hand into his pocket, but found it empty. Promising to help her as soon as he could, he went on into his room.

Here Antony paused and looked at his students sitting comfortably around the warm room and indicated the paintings the Methodist restorers had hung on the paneled walls. "In Wesley's day, the walls were hung with pictures as well. And they seemed to accuse him. 'It struck me,' he recorded in his journal, 'Will thy Master say, "Well done, good and faithful steward," Thou hast adorned thy walls with the money which might have screened this poor creature from the cold! O Justice! O Mercy! Are not these pictures the blood of this poor maid'?

"To my knowledge it isn't recorded that Wesley sold his pictures, but it's hard to imagine that he would have done anything less.

"Perhaps Wesley's mind was on this or some other aspect of the self-examination he so strongly urged when he dismissed the last of his Greek tutorial students early on a Friday afternoon."

His stomach growled and he glanced at the timepiece on his mantle. Not yet three o'clock. Hungry as he was, though, he would not break the fast he and his companions undertook every Wednesday and Friday. In a short time they would meet in William Morgan's rooms in Christ Church for their nightly study of the Greek New Testament to be followed by a light supper. He would leave now and take some exercise walking around Christ Church Meadow.

He had not been getting enough exercise of late and he was a great walker. Just two summers ago he and Charles had walked the seventy-five miles to Epworth to visit their family and help their father with his parish work at St. Andrew's Church. The fond memory of being in the heart of his close, intellectual family was interrupted when he saw William Morgan approaching him in some anxiety. "William!" He called in greeting.

Morgan's furrowed brow lightened when he saw his friend. "I have just come from visiting a condemned wife-murderer in the Castle, Ponson by name. It is a desperate case. He will soon be executed and he is in much anguish of soul.

"Will you return with me?"

"By all means. But let us get Charles to go with us as well."

In a short time the three men stood outside the former Medieval castle that now served as Oxford's jail. The crumbling tower atop the green mound of a hill loomed a dismal hulk under a grey sky. Christ Church College, which owned the prison, leased it to wardens who profited by charging prisoners for their board and lodging. A gallows stood beside the tower, where the unfortunate Ponson would soon see his end.

Morgan approached the Ordinary, a son of the Etty family who ran the prison for the college. Although the Ordinary served as chaplain to the souls incarcerated within the walls only the fact that he stood outside distinguished his appearance from those in his care. If anything the chaplain looked meaner and more disreputable than many of his prisoners. "You shall not obstruct our entrance, Mr. Etty. The God of all compassion shall make an entrance for us so that our acts of mercy may continue." As Morgan accompanied his brave words with the clink of coins, the three men were allowed to pass.

Ponson was not alone in the condemned cell, but the other prisoners drew back as the turnkey pulled the iron door open to allow the visitors entrance. Ponson, though, rushed forward and threw himself on his knees, grasping Morgan's legs. "I don't want to burn!" He was shaking so hard he almost pulled Morgan off his feet. "'angin's bad enough. But not eternal damnation in 'ell afterwards."

John stepped forward and pulled Ponson to his feet. He addressed the terrified man in his softest voice, speaking more kindly even than he had done to the urchin Mary Hobsey a few days before. "My friend, let us tell you what joy can await those who enter into the presence of their Lord."

The prisoner continued to tremble, but seemed calmer as Wesley continued, inviting him to come to Jesus, the sinner's friend. As he spoke, the man's countenance lightened, but there was time for no more as the iron door clanked open and the warden stood before them, filling the passage with his straddle-legged stance, his size increased by the heavy boots and leather jerkin he wore and the black, greasy hair that fell to his shoulders. His hand on his sword hilt, he growled to the prisoners, "The dead warrant just come down. Execution in the mornin'. Look to yer souls."

"From that day the Oxford Methodists added regular

prison visiting to their list of spiritual exercises," Antony concluded. His students snapped their notebooks closed and began talking about how they would spend the rest of the afternoon.

Antony gave a half-suppressed sigh. His work was finished. He now had nothing to distract him from worrying about the debate.

Sixteen

Antony sat at the long table to the right of the podium and looked around the room. He felt overwhelmed with the weight of the learned discussions that had been held here through the years. The dark wood gallery running around the deep red walls seemed filled with the ghosts of hearers who had come to cheer—and to mock—erudite speakers through the years. Tonight the long benches, resembling church pews, which crossed the wooden floor before him were filling with a lively audience. Chatting among themselves, they filled the benches. A few even looked his way and smiled. He wondered how soon the smiles would turn to jeers.

He forced himself to focus on the row in front of him, filled with faces he knew would remain stalwart. Felicity winked at him and gave him a discreet thumbs-up. Yes, Felicity and the others would be loyal. Even if they were disappointed with him.

Gwena made her best leading lady entrance, swinging open both of the double glass doors at the back of the room and bestowing gracious nods on any who looked her way. Two girls sitting on the aisle recognized her and squealed and applauded. She paused and shook their hands before moving on with a little wave to the rest of the room. Two men followed in her wake: Derrick, who had evoked the offhand remark that had landed Antony in this position, dressed in a dark suit with a red and black striped shirt and a tall, fair-haired man whose aristocratic features and bearing seemed to set him apart from everyone else in the room. Apart and above.

Antony rose to his feet as Gwena approached. "Well done, Squib, I knew you wouldn't let me down." Although her voice betrayed just the slightest note of relief which said she had been afraid he might do exactly that.

Antony winced at her use of her childhood name for him, and at the thought that he might yet let her down—or at least himself—but he put on a brave smile as he walked around the table to shake hands with Derrick.

"And this is your honourable opponent, Allyn Luffington. Allyn, the Reverend Antony Sherwood." The men exchanged polite greetings and shook hands. Allyn's grip was cool and distant. Antony was aware that his own hand was warm and moist.

From there on the evening was something of a blur to Antony. The student chair of the society, a young woman in a black dress and black boots with long brown hair and a copious amount of silver jewelry, welcomed everyone, introduced the speakers—each of whom received a polite round of applause—and explained the rules of the evening. Since this was a chamber-style debate each speaker would deliver his address and the audience would be allowed to respond, but there would be no formal vote at the end as there would be in a competitive debate. Antony supposed that made him feel marginally better.

"And now, gentlemen, the motion is before you: 'This house is resolved that God does not exist.'"

Oddly, it seemed to Antony, since the resolution was stated in the negative, Luffington was upholding the affirmative position. But Antony was quite happy to have the opposition speak first. He took out his pen preparatory to making notes. Luffington began with the *A priori* argument that it was illogical to believe in the existence of a being that could not be proved by any of the five senses—with which His believers claimed He Himself had gifted them. "Illogical in itself." He gave a slight wave of his hand as if the debate could end right there. "A God so omniscient, omnipresent and omnipotent, we are told, that He," each pronoun reference to the deity was pronounced with a puff of air as if to capitalize the H, "sees the smallest sparrow fall, and yet He can't be bothered to prove Himself to His creatures."

He then moved on to the A *posteriori* claim that the world, by its very nature is other than it would be if God existed. "And so, once again, the simplest of logic teaches us that there cannot be a God."

The problem of evil, Antony scrawled across the top of his notepad, resisting the impulse to shake his head. Of all the atheistic arguments, this was the most weighty, the one that had been around for longest, had the most words written about it. In a way the premise was incontrovertible. Evil did exist. One was surrounded with daily proof.

And Luffington, a smooth and engaging speaker went on to detail the illogic—that word again—of an all powerful, benevolent God who would allow children to starve, young mothers to be ravaged by terrible disease, young men to die in war.

Antony ran his hand through his hair, pushing it back from his forehead and letting it fall like spillikins. Where did he start? At creation, with the concept of a God who wanted children, not puppets, even if his children made bad, even disastrous choices? At the fall, where man chose to disobey?

"And for my final exhibit, let me share with you a story that is even yet unfolding right here in Oxford. Monica, the Mother Superior of a house of nuns in Fairacres, just down the Iffley Road, a woman of a lifetime of charitable works and prayer, of devotion to her God, was found last week floating face down in the Isis. God could have prevented her careless step that led her into the water, you might be thinking. But then, even a very good person can be guilty of an incautious moment. Neither her fault nor God's—these things just happen." He paused for dramatic effect.

"But let me assure you, it was nothing so simple. Before we knew the fate of Mother Monica the case came to my attention in a most graphic way when a young lady visiting the Ashmolean Museum," his gaze swept the audience, but didn't linger on Felicity, "discovered a newly crimsoned reliquary in our Treasures of Heaven exhibit." The audience drew in a collective breath. Antony saw Felicity shiver and pale.

"A severed foot in the shrine that had once held a medieval relic. Grisly, yes. But not the first, for I am told that a few days earlier a disembodied hand had been found, coincidentally," did he put just a touch too much emphasis on that word? "by the same young woman, again in a shrine reserved for objects of devotion." Now Felicity wasn't the only one in the room to shiver and look slightly ill. "Yes, Mother Monica's body parts. And still the police have not found the perpetrators of this outrage against a holy woman whose whole life was lived in devotion to her supposedly all-knowing, all-powerful, all-loving God.

"A God who allowed the body of his devoted follower to be hacked to pieces before she was strangled, then her body stored in a filthy lockup and disposed of in a river. If this God does exist who would choose to serve Him?

"Gentlemen and Ladies, I rest my case." He took his seat with a sketch of a bow and a barely suppressed air of triumph.

Now all eyes were on Antony. He picked up his notes and, with a great force of willpower walked to the podium. He cleared his throat and opened his mouth. But no words came out. He drew breath to try again, but then he knew. He pushed his notes aside, looked out over the crowded room, then turned to his opponent. "I thank my worthy opponent for telling the story of Mother Monica in such a moving way. And this lady is only the latest—or perhaps the closest to us—of the countless victims of crime, violence, injustice—of man's inhumanity to man—that constantly surround us.

"So I would like to ask that we take a moment of silence for the victims of all such evil. If you would just bow your heads with me to pay your respects for all who suffer in this imperfect, fallen world in which we live." Every head in the room bowed in a profound silence.

It occurred to Antony that he might do worse than simply have his audience spend their time in silence, allowing each person time to look into their own soul. But he didn't have the courage. "Thank you." Heads came up. Eyes fixed on him. "I'm not a debater. I'm a storyteller. So I am going to tell you two stories this evening. Stories, like that of my worthy opponent that took place right here in the hallowed ground of Oxford.

"Stories, my opponent will point out, of injustice and suffering. But I would contend that the proof of the pudding is in the eating and the proof of any belief system is in the living – and the dying. The question is not does evil exist? but rather, is good stronger?"

He then recounted, with dramatic detail worthy of his actress sister, the executions of Latimer, Ridley and Cranmer. "And we can ask, did their deaths light the inextinguishable flame Latimer promised? Look around you. The faith continues. The church still exists. The flame flickers, I'll admit. But it is not quenched. If it were, we would not be having this debate."

Then he told the story of the Holy Club. "These men, who were later joined by many women, saw the poverty, the hunger, the suffering around them and saw it as their God-given job to do all in their power to correct it. At the end of a long life well lived, John Wesley died in his own bed with his friends and coworkers around him. I'll close with his last words: 'The best of all, God is with us.'"

Antony took his seat to polite applause, although the one glance he allowed himself at the bench where Felicity and his students sat told him they weren't at all lukewarm. The moderator then opened the discussion to the audience. The question seemed to come down to disputing whether Cranmer, Wesley and their followers were acting in accord with a higher power or simply on their own volition. As was to be expected, the weight of opinion fell to the humanists, but Antony, who remained quiet during the exchange, felt like giving his own cheer when Felicity asked those who were bewailing the preponderance of evil how they explained the presence of good in the universe.

Overall, he felt, it could have been worse. They convinced no one, of course. But perhaps they had given people something to think about. He could ask no more.

Seventeen

"I was so proud of you." Felicity accompanied her words with a bright smile to give them emphasis, because, judging from the dark circles under his eyes, she was quite certain Antony had spent most of the night replaying the debate.

He didn't seem to have heard her. She started to repeat herself, but just then the bus arrived. The priority for their morning was to visit Sister Gertrude who had been moved to the convent infirmary yesterday. When they were settled in a front seat, though, he gave a curt nod that told her he had heard her.

"Thank you," he said it almost dismissively. "But I've been thinking about something Luffington said."

Felicity nodded. Just as she thought. A whole night thinking *I should have said this... If only I'd thought of that...* "Antony," she began.

But he ignored her opening. "The details he gave about Monica's murder. I didn't realize the police had established that the mutilations were done while she was still alive."

Felicity shuddered. "I was hoping that wasn't so, but I had suspected it all along. I don't think parts from a dead body would still bleed. And there was fresh blood on the reliquaries." She could have given in to bewailing the horror, but she bit her lip and carried on. "I suppose Luffington figured out the same thing when he saw the shine in the

Ashmolean display. That was what alerted me."

Antony nodded slowly. "Yes, I expect you're right. But how did he know about the 'dirty lockup,' as he said?"

"I suppose it could have been in the news. I haven't seen a paper or the telly for days. Or he may be working more closely with the police than we realized. But most probably he was just carried away with the flow of his own rhetoric.

"Oh!" She grabbed Antony's arm. "I didn't tell you. Luffington. I saw him at St. Mary Mag's yesterday. Only I didn't realize who it was until I saw him at the debate."

Antony turned to her on the seat. "You what? Our evangelistic atheist was in church?" He paused. "Oh, probably researching the 'enemy'."

"No, no, nothing like that. I mean outside the church. I ran into him — almost literally. He was coming down from the bell tower and going out for a run or something before the closing peal. I think he must be one of the university ringers. Is that possible?"

"Quite possible. It's not necessary to ascribe to any faith to be a bell ringer. It's a popular hobby and purely social."

"But he isn't a student or anything."

"Oh, I see what you mean." He shrugged. "Probably a life member or something."

The bus arrived at the stop for Fairacres so Felicity didn't bother mentioning that Luffington had also leered at her in Christ Church Meadow. Or had he? Maybe it was just his perennially superior manner.

They met Dorcas on the way to the infirmary. "Oh, no, she's not in there. Insisted on getting back to work at the Press. Of course there is so much to do." She shook her head. "Such a shambles. I sent Sarah with her and Sister Hannah. I don't know if you've met her, but Hannah is very reliable and I've asked her to stay close to Gertrude until we find out what's going on. It's so worrying."

The door of the Press stood open. A young woman was sweeping just inside. "I'm Sarah, the telephone sister. Except I'm not a sister yet." She touched her white novice's veil. Felicity introduced Antony and they went on in. In spite of the fans the sisters had set to pull in fresh air from every window and doorway, the Press still reeked with the acrid smell of smoke and burnt oil. Antony turned immediately to helping Sister Hannah with a stack of files she was struggling to shift. Felicity went on into the office where she found Gertrude sitting at her desk, examining a pile of sodden, smudged papers. "Sister Gertrude, should you be doing this? Shouldn't you be resting?"

Gertrude looked up. Her normally round cheeks were hollowed and she had a smudge of soot on her nose, but the eyes behind her tortoiseshell glasses were bright. "No, truly. I'm fine. Just a tiny headache. I hardly notice it." As she spoke, she rubbed her forehead and left a black streak beneath her veil. "I'm very lucky, really."

"And you don't have any memory of anything? Who attacked you? Or what you told them?"

She shook her head. "Like I told the police. If I saw anything, I don't remember. It's all a blur. I certainly don't remember what I said. I assume it must have been something about the manuscript, and apparently I would have answered anything I was asked. Probably in great detail." She grinned. "I didn't realize I was such a chatterbox. But, really, I don't know anything I wouldn't have freely told anyone who asked."

Felicity looked around the disheveled office. "What a mess. But it doesn't look as though much actually burned."

"Just this horrid oily black soot on everything. To tell the truth, the firemen made the most mess. Everything was soaked with water—and since we have so much paper here…"

"So there was no actual fire?"

"It seems they—he, whoever—dropped burning rags soaked in creosote through the side window—the one sheltered by the hedge where no one would have seen them. There was some burning there, but mostly smoke."

"But why?"

Gertrude spread her hands helplessly. "That's what the police keep asking. Maybe to get me to run out—which I apparently did, and then was grabbed and taken to the summerhouse. Maybe so they could run in and search our files. Maybe just wanton destruction… Who knows?"

"You keep the door locked when you're in here?"

"Always. When I'm working alone."

"I don't suppose you can tell if anything has been stolen?"

Gertrude surveyed the chaos with an ironic smile. "If only." She turned back to her desk. "And the worst part of it is that it will be ages before I can get back to Frideswide."

Felicity was pleased to be able to give her one piece of hopeful news. "At least we can help a bit there. Antony is taking his seminar group to Binsey so I can work on the background you said you wanted. I'll make some notes. Just impressions of what it's like today. Would that help? Would you like some pictures of the well? I could take some on my phone if you like."

Gertrude brightened. "Oh, that would be very helpful. Actually, though, if you wouldn't mind," she bent over and pulled out the bottom draw of her metal desk. "Fortunately it was in here, so, unlike our computers, this was protected from the water." She pulled out a serious-looking Nikon. "We purchased this a few years ago so we could get high resolution pictures for publication. This is so good we can even photograph documents. I photographed the Frideswide document before I sent it out."

"Great. Just show me what to do."

"Smile!" Felicity said when Antony walked in a few minutes later just as she was practicing focusing the lens. She snapped, but there was no flash.

"Oh, sorry. I forgot to show you that." Gertrude made the adjustments to the camera settings while Felicity explained the project to Antony.

Unanswered questions notwithstanding, Felicity was heartened to see Sister Gertrude doing so well. In spite of the chaos, she had no doubt but that the Press would be up and running again in record time. And now Felicity looked forward to being able to contribute to the Frideswide book in another way with some photos.

They had lingered longer at the convent than they had

expected and after waiting some time for the bus they finished by practically running the last bit to arrive—out of breath and a few minutes late—at the Bodleian where Antony's charges had spent the morning researching the various papers they would write on topics related to the Oxford in Christian History theme of their seminar.

Antony surveyed his group with a frown. "Has anyone seen Marc? He was supposed to meet us here." He looked at his watch.

"Wasn't he at the library?" Felicity asked.

"No, he's doing C. S. Lewis, so he took the bus to Headington to see The Kilns." As he spoke his phone rang. "Right then. You stay there. We'll come to you. Not a problem." He returned the phone to his pocket. "Bus was late. We'll meet him at Carfax. It's a bit out of our way, but it'll give us a chance to take in an extra site."

As Antony turned to lead the group across the street Sheila, swathed in flowing cape, scarf and full skirt, fell into step beside Felicity, her cane tapping on the pavement with every step, but not slowing her down in the least. She began talking about the hymns of Charles Wesley, which she was doing her essay on. "You know he wrote at least six thousand hymns, some say the count is closer to eight. I've decided to focus on his 'Hymns for the Lord's Supper.' I really hadn't realized before that the Wesleys were such high churchman."

Felicity smiled and agreed, taking in as well bits of the conversation behind them as Brian talked about John Henry Newman, "Did you know Newman was an Evangelical when he was appointed vicar of St. Mary's?"

"No! Who would have thought?" Gareth laughed. "Well, no one could have accused Laud of that when he was appointed Chancellor of Oxford. I found out that before he became Archbishop of Canterbury..."

"'O the Depth of Love Divine' may be his greatest," Sheila continued with her topic and began singing in a quite lovely light voice, "Who shall say how bread and wine God into us conveys! How the bread his flesh imparts, how the wine transmits his blood..."

Felicity let her mind wander, thankful that her Saint

Frideswide work was finished.

Marc was waiting for them at his appointed place with a shy, apologetic grin. They continued on up Queen Street, now with another voice informing any who cared to listen about his morning's research. There was no doubt Antony's students were thoroughly immersed in their topics.

A short time later Antony came to a stop before a high green mound. A dirt path zigzagged to the top and a few trees dotted its side. A square tower rose to the back and beyond that stood a shorter, crenelated, round tower. "Oxford Castle," Antony announced. "St. George's Tower," he pointed to the tall stone structure, "was built in the twelfth century to guard the west gate of the city. After the Civil War, the castle became the local prison. If we had been here in the eighteenth century we might have seen our Holy Club members going about their ministry visiting the captive spirits."

At first Felicity thought her imagination was playing tricks on her. She blinked to be certain she hadn't conjured up the sturdy cassocked figure walking toward them from behind the mound. Surely—

Antony raised his hand in greeting and she realized who it was. "Father Ben. What are you doing here?" she asked when he approached.

"Prison visiting," he replied with a smile.

"Really? You mean just like the Methodists?"

He laughed. "No, I mean visiting. Like a tourist. Or a pilgrim. More of a personal journey. The prison closed in 1996. It's a hotel today." He gestured toward the renovated building beyond the Medieval wall. "But actually, in my undergrad days a group of us from the Christian Union did undertake a spot of visiting prisoners. It was probably good for us, although I don't know how much good it did the prisoners. I was rather reliving those days."

"We're on our way to Binsey," Antony said.

"Ah, St. Frideswide's well." Ben's voice rang with a note of nostalgia. Apparently that held memories for him as well.

"Would you care to join us?" Antony asked.

Ben accepted readily and when they headed up Walton Street he assumed somewhat the role of guide. "Jericho, this area is called. I served my title here at St. Barnabas." He pointed to the west where the top of an Italiante campanile showed above the rooftops.

"Rather nice area now. It was just shedding its red light district reputation when I was here. Originally Jericho was outside the city walls and provided a place for travelers to stay if they arrived at Oxford after the gates were closed. Then industry grew up because of the canal. Most famous as home of the Oxford University Press now, of course." As he spoke they walked along the side of the impressive gold sandstone building and passed Great Clarendon Street.

But Felicity's mind was on something entirely different. Jericho was where that adventurous schoolboy had found the relic of Margaret Clitherow. Surely it was just a coincidence that Father Ben was intimately acquainted with the area. Felicity scanned the canal bank as they approached it but only her excited imagination revealed a shriveled hand protruding from a pile of smoldering leaves.

She forced herself to shake off the image as they crossed a bridge that spanned both the canal and train track and set them on a footpath across a wide green meadow. "Port Meadow." Ben waved his arm at the green expanse. "It's called Oxford's oldest monument because it has changed little since prehistoric times—still unplowed. King Alfred gave it to the Freemen of Oxford for their help in defending the city against the Danes."

Felicity quickened her pace to bring her aside Antony. She slipped her hand into his and together they pulled aside as Ben took the others on across the meadow. "What a beautiful day." She felt the sun warm on her head. And the day became even more beautiful, and warmer, when Antony took her in his arms and kissed her.

They grinned at each other for a moment, both feeling like naughty school children. Antony sighed and looked at their departing group. "Back to work."

They caught up with the others on the far side of the meadow at a high-arched bridge painted a vibrant magenta. The students were gathered around Father Ben who was taking obvious pleasure in his role as tour guide. "This part of the Thames is known as the Isis and this particular bit is where one Charles Dodson and his friend were rowing with three small girls when young Alice asked Dodson to tell them a story to make the time pass more quickly. Hold that thought and more shall be revealed." He whirled and strode on over the bridge.

Felicity and Antony followed along, hand in hand, mirroring Clare and Brian's hand-holding. Here the path followed the bank of the river, then across another green field until they came to a cluster of buildings surrounded with an autumnal glory of golden trees. With as much confidence as if he did it every day Ben pushed through a gate at the bottom of a large garden. As they advanced up the walk Felicity realized this was not the grounds of a private home as she had first thought. "Oh, it's a pub!" She was quite relieved that they hadn't trespassed because the people she saw sitting at tables scattered around the lawn certainly gave the impression of a private party.

"Yes, indeed," Ben agreed. "The Perch. Said to be where Lewis Carroll gave his first reading of *Alice in Wonderland*. Ben led the way across the patio and into the building. He suggested they order what refreshment they might like and enjoy the hospitality.

Felicity readily agreed. She chose chicken pate on rustic bread with pickles and left Antony to bring it to her while she sank into a garden chair next to a flower bed with yellow butterflies flitting among the purple asters and bees buzzing around the Michaelmas daisies.

She was so relaxed that without the camera hanging around her neck she might have forgotten that she was there on an assignment.

When they had finished their leisurely lunch their self-appointed guide took them back through the pub, along a lane between green fields toward a cluster of houses, some stucco and some stone, all looking very old to Felicity's American eyes. "These are all listed buildings." Ben confirmed her thoughts. "A few years ago Christ Church College, who owns the village, proposed to double its size by building seven more accommodations. The idea caused such an uproar they withdrew the plan and Binsey remains its peaceful bit of Olde England."

The lane now stretched out before them, a pleasant stroll between golden trees and wayside bushes with crunchy leaves under foot. Around every curve Felicity expected to see the tower of an English country church rising through the branches, but only plowed fields and pastures dotted with sheep stretched beyond the brambles. "How far is it?" She asked their guide.

"A little over half a mile. Ten minute walk or so," he replied with his perennially jovial air. She wondered if some of his nonchalance had been acquired in his years living in the Caribbean.

"Strange — to build the church so far from the village."

"No, no. Church was built first — in Saxon times. As an oratory by Frideswide, if you believe the legends. It became a priory in medieval times. Apparently there were houses all along this lane then. Either the village was larger in those days, or it moved."

A few more minutes of walking brought them to a thick cluster of trees. Through the drooping branches of an enormous evergreen Felicity glimpsed the sturdy stone church with its recessed lancet windows and a flat tower supporting two bells. The wide churchyard was covered with luxuriant, unmown grass dotted with leaning tombstones. Picturesque, but slightly spooky. A place she might think twice before visiting on Halloween.

The door inside the small porch was unlocked and they entered the sanctuary through a wide golden arch that spanned the whitewashed walls. Ben put his hand on the arch. "This is the earliest datable stonework in the church. Its zigzag pattern makes it Norman. Probably late twelfth century." Felicity snapped several photos, one of the expanse of the arch and some close-ups for Sister Gertrude. Then went on into the nave to examine the lead-lined font-bowl, which Ben was pointing out as also dating from Norman times.

"The present church was built on the site of a Saxon church," he assured them, "so its association with Frideswide is very possible. The well made it a place of pilgrimage for centuries. Henry VIII is known to have visited. We are told that 'the very pavement was worn away by the knees of the pilgrims,' and that restored cripples hung their crutches around the church to testify to their cure."

Felicity wandered around the small sanctuary, taking pictures of the antique pump organ, the oil lanterns hanging over pulpit and reading desk, the altar and reredos. She was undoubtedly getting far more than Gertrude would need, but this would give her choices. One of the outstanding features of the church was the open ceiling, showing the ancient weathered beams supporting the roof. The space between the timbers was painted a lucent turquoise blue that highlighted the silvery tones of the wood and suggested the very heavens shining through on the congregation.

Felicity took shots from several angles, then, wanting to do the ceiling full justice, lay down in the wide aisle between the rows of high-backed wooden pews and pointed her camera straight up. "That's extreme devotion to art." Felicity lowered her camera to see Father Ben standing over her smiling. He extended his hand in an offer of help. Felicity handed him her camera and scrambled to her feet.

"Not art. Duty."

"How many shots have you taken?" He asked.

She checked the number on the digital display. "Not sure. This says 75, but I haven't taken that many. Sister Gertrude had some on here already." Felicity looked around and realized that Antony and the others had gone out into the churchyard. Now the space that had seemed so peaceful and hallowed with soft light felt cold and isolated. With an urge to fill the silence she told Ben about her photography project for the Fairacres Press as she headed for the door.

"That's interesting." He raised a heavy dark eyebrow in query. "And what discovery have you made about Frideswide?"

"Nothing particularly new, I fear. Although I suppose unearthing a manuscript of impeccable provenance that supports the other known accounts adds weight to the Frideswide story."

"Ah, and what is the provenance?"

She considered for a moment, but couldn't see any reason not to tell him. It would all be public when the booklet was published. "The Sisters of the Holy Paraclete found it in their archives. It came from their house in Leicester. I suppose that's what makes it most interesting."

Ben agreed instantly. "Yes, with Algar's lands in Leicestershire, it suggests authenticity for the whole legend. Do you suppose Algar could have repented of his villainy and ceded lands to Frideswide?"

"In gratitude when Frideswide's prayers for his sight were answered?" Felicity suggested as they made their way out into the sunlight of the churchyard. "Possible, I suppose. Unless you accept the version that he died straightway. There are so many versions." Felicity sighed.

Ben was quiet for some time. "If Algar did make a land grant I suppose it could arguably belong to Christ Church College, as all the Binsey lands still do."

"You mentioned that earlier. It seems strange to me. How did that happen?"

Ben laughed. "The reformation happened. Frideswide's nunnery—the one she established in Oxford—had become an Augustinian friary in the 1100's. The friary owned all the lands that had been Frideswide's. Cardinal Wolsey dissolved the friary to establish his Cardinal College. When Wolsey fell out of favor, Henry took over and named it Christ Church." He shrugged. "Logical enough when you know the history."

"And those claims are still valid today?" Felicity said it almost under her breath. So did that mean the charter she found could still be legal?

"Oh, quite legal." She jumped as if Ben had answered her mental question, then realized he meant the claims of Christ Church. She had the feeling Ben was preparing to ask her another question, but she hurried on toward the voices she heard around the corner of the churchyard.

She found Antony and the others standing around a rectangular hole in the ground about the size of a doorway. The white cement border around the opening was strewn with somewhat wilted posies of autumn flowers. Clusters of golden chrysanthemums, deep red dahlias, vivid yellow marigolds covered the low wall and small pots on each side of the steep stairway descending into the well were filled with zinnias of every color. "Oh, what is it?" Felicity asked.

"St. Frideswide's well," Antony replied.

"Do pilgrims bring offerings?" The flowers puzzled her.

"There's apparently been a blessing recently. It's frequently done at holy wells. Most likely for St. Frideswide's day."

"Of course." Now Felicity realized. That had been the beginning of this whole affair—the grand patronal festival around Frideswide's shrine in Christ Church Cathedral. When everything had gone so wrong. She shivered in spite of the sun filtering through the trees surrounding the well.

The story Antony now told his students was a somewhat different version from the one Felicity was most familiar with—more in keeping with the miraculous nature of the well. "Frideswide fled to Binsey to escape a forced marriage to a King Algar of Mercia. His pursuit of her was halted when he was struck blind, but Frideswide's prayers brought forth a healing spring, whose waters cured his blindness."

"Yes," Ben moved into the foreground again. "In medieval times this became well known as a treacle well and pilgrims flocked to it. 'Treacle' meant an antidote to poison, so a treacle well was a healing well. And—remember, I told you you'd be hearing more about Alice?—that's the source of the Dormouse's tale of Elsie, Lacie and Tillie living at the bottom of a treacle well.

Most of his listeners returned blank looks, but Felicity cried "Yes," as the childhood memory of reading a favorite book came back to her. "Three young girls who lived on treacle, and drew pictures of things beginning with M. And this is the well. How amazing—Saint Frideswide and Alice in Wonderland all coming together."

Antony smiled, "Yes, and some, like our friend Luffington would say there's no difference between the two."

"Father Ben, how did you become such an expert on Alice?" Felicity didn't add that it seemed a surprising enthusiasm for a priest.

"At my mother's knee, you might say. She was an Alice

enthusiast. But more recently, I found the tales most useful entertaining orphans in Barbados." He sketched a bow. "Well, this has been delightful, but I fear I must bid you farewell here. I've promised myself to walk on to Godstow. I want to see the abbey this afternoon."

He stopped and turned when Clare asked, "But what about the poplars?"

Her question was directed to Antony, but he passed it to Ben with the explanation, "Clare is doing Gerard Manley Hopkins for her essay."

"I saw the manuscripts of 'Binsey Poplars' in the Bodleian this morning. They just purchased the most recent autograph copy last spring. They already had four earlier drafts. It's so amazing to see it in the poet's own hand.

"Of course, I know they were cut down. That's what he was writing about: 'All felled, felled, are all felled; / Of a fresh and following folded rank/ Not spared, not one.' But I thought they had been replanted."

"Yes, indeed," Ben replied. "After the poem was first published in 1918. Sadly, a storm early this century made it necessary to cut them again. Poplars aren't particularly long-lived trees anyway. But fortunately, they have been replanted once again and they grow quickly. I'll point you the way. It's the opposite direction to where I'm headed."

He led the way out of the churchyard, but Felicity hung back. Antony turned when he reached the corner of the church. "Coming Felicity?"

"In a minute. I don't have any pictures of the well yet and it will interest Gertrude the most."

"Fine. I'll wait with you."

He had taken three steps toward her when Ben called him back. "Can you help us Father Antony? Just how strongly was Hopkins influenced by the Pre-Raphaelites?"

Antony hesitated. Felicity waved him away. "Oh, go on. It's your job, after all. I'll catch you up before you get to the river."

She was immediately absorbed in her work, hearing only the soughing of the breeze in the trees over her head, the sounds of birds and insects and an occasional gentle baa from the sheep in the adjoining field. Working with a sense of peace inspired by the setting she took several shots showing the well with its overhanging trees, then with the church in the background before moving in to capture it more closely. She knelt at the top of the stairs to photograph the sharply pointed gothic opening to the well itself. Then she noticed the inscription at the back:

S. MARGARETÆ FONTEM
PRECIBUS S. FRIDESWIDÆ UT FERTUR CONCESSUM
INQUINATUM DIU OBRUTUMQUE
IN USUM REVOCAVIT
T. J. PROUT ÆD. XTI ALUMNUS VICARIUS
A.S. MDCCCLXXIV

She snapped a close-up picture, then took a notebook from her pocket and scribbled a hasty translation:

T. J. Prout, alumnus of Christ Church, Vicar (of St Fridewide's), brought back into use St Margaret's well, made to flow by the prayers of St Frideswide, and for long collapsed and fouled. A.D. 1874.

She descended the final few steps into the well. Just one or two shots of the water itself, then she would hurry on to catch up with the others. She knelt on the rough stones and ran her hand over the tiny green plants growing over the lip of the well. Small offerings of flowers had been left on the shelf behind the circular well opening — a bundle of dried lavender, a few roses, and, tied with red ribbon, a posey of wildflowers atop a note. A prayer request, perhaps? Felicity had heard that pregnant women often requested the prayers of St. Margaret of Antioch to whom Frideswide had prayed for help and to whom the well was formally dedicated, although most called it St. Frideswide's well.

The space was so small it was impossible to get a good angle for her shot. She inched forward, leaning her whole body over the well. At that moment she felt the strap fall from her neck and the camera jerked from her hands.

She gave a startled cry and started to turn, but the next thing she knew, she was seeing stars. The world spun and she fell face downward into the well.

Eighteen

All Hallow's Eve

"I was only in the water for seconds, I'm sure."

"And you're certain you aren't hurt?" Antony asked for the third time.

"I'm certain. But I'm awfully glad you came back for me." She had made it as far as the end of the churchyard before sinking onto a mossy rock. She wouldn't have wanted to have to walk all the way back to Oxford alone. "We should catch up with the others." She attempted to struggle to her feet.

Antony tightened his arms around her. "Sit. I rang the police. They'll be here soon."

"Police? Surely that wasn't necessary. They have enough to work on right now."

"Felicity, you're hurt. Your head is bleeding." The control with which Antony spoke must have cost him dearly.

Felicity touched the lump on the side of her head and gave a rueful grimace. "I did this myself. Gave it an almighty whack on the back of that arch. I wanted to give whoever grabbed my camera a good run for his money, but there was no one in sight when I got up." She groaned. "And now I've lost The Press's camera. I'll have to buy them a new one."

"The camera was probably insured, but I wonder about the pictures."

Felicity frowned. "I just took shots of the church and the well. Nothing any tourist couldn't have done. You don't think that's what they were after, do you? I thought it was a simple mugging."

"I'm certain that after everything else that has happened the police will agree that a 'simple mugging' would be too much of a coincidence."

And when they arrived a few minutes later PC Evans and Sergeant Thompson took the report most seriously, indeed. "And you didn't see or hear anything?"

"I had my head in the well, concentrating on my work."

He turned to Antony. "And you were where?"

Antony explained about their group walking on toward the river. "I shouldn't have left her."

"You weren't to know, sir. And you didn't meet anyone on the path or notice anything out of the ordinary?"

Antony shook his head.

"And all your group was with you the whole time?"

"Yes. Absolutely."

"No one fell behind or anything?"

"What are you suggesting? None of my students would do such a thing." Antony's voice rang with indignation. "Father Ben pointed us in the direction of the poplars Clare wanted to see, and we headed straight there. I was the one that turned back when I thought Felicity had been gone too long. And I'm so thankful I did." He reached over and took her hand.

"And Ben?"

"He went on to Godstow Abbey. He took a shortcut he remembered from his student days."

Sergeant Thompson noted that in his book.

"Sergeant, you can't possibly—" Felicity began but at that moment Ryan Evans strode across the churchyard holding a black object dangling from a cut strap.

"Look what I found in the hedgerow. I take it this is the stolen camera?"

"Oh, wonderful!" She stretched out a hand toward it.

"No, no. It will be returned in time, but we'll need to check for fingerprints."

"Oh, of course. But I'm so glad you found it."

Felicity wanted to go straight to the Fairacres convent and tell Gertrude all that had happened, but, in spite of her protests that she was unhurt, Sergeant Thompson insisted they take her to the Accident and Emergency room first. So that by the time they returned to the Seminar House, in spite of finding a message to ring Dorcas waiting for them, it was far too late to do anything but scratch together a hasty supper from the tinned soup they found in the cupboard of the little kitchen their house offered, and go to bed with all of their questions unanswered.

It wasn't until Felicity was in bed that she would allow herself to admit that she did, indeed have a splitting headache. She didn't want Antony to worry and she most certainly didn't want him to insist that she spend a day resting or — worse — that she go back to Kirkthorpe. She had no intention of leaving Oxford until she knew what was going on. With the help of her spiritual director she had been working on controlling her stubbornness and felt she was making strides to conquer her rashness, but there were times when determination was called for.

And besides, tomorrow would surely bring the answers they sought. Apparently today would have if they had returned in time. What else would Dorcas be calling about? The police had found who had murdered Monica and the sisters were planning her requiem. That must be it.

Finally they would have answers for everything that had happened. Thank goodness the police had solved the mystery, because no matter how she examined it, she couldn't see any reason for anything.

Felicity was just sinking to sleep when she realized that tomorrow was All Saints' Day. That meant that tonight was All Hallows' Eve — Halloween. What a far cry this night had been from the lighthearted evenings of her childhood, going trick-or-treating around their neighborhood in spooky costumes with her brothers. It seemed a lifetime ago.

Nineteen

All Saints' Day

And late the next morning when Felicity and Antony returned to Fairacres, Felicity had the feeling that her former existence was not only a lifetime ago, but that it must have occurred on another planet. She was now in her second year of theological college—which meant she had been living in a monastery for more than a year. In this time she had experienced all the liturgical feasts and solemnities that she had been only vaguely, if at all, aware of in her very modern American former life. And she thought she had adjusted to— even learned to revel in—most of the observances.

But when they arrived at the convent expecting answers to the mysteries that had shadowed these past weeks, only to find that, far from having any solutions, Dorcas had simply been issuing an invitation for them to join the community for their All Saints Eucharist, Felicity felt as bemused as Alice must have felt after falling down her rabbit hole. They were surrounded with questions. Where were the answers? Why wasn't anyone doing anything? Couldn't they think of anything more productive than praying?

Felicity opened her mouth, but before she could speak Sarah entered, her face as white as her white novice's veil. "Sister Dorcas, forgive me, but—"

"Yes, Sarah, what is it?"

"Pusey House rang. The police were just there. They've taken Father Benjamin in for questioning."

"Father Ben? Whatever for?"

Her eyes grew wide and round. "They seem to think he murdered Mother Monica."

"What nonsense. I'm sure it will all be straightened out." Then Dorcas's brow furrowed. "Oh, dear. That does leave us without a celebrant." She turned to Antony. "Father, could we possibly impose on you?"

Antony agreed readily.

"Thank you. You'll find Sister Thérèse in the sacristy. Sarah, will you show Father Antony the way?"

Felicity wanted to cry out for him to wait. They needed to talk. Surely the police were wrong, but they must have found some strong evidence to take Ben into custody. Still, Father Ben? Was it possible? She ached to talk it over with Antony, but he was already out the door.

"My dear, I am sorry to leave you, but would you excuse me? This has been something of a shock and there are things I need to see to."

Felicity merely nodded. Sister Dorcas's exit left nothing for Felicity to do but to find Sister Gertrude and confess the fiasco of the day before.

She walked slowly toward the Press, her eyes focused on the path before her. The sound of a quick step approaching made her look up to see a flutter of brown robe and the nun she was seeking coming toward her. She had the feeling Sister Gertrude would have embraced her had not restraint overcome her at the last moment. "Oh, I'm so glad to see you are well. Are you truly unhurt? After all that's happened I should never have let you go out on my behalf."

Now Felicity did hug the nun. "Yes, I'm quite all right. But how did you know? I was coming to tell you. I'm so sorry. I made such a shambles of what should have been a simple task. And it may be ages before you even get your camera back."

"No, no. The police were here this morning. The camera is quite undamaged. Well, except for the cut strap, but that's of little concern. I am sorry we lost your pictures. I'm sure they would have been lovely, but—"

"Wait. Do you mean you have it back already?"

"Yes." She sighed. "Unfortunately, the hoodlum removed the memory card, but as long as you're all right, that's all that really matters."

"My pictures can be retaken, but what else did you have on the card?"

"Just the photographs I took of the Frideswide document. We'll want to include at least one facsimile page, perhaps more in the publication."

Felicity wanted to ask more but the bell from the chapel tower called them. She wanted to tell Gertrude about Ben but she wasn't sure she was at liberty to do so. So she walked to the chapel with her head swimming with questions and protests.

And as always, the quiet of the chapel drowned the tumultuous noise in her head. How different this service was from the grand feast day service she recalled from the year before at the Community of the Transfiguration. But they still opened with the traditional hymn: "For all the saints who from their labors rest..." She thought of all the stories she had heard recently of those who had labored here in Oxford. How lovely to think of them now at rest.

> Thou wast their Rock, their Fortress, and their Might;
> Thou, Lord, their Captain in the well-fought fight;
> Thou, in the darkness drear, their one true Light.

The rhythm of the melody and the powerful images of the words filled her mind.

> "...We feebly struggle, they in glory shine..."

Her voice strengthened as she sang:

> And when the fight is fierce, the warfare long,
> Steals on the ear the distant triumph song,
> And hearts are brave again, and arms are

strong.

She felt buoyed by the concept of the saints triumphant rising in their bright array to the streaming of a yet more glorious day.

Then they knelt for the litany of the saints, recalling the saints and martyrs on whom Christianity had been built, asking their prayers as one would ask any friend to pray for them. And then praying:

> *"Lord, save your people..."*
> *"From all evil, from all sin..."*
> *"Lord, save your people..."*
> *"From your wrath,"*
> *"Lord, save your people..."*
> "From a sudden and unprovided death..."

The list went on, but Felicity's thoughts were fixed on Monica who had not been spared a sudden death. At the end of the litany Felicity sat for the readings and was amazed at the calm, almost joy, with which Dorcas read Saint John's vision of the saints in glory:

> *"And the city had no need of the sun, neither of the moon, to shine in it: for the glory of God did lighten it, and the Lamb is the light thereof. And the nations of them which are saved shall walk in the light of it: and the kings of the earth do bring their glory and honour into it... And he shewed me a pure river of water of life, clear as crystal, proceeding out of the throne of God and of the Lamb. In the midst of it was there the tree of life... And there shall be no night there; and they need no candle, neither light of the sun; for the Lord God giveth them light: and they shall reign for ever and ever."*

Felicity felt that for the first time in days she could truly mean it when she entered into the response, "Thanks be to God."

Antony rose to give the homily. Felicity was so impressed. He had been given only a few minutes to prepare and yet he spoke with no notes. "We live in a day in which people don't die. They 'pass on' or 'cross over.' We no longer have funerals. We have 'memorial services' or 'celebrations of life.' All in an attempt to deny the fact of death.

"But here, in these days dedicated to All Saints and to All Souls we have time set aside for remembering the dead, and contemplating our own deaths. We are given time to deal with the reality of death—our own, as well as the death of others. In these days we are to bring death and the dead into the light; to mourn, but not to despair; even more to celebrate what needs to be celebrated. Most of all we are to see life as a gift and death as a new beginning."

As soon as the service was over Felicity wanted to rush to Antony to tell him how greatly she agreed with his sermon and how much better she felt. Only two things stopped her. One was the simple fact that Antony was still in the sacristy, and the other was the fact that she couldn't really put Monica's death behind her and move on. Not until she was certain Father Ben was guilty and she understood why.

She left her little side chapel with slow steps, asking herself again and again: Had Ben snatched her camera at the well? Had Ben been the dark figure she glimpsed running from the drugged Sister Gertrude? Was it possible that a man who had ministered for years in a mission orphanage could have committed such a brutal murder? And if so, why? Why? Why?

She was concentrating so hard she almost cried out when she became conscious of a dark-suited man walking in step beside her. "What? Sorry. Did you say something?"

The slight, baldheaded man smiled, making his sandy mustache bob. "Only twice. I'm not very forceful, I'm afraid.'

"Sorry. Afraid I was deep in thought. What can I do for you?'

"I asked if you could direct me to Sister Gertrude."

"Oh." Now Felicity looked at him properly. In spite of his self-effacing manner the man had an air of scholarly intelligence which seemed to be underscored by the leather brief case he carried. Was this Gertrude's legal historian? Perhaps she shouldn't ask. But the possibility of getting some answers was encouraging. "She should be coming out of church any minute. I'll see if I can find her. Who shall I say?"

"Charles Ross," he supplied. "She asked me for advice on some papers." He indicated his brief case.

"Yes, wait here." Felicity darted to the main door of the church and, as she hoped, caught Sister Gertrude as she entered the narthex from the chapel. "A man, Charles Ross, is waiting to see you."

"Excellent. Come along. I know you'll be interested."

Ross was, indeed, the expert Gertrude had sent the charter to. She introduced Felicity as the one who had made the translation and suggested they settle in the parlor as her office was not in working order yet.

Ross drew out Felicity's translation. "You did a fine job."

Felicity smiled. "Thank you. I thought I knew most of the words, but I didn't understand the legal er—ramifications."

"What are the ramifications is precisely the question. The document is actually quite straightforward and in keeping with charters of its type drawn at that time." He looked at Gertrude. "You asked if there was any way this charter could be effective today. Of course, it would have to be authenticated and undoubtedly would be tried in court. It's all tenuous, but I would say someone making a claim could at the least make an interesting argument and possibly prevail. Let me call your attention to this phrase," he pointed to Felicity's translation 'reversionary interest', "which I must say I checked against the original and you translated quite properly."

Felicity gave a sigh of relief. Since she had no idea what the term meant she was very pleased to have done it correctly.

"A reversionary interest means that conditions are set forth for the terms of the grant. If the terms are not met, then the property reverts to the original owner."

Felicity recalled the bit of research she had done on the abbey built on this land. "Yes, the monastery was required to 'continue in good fettle.' I assume that insolvency would be considered a breach of that."

"Correct." Charles Ross looked pleased with his student.

"But that was before the reformation. Surely everything changed then regarding monastic lands," Gertrude said.

"Indeed. I'm not suggesting it would be an easy case, just that there would be arguments on the side of anyone wanting to raise the issue. You see, the charter also contains a covenant that runs with the land. This means that the requirement affects the title ever after."

"Like mineral rights?" Felicity suggested. "At least in the States one can sell land but retain the mineral rights for their heirs."

Ross nodded. "It's similar here. With certain exceptions. That's a very good example. Well, I think this is all I can tell you." He drew the box containing the original from his brief case. "I do urge you to be very careful with this document. If you should be thinking of bringing a claim on behalf of the descendants of Radulfus of Anstey," his smile showed the unlikelihood of such an action, "it would be necessary to have the original document. Even such an excellent translation as yours," he nodded at Felicity, "would have no standing.

"But I should just mention that if you're trying to ascertain the monetary value," he continued, "the simplest answer may very well be in the value of the document itself."

Gertrude gave a startled laugh. "Goodness. We just wanted to publish a rather academic pamphlet. It's what we do. There's very little monetary value in that, I can assure you. The original doesn't even belong to us. It's on loan. And the sooner I can return it to its owners the happier I'll be."

"Well, I'm not an expert in valuing antiquities, but I happen to know that a charter of similar dating, and of less interest than this, recently sold at auction for well over £150,000."

He handed the box to Sister Gertrude with both hands. "I do advise you to be careful."

Twenty

Antony blinked at Felicity. "Let me get this right. That charter made in the troubled reign of King Stephan—" He paused, struggling to bring back his schoolboy history. *Stephan, grandson of William the Conqueror, crowned 1135...* "You're saying there's a possibility this could still be in effect?"

"I didn't say it. Sister Gertrude's legal historian said it. I know it sounds unlikely."

"It certainly does. Twenty-five hectares—something like sixty acres, I think—including a city park and a ruined abbey." He shook his head.

Felicity refilled their teacups and they leaned back in the cushions of the lounge at their lodging. It was a blessedly quiet moment as all his students were out or in their rooms working away on their essays. "So, assuming the mayhem of the recent days has something to do with this charter, we need to know who could possibly benefit from it."

"Beyond a limited publication by the Fairacres Press," Felicity added. "Are you thinking that an heir to this Radulfus—or Ralph as he would be called now—is still around and wanting to make a claim? If so, why the skullduggery? Just hire a lawyer—or whatever— and get on with it."

"I agree. Still, I'd like to know what's become of the line.

They would probably have that at the National Archives or Public Records Office—whatever they call it now. One might even be able to access some information online. Or some book might..."

"Yes!" Felicity jumped at the suggestion. "Maybe even the Bodleian. Do you think you might...?"

Antony's mobile rang. He gave Felicity an apologetic look and answered.

"Aunt Beryl, yes, what is it? You sound upset."

His heart sank at the tightness in her voice. He could see the deepened lines in her thin face and sensed her hands clenching the phone as a lifeline. He was picturing her standing in the dark hall of the Victorian terrace house where he had grown up, the phone still on the small black oak table where it had always been. "It's Edward."

It took him some time to draw the facts from her. Another heart attack. The ambulance just gone. Yes, Mrs. Bolton next door could take her to the hospital. She was quite all right, thank you. The distance was back in her voice. "I just thought you should know."

"Yes, of course. Thank you for ringing." He took a deep breath. "Aunt Beryl, I'll come as soon as I can."

"No. I know you're busy. I don't want to inconvenience you."

Inconvenience? These were the people who had raised him. He must have been far more than an inconvenience to them. "Don't talk nonsense. I want to be there. I'll let you know when I've sorted something out. And I'll let Gwena know. Perhaps we can come together." He added the last without thinking but when he heard the words he knew what a nonstarter the idea was.

"And, Aunt Beryl, I'll be praying."

Whether her sniff suppressed her tears or expressed her opinion of the value of his prayers he didn't know.

He looked at the time before he put his phone back in his pocket. Not quite half four. Gwena wouldn't be at the theatre yet. "Felicity," he said. "I need to go see Gwendolyn." He then told her about Edward.

"Sure." She set her teacup down. "Do you want me to go

with you?"

"I would love it. But I think I need to do this alone. You don't mind do you?"

"Of course I don't mind. I'm thinking of doing something totally frivolous." She stood up and reached for her bag. "I hadn't told you yet—I'm going to be an auntie. I got an email from mother. Charlie and Judy are expecting a baby next March. So I'm off to Alice's Shop to buy the sprog something entirely useless. It's sure to be the only non-digital gift the child gets."

They walked out together and parted at Banbury Road. Gwena had given him the address of her digs, but he had never visited her there. And why was he doing it now? he asked himself. Surely it would be just as well to ring her. She probably wouldn't even be in. He halted. He could join Felicity at Alice's Shop. They would have a delightful afternoon browsing books and Victorian replica toys.

He started to turn, then stopped. No, he had run from far too many things in his life. Surely he could face his sister.

When he banged the fox-head knocker on the door of 623 Canterbury Road, he was still unsure he had made the right decision. And he was less sure when he saw the scowl on his sister's face. "Squib. What are you doing here?"

At least she stepped back and let him enter. She led the way into a drab parlor furnished with grey furniture and plopped into the nearest overstuffed chair, indicating that he might as well sit down too. "Aunt Beryl rang," he began. "Uncle Edward has had a relapse. It sounds serious. I thought you should know."

"Right. Thanks. Now I know."

"Gwen, I, er—I told Beryl I'd go up as soon as I could." She nodded to indicate she had heard his words, then returned to studying her nails. "I told her I'd ask if you would come with me."

She gave a hoot of laughter. At least he had her attention now. "Whatever possessed you to say that? I can't leave. I have a show to do. It's fine for you. You aren't doing anything important anyway—you never have."

He knew that would be her answer, but something

spurred him to argue. "That's not what you said when you needed me as fodder for you debate."

At least the derision was gone from her voice now. "Not my debate." She paused. "Besides, you weren't fodder. You held the side up rather well."

He was so surprised he gaped at her. Her conciliatory words gave him the courage to try his request again. "Gwena, please reconsider. I know they were remote, uncaring even maybe, but they did—"

She jerked upright in her chair, eyes blazing, any attempt at appeasement gone. "*They* were remote, uncaring? Beryl and Edward? You've got to be kidding! How did you even notice?"

"Huh? What are you talking about?"

"You were the remote, uncaring one."

"Gwen—"

"Where were you when I needed you? Didn't it ever cross your mind that I might want to talk to my brother? Might even need advice?"

His mouth fell open, but no words came out.

"Yes, Beryl was all about efficiency and being proper. But that was better than you. You were absent."

Now he found his tongue. "Absent? I was always there."

"Physically, maybe, but a million miles away mentally. You always had your head in a book."

The truth of that struck him. Reading had always been his escape. Books had kept the dark and the cold at bay. He had been so consumed by his own need that it had never occurred to him that his sister—older, gregarious, self-assured as she always seemed—could need anything.

The room slowly fell silent as the echo of her angry words, pent up for more than twenty years, faded away.

"Gwendolyn, forgive me." What else could he say?

She gave a little shrug, then got to her feet and walked to the door. He followed. "I'll let you know about Edward."

"You do that." She shut the door behind him.

He stood on the pavement looking at the door. Was it true? Was the coldness and isolation of his childhood his own fault? Had it not been his family who shut him out, but he who excluded them? If so was it possible to make amends? He had apologized to Gwen. Surely that was a start. Did Beryl feel the same way? How could he possibly make it up to her after all these years? Should he go to Blackpool now? Or would that be overreacting? After all, Beryl had her neighbor and her vicar. And he had promised to celebrate at the All Soul's service tomorrow.

Pushing away the thought that he was making excuses, he turned and walked briskly down the road. Might as well do something constructive. He felt in his pocket to be certain he had his reader's card with him. He would stop at the Bodleian and see if he could unearth anything about this Radulfus of Ansty that Felicity wanted to know about.

After taking a few moments to orient himself he started with a general reference book on the aristocracy. William the Conqueror had introduced the rank of Baron in England to distinguish the men who had pledged their loyalty to him, it explained. Antony skimmed a great deal of information as to how barons were chosen and what their duties to the king were, primarily providing knights for battle and attending councils. But this was little to the point.

Another book provided a list of baronies, telling which were extant and which extinct. If Ansty was listed and extant... Ah, here it was: Abeyant 1964. What did that mean? Back to his first volume which explained that a barony was declared to be abeyance when the right to it is not vested in any one person, but awaits the appearance or determination of the true owner—as when there is no male heir and more than one female heir.

He read on, learning that a barony could pass to daughters only if there were no sons. Interestingly, under inheritance law, sisters have an equal right to inherit with no special inheritance right due for an eldest sister as there is for an eldest son. The next sentence caught his attention. He read it again to be certain he had it right: Thus, it is possible that two or more sisters (and their heirs after their deaths) have an equally valid claim to the title; in such a case, the title goes into abeyance. The abeyance ends when there is only one remaining claimant due to deaths of the other claimants.

Goodness, that made it a tontine.

With that background he felt ready to tackle *Peerage & Baronetage*. Since the barony had gone into abeyance in 1964 he assumed he would need the edition for that year. The librarian helped him locate the volume in the reference section and he carried it back to his table. Antony had never had reason to consult such a work before. It took him several minutes to orient himself, especially getting familiar with the long list of abbreviations. It was almost like reading a foreign language. He smiled at the note that the surnames and Christian names of married daughters, sisters and aunts were given in a separate section. It was interesting that aunts were given special mention, but Felicity would doubtless have flared at the idea of women being listed separately from their male counterparts.

There it was, at the top of the second page: George Beaumont, 22nd Baron Ansty, d. 1964, 2 dau. He turned to the back for the section dedicated to females of the line. And here they were: Beaumont, dau of George: Margaret b. 1948; Phyllis b. 1952. He made a note of his findings and left the library feeling quite smug with the success of his sleuthing.

Until he asked himself what it proved. He was still mulling it over, trying to find a possible application for his knowledge of the Barony of Ansty, which was presumably the rightful owner of the document Felicity had translated. Or was once the rightful owner until some long-ago ancestor was having a good spring clear out and donated the account of the saint's life to the nearest abbey. Perhaps in exchange for prayers. Or perhaps it had been disposed of at the reformation, the baron of the day not wanting to be found tainted by a popish document.

He still couldn't see how anyone could hope to benefit from Monica's murder or from stealing the manuscript. Any such actions on an heir's part would preclude their benefiting from anything that would otherwise be rightfully theirs.

He was still musing when he arrived back at their lodgings and found Felicity in the lounge, bursting to show him her treasures. "Look, I got this bag with all the Wonderland characters on it—it'll make a great diaper bag. And a cuddly

Dodo bird. Feel how soft it is." He gave it an obedient squeeze. "And this darling Alice locket for Judy and, ta-da—" She pulled out a silver pocket watch with a white rabbit on its face. "My head-in-the-clouds brother is always late for everything. This is so perfect."

"I thought he was high tech only."

"That's what makes it so perfect. His sense of humor is very retro."

Antony admired her purchases, then told her about all he had unearthed at the library. "I made some notes. Wanted to be sure I had the names right." He handed her a sheet from his notebook.

"Hm. Very interesting. So would this Margaret or Phyllis would have a motive to cause trouble over the charter?"

"Maybe one of them wants to end the abeyance of the barony."

"Wants to become the Baroness Ansty?" Felicity thought for a moment. "It certainly has a nice ring to it. But I can't see how stealing the charter would help her position."

"If she wanted to claim—what was it Charles Ross said?— Reversionary interest in the lands her twenty-second or so great grandfather deeded away?" Antony shook his head. "Maybe you should tell Sergeant Thompson all that tomorrow."

"Me? What's wrong with you telling him? You unearthed it."

Antony sighed and just stopped himself running his hands through his hair. "I need to go to Blackpool. But that's another topic. Let me put the kettle on first."

Felicity turned to repackage her shopping as Antony disappeared into the little kitchen. She was just finishing when Brian and Clare came in hand-in-hand talking about the bell ringing practice they had attended. "I hadn't rung since I was at Brasenose," Brian said. "Wasn't sure I could go the pace, but I guess it's like riding a bicycle."

"He was brilliant." Clare gave a toss of her long red hair

and beamed at Brian.

"So you'll be ringing for All Soul's?" Felicity asked.

Brian nodded. "One of the band dislocated his shoulder playing squash so a friend from the old days invited me. I love being back at it."

"And I loved watching," Clare added. "Brian volunteered to help muffle the bells tomorrow and I get to go along and see that, too. I've been hearing church bells all my life but I never really knew anything about them."

Felicity smiled. "That's so cool. I remember doing that when I was here. I loved it. Even if the spider webs in the rafters were a bit of a drawback." She wiped her hand across her face at the memory.

"Why don't you come with us?"

"I'd love to." Or would she? She had spoken without much thought. Now she considered. Her carefree memories of student days were replaced by a far more sinister, more recent specter. She hadn't been up in a bell tower since last spring. Did she really want to do that again? She pushed away the panic that started to rise in her throat and stiffened her shoulders. Yes. If she was afraid of it, that was exactly what she should do. Go up again with her friends where there was no chance of repeating the terrors of last time.

Antony returned bearing a tea tray. "I heard voices so I brought extra cups. Want a cuppa?"

Clare and Brian declined and departed. Felicity took the cup Antony poured for her and sat next to him on the sofa. "Right. A new subject, you said."

"Gwen..." he began, then floundered.

"Wasn't open to the idea of going to Blackpool with you?"

"To put it mildly. That's not the problem, though. Of course she has a show. I should have thought of that. The thing is—she had a whole different perspective on our childhood. On me, to be precise."

Felicity frowned. "I can't imagine you being a difficult child or a stroppy teenager."

"It would probably have been better if I had been. Apparently I shut everyone out. All the coldness I blamed on them—it seems it all came from me. At least, to hear her tell it."

"Oh." Felicity's silence indicated that she could imagine the validity of that perspective. Then she set her tea down and reached for his hand. "But Antony, that's never true. Things like that are never one-sided. I understand that Gwen was hurt, felt let down, when you weren't as mature and supportive as she would have liked. But she was four years older than you. Did she ever reach out to you? Ask for your help?"

Antony spent several moments groping through childhood memories, reliving scenes he hadn't visited for years. Times he thought far best left locked away. There had been moments... Gwena coming into his room when he didn't look up... Flickers of conversation that he didn't respond to...perhaps he hadn't listened—hadn't really heard her. At last he shook his head. "I simply don't know. I know I always had my head stuck in a book." Odysseus, Arthur, Taran Wanderer, Richard Hannay—they were all more vivid in his memory than his sister.

"I can believe that. But it's not too late. You can start building bridges now. Look at my mom and me. I've come to understand her so much better since that business in Norfolk. We aren't best buddies yet, but we do keep touch now, and I'm truly looking forward to seeing her at our wedding."

"Yes, that's brilliant. I'd like to think Gwen and I could get that far."

"And what about Beryl and Edward?" He groaned as she prodded the other sore spot.

"They need me," he said at last.

"Go."

Her one word directive hung in the air as if it were a flashing light. He really didn't have an excuse. If he left in the morning he could be there just after noon. His students were all settled into their independent studies. The priest at St. Mary Mag's could easily replace him at the All Soul's mass. There was only one thing—"Felicity," he turned to grip her shoulders and looked straight into her eyes. "We still don't know what is going on here. Be very careful."

Twenty-One

All Souls' Day

The commemoration of All Souls' Day dawned a crisp, golden November morning. Perfect for a run in the University Parks. Felicity pulled on jeans and running shoes. She and Antony had, the night before, said their good-byes for their few days apart—Antony leaving her with a long list of mother hen do's and don'ts. Among them, "Don't go off by yourself." She considered knocking on Clare's door and inviting her to chaperone her jog, but from the silence in the house, Felicity was quite certain she was the only one yet up.

She thought of ringing Gwendolyn. She would like to talk to Antony's sister again. Maybe she could help with the bridge building that needed to be done. She glanced at her watch. No, ringing an actress at 8:30 in the morning probably wasn't the best first step to building a bridge. She went out into the morning, filling her lungs with fresh, moist air. Once across Norham Gardens Road, she stopped to do a few bending and stretching exercises, then set out at an easy lope along the gravel path toward the river. Beyond the bushes bordering the path, a light morning haze hung over the grass, the sun making the dew on each blade sparkle like a diamond. Felicity couldn't remember experiencing a more glorious morning.

And if she had felt guilty about ignoring Antony's

stricture, she needn't have. She was hardly alone. A group of uniformed schoolgirls walked toward her, giggling. An elderly gentleman passed on the other side, propelled by the three Dachshunds whose leads he held. Ahead of her a young woman jogged, her long red ponytail bouncing with each step. Then Felicity realized who owned that bright head of auburn hair. "Clare," she called.

The jogger slowed and Felicity caught up. "Hi. I thought I was the first one up in the house. Other than Antony, of course. He left before I was awake."

"Oh? Where did he go?"

Felicity explained about the family emergency. "He said he was confident you could all carry on with your work without him. He said he would ring the priest at St. Mary Mag's to give the seminar about All Souls'. Although I'm probably the only one who isn't up to speed on all the history."

"I doubt it. Some of us were raised in all the traditions, of course, but Brian said it's all pretty new to him."

"But he's a bell ringer."

"Oh, sure, he's done it all. I just don't think he ever asked why they were doing it. Until recently, of course."

The path curved to circle a small pond where ducks swam and dove for food among the water lilies. A small island in the center of the pond provided safety for their nests. Clare slowed as they approached a brown, wooden bench. "I'm sorry. Do you mind if I take a break? I had already lapped the cricket ground before we met." She sank onto the bench. "But you go on, you're just starting."

Felicity sat beside her. "That's all right. I just wanted fresh air more than exercise. What I really need to do is to get back to my exercises. I used to be religious about maintaining my barre routine."

"Oh, are you a ballerina?"

Felicity laughed. "I had ambitions. Until I grew to be five foot ten. When my partner did a lift and my feet were still on the ground, I got the message."

"And now you're going to be a priest?"

"I thought so. Going to set the world right. Single-handedly." She gave a rueful smile. "Then I was going to be a nun. Very romantic. Like Maid Marian." She put her hands together in a pious gesture. "But I was more like Maria in the 'Sound of Music'." She sighed. "Not sure now what I'll do with my theology degree. What about you?"

Clare shook her head. "I'm undecided, too. I've actually thought about...shall we say working abroad? Being a missionary sounds so didactic."

Felicity laughed. "Like being a nun?"

They grinned at each other then Felicity asked, "Were you and Brian an, um — item before?"

Clare's grin turned decidedly saucy. "I'd noticed him, certainly. Who wouldn't with that white hair and purple trainers? But since I'm on NOC we only get to Kirkthorpe a couple of times a term, so there wasn't much chance for a relationship to develop." She paused. "I can't help feeling a little guilty, though, I mean — if I am supposed to be a missionary..."

"Yeah, I know. No one plans these things. Don't feel guilty. Just go with it and see what works out."

They sat together for several moments enjoying the sun on their heads and their warm thoughts.

Until Clare's smile faded and she abruptly changed the subject. "Have they learned anything more about that murdered nun we found in the river?" She gave a small shiver at the memory.

Felicity was glad of the question. It seemed it always helped to talk to someone when you were looking for a solution, even if you only came up with more questions. "I don't have any idea what the police have learned, but I'm convinced it has something to do with that manuscript I worked on."

"Really? How?"

A nanny leading two small children walked past them then paused to throw breadcrumbs to the ducks in the pond.

Trying to make sense of it herself, looking for links in the story, Felicity told Clare about the legal historian who believed the charter might possibly have some validity and about Antony's research about the barony being abeyant.

"So you're thinking the heirs of this baron might have

killed, what was her name—Sister—no, Mother Monica?" Clare frowned. "How would that help them?"

"That's the problem. I have no idea."

"Do you know who they are? The heirs?"

"Apparently, Margaret and Phyllis Beaumont. Except, of course, they've probably married, so it's probably not Beaumont anymore."

"Shouldn't you tell the police?"

"I suppose so. Antony said I should. I'm not at all sure, though, that the Thames Valley Police either want or need to be told their job." She grinned. "I've seen Inspector Morse on television."

Clare nodded. "Me too. Loved it."

"Besides," Felicity was more talking to herself now, "I doubt that anything so convoluted is necessary. Sister Gertrude's expert said the manuscript itself would have considerable monetary value. Perhaps in the neighborhood of a hundred and fifty thousand pounds."

"Do you think that's why you were mugged at the well?"

"I've no idea." They sat in silence for some time watching the two little boys feed the noisy ducks. When the nanny's bag was empty they moved on.

Clare jumped to her feet. "Oh, I sat too long, my muscles are stiff. I need a hot shower. I'll see you at St. Mary Mag's at one." She was off with a wave, her ponytail bouncing as she jogged away.

Felicity sat on, thinking again of what she had laid out to Clare. Assuming she understood it properly, if George Beaumont had had only one daughter she would now be the Baroness Ansty. And if one of the daughters died, the other one would inherit the title. Unless there was now a male heir? What did Antony say he had read? That the title became abeyant when two or more sisters (and their heirs after their deaths) have an equally valid claim to the title? But what did that mean? She wished she knew more about English inheritance law. 'Remember, you're not investigating this,' Antony's stern voice reminded her.

A little chill rippling the length of her spine told Felicity that Antony was right. She really should tell Sergeant

Thompson what Antony had uncovered and leave it to him. Even if he laughed at her. She pulled her phone from her pocket, then realized she didn't have the number. It hardly seemed worth a 999 call.

Now she indulged in the run she had set out for in the first place. She held her head up, drawing in deep breaths of the morning air in rhythm to the movement of her feet. It felt so good to stretch her legs. Then the luxury of a hot shower. She even allowed herself time to fry an egg for breakfast. Sheila stuck her head in the kitchen door just as Felicity was considering a second cup of tea. "Going to the lecture?"

"Oh, yes, just a minute." Felicity put her dishes in the sink.

Once outside Felicity considered suggesting they cut across the park, but thought the pavement would be easier walking for a woman with a cane. As if following her thoughts Sheila remarked, "I expect you've been up for hours. I should have been at my reading, but I'll have to admit to having a bit of a lie-in. The seminar is wonderful, but it's quite a pace for a mature student." She gave a youthful smile that made her eyes twinkle and her wrinkles disappear. The rest of the way she talked about how interesting she was finding the seminar and what a wonderful lecturer Father Antony was. Sentiments that would get no argument from Felicity.

The others were standing on the porch when they arrived. Sheila apologized for keeping them waiting, making a slight nod toward her cane. Everyone insisted it was no problem. The parish priest welcomed the latecomers and invited everyone to come inside and take a front pew while he perched on the altar rail. Along with the others Felicity drew out a notepad and pen. She wouldn't have had to take notes since she wasn't taking the seminar for credit, but she was interested in the history and meaning of the day. "Beginning in the tenth century, it became customary to set aside another day as a sort of extension of All Saints for the Church to remember the faithful departed not officially declared saints. It's also a day for particular remembrance of family members and friends." Father Peter tossed his fringe of brown hair, making him look extremely young for one in charge of such a prestigious church.

"The day is kept in various ways in different countries. In Mexico The Day of the Dead is a national holiday. Families remember their departed with processions and with picnics in cemeteries, usually eating a favorite dish of the departed. In England the official name is Commemoration of the Faithful Departed—which I think you'll agree doesn't have quite the same ring to it." He paused to give his boyish grin.

"However the day is kept, though, it shows the fascination and deep concern that human beings have always had regarding death and what happens to the dead. This is especially appropriate to Christianity because death and questions of the world to come stand at the very heart of our faith. After all, the death of one man and his resurrection are the centerpiece of Christianity and inform our beliefs about the state of the dead and the future of all mortals."

He went on to explain some of the traditional prayers and practices they would experience at the service later that day. "The most distinctive part being the *Dies Irae*. I'm delighted that our choir will be doing the setting from Mozart's *Requiem*. It's my favorite because it so portrays the urgency of a soul awaiting judgment."

The discussion became more general when Sheila spoke up. "My mum always made soul cakes when I was a child. I loved them, but I didn't really know what it was all about."

Father Peter nodded. "A nineteenth century tradition. Probably a forerunner of trick-or-treating. Children would go from house to house, singing and asking for a cake in exchange for a prayer. You probably know the song: *A soul! a soul! a soul-cake! Please good Missis, a soul-cake!*"

Several joined in the lilting tune. Their lecturer dismissed them after a few more questions and Felicity joined the others preparing to leave. "Aren't you coming up with us?" Clare reminded her, nodding toward the door to the bell tower at the back of the church.

"Oh. Yes. Right." Felicity swallowed and reminded herself of the assured safety of the undertaking. She took a deep breath and pasted on a smile. She had been about ten years old, riding horses with her brothers on her uncle's farm when, with her usual fearlessness and determination to outdo her older brothers, she gave her docile mount a hearty kick to spur him to action. Felicity rubbed her bottom as she recalled the pain of hitting the ground hard when her horse galloped off. She could even smell the dust that filled her nose and mouth.

Charlie, the brother closest to her in age, led Old Smoky back to her by the reins. 'Up you go,' he said firmly. She had drawn away, but Charlie was adamant. 'If you don't get back on you may never ride again.' She got on.

That was her problem. She hadn't gone up again after being attacked in the bell tower of St. Helen's, Ranworth. "Right, then. Back on Old Smoky," she muttered and ascended the slick stone, pie-shaped steps curving up the tower.

"Watch your step," Brian called back.

But there was no worry. The tower was well lighted and she was in the company of friends. At the top of the climb they came out into a pleasant room, its walls painted shiny red and white covered with pictures and plaques commemorating various peals rung there. A circle of ropes with their striped hand grips, hung from the bells above, carefully looped up for safety. Brian picked up a pile of thick, brown leather pads from a chair in the corner. They were varying sizes of oblongs with a heavier black circle in the center and black straps dangling from each end.

"One more level." Brian started up a wooden stairway in the corner.

Felicity followed Clare. When she emerged into the bell chamber Felicity found herself on a narrow ledge running around the bells. She pushed back against the wall, recalling leaning over the railing in that other tower, peering down on the great, iron bells supported on their heavy timbers, and realizing that if crashing onto several ton of cast iron didn't kill a person, the fall to the floor below certainly would. But the worst had been that Antony, whom she had been so sure she would find in the tower, was not there.

Feeling the emptiness she forced herself to picture him safely in Blackpool, being served tea and muffins by his aunt, as he surely was at that moment. Brian switched on a light and far below in the recesses of the church the organist began practicing, a few of his more magnificent chords reaching the tower with reassuring solidity. With a determined lift of her chin Felicity put her qualms behind her. *That was last Easter; this is now, she reminded herself.*

"Ten bells," she commented.

"Yep, a full peal," Brian agreed, as he made his way along a narrow beam to the smallest bell carrying the littlest of the muffles. He squatted down and reached up under the bell, giving a growl of disgust at the awkward position the maneuver required. He adjusted his posture, pulled the clapper toward him and buckled the top strap of the muffle around the ball of the clapper.

"Only one side?" Clare asked.

"Full muffle only on the death of the monarch." Brian finished the second buckle and stood up. "For half muffle we muffle the backstroke. That makes the handstroke sound bright and the duller backstroke emphasizes the echo effect."

He returned to his work, rechecking to be sure the straps were tight and secure. "It'll ruin the whole effect if one of the muffles comes loose."

After the second one Clare asked, "Wouldn't it be easier to reach them if you turned the bells up?"

Brian gave a jerk of a nod, his white-blond hair seeming to glow in the dimmer light of the bell chamber. "Easier. But dangerous. One slip and the bell could go down and take me with it. These babies weigh eight or nine hundredweight each."

Felicity, observing the procedure silently, gave a small shudder.

Brian continued around the catwalk balancing on the planks between the bells, going from smallest to largest bell. But he stopped when he got to the last one. "Aren't you going to muffle it?" Clare asked.

"Al said to leave it unmuffled. The tenor isn't usually muffled. Especially since we'll be tolling before the service." Brian came back to them on the ledge and they descended together.

Once they were completely out of the tower and back in the sanctuary with the reverberations of the organ practice washing over them, Felicity was amazed at her reaction. She should be relaxed. She had fought with an old ghost and laid it to rest. She should feel triumphant. She could now go up any tower in the country with no fear of a shadow uncoiling from a dark corner and jumping at her with a rapacious leer.

But she wasn't relaxed and she wasn't triumphant. Somehow reliving her earlier experience confronting evil had made her angry. Angry with thieves and rapists and murderers and all the barbarity in the world. If All Soul's Day was intended to make people come to terms with death, it hadn't worked for her. Maybe Allyn Luffington and his student atheists were right. What was God thinking to let such atrocities go on in his world? And she hadn't even started yet on war and starving orphans and mutilated nuns.

Without another word to her friends Felicity marched out of the church and up Banbury Road with a furious stride. She didn't turn right when she came to the Parks. She had no desire to go back to her room. Instead she turned to go to Gwena's lodging. It wasn't until she had given the knocker its third sharp rap that she thought to wonder what she was doing there. But then it was too late. The door opened. "Felicity, what a surprise."

She stepped in at Gwena's invitation. "I, um—just thought I'd tell you I'm sorry about your uncle."

Gwena nodded. "Yeah, me too. And when you hear from Antony—I suppose he's gone to Blackpool?" Felicity nodded. "Tell him I'm sorry I popped off at him. I was right, of course, but I could have been more diplomatic about it."

"I will." She couldn't think of anything else to say.

Gwena frowned at her. "Are you all right? I'd offer you a cup of tea, but I need to get to the theatre."

"No. Yes. Er—I mean I'm all right." She wasn't, but what could she say? "Sure, I know you need to go. I won't keep you. I was just passing—sort of," she added in the interest of honesty.

Now what? she wondered when she was back out on the pavement. A pub, maybe? But going to a strange pub alone sounded more dismal than going to church where she was meant to be.

Then the tolling started. A single, deep tone vibrating

above the trees and rooftops. Then silence. The air still
quavered, but even the normal sounds of a busy city seemed
stilled. She held her breath. After a full minute that seemed
like an eternity, the tolling came again. The sonorous, rich call.
The somber tone of the tenor bell pulled her forward at a
measured pace, each echoing ring soaring onward into silence
before the next.

Almost sleepwalking she crossed the street back to the
little island where the church stood, but she did not go in.
Instead she climbed the steps of Martyrs Memorial and sat at
the base, listening to each knell. Each toll felt as if the clapper
were striking her with a ring for those departed she had been
thinking of lately: The Oxford martyrs, Mother Monica,
Antony's uncle…

At first she thought the vibration in her pocket was an
extension of the resonance from the bell tower above her, then
she realized it wasn't. She pulled her phone from her pocket
and considered not answering. She didn't really want to talk,
even to Antony. And he would think she was in church. But at
last she responded with a simple, "Yes?"

"Felicity, are you all right?"

She wanted to yell at him. How could he ask? No, of
course she wasn't all right. Nothing was right. We lived in a
fallen universe and evil was winning. Didn't he know? She
sighed. "Yeah. Fine. Just tired." She made a Herculean effort.
"How are things there?"

"Edward is unconscious. Not likely to waken, actually."

She knew she should say she was sorry. But the depressing
news seemed so in keeping with her thoughts on death and
devastation, it was almost comforting.

Antony continued, "Beryl is amazing. She's steadier than I
am. She talks a lot about what a good man he was, what a
good life they had together… Now I see her demeanor as good
sense, not coldness. If only —"

"Yeah. If only the world were different. I get it." It wasn't
until after they rang off that she remembered she hadn't given
him Gwen's message. She started to ring back, then saw that
her battery was dead. It was such a perfect symbol of the
world around her she almost threw her phone down in

disgust.

And then the tolling stopped. Felicity shivered. November evenings were cold. And dark. Light spilled from the open church door ahead of her and an organ prelude drew her forward. If it had been in a major key she would have been repulsed, but the minor notes so matched her own mood, so nearly spoke her own thoughts, that she couldn't turn away. She entered the church and took a seat about half way down the aisle. She noticed her friends sitting together nearer the front, but she had no desire to join them. She would experience this on her own. A service for the Dead—for all who had died, for all who would die. As she would someday.

She looked first at the alter: the unbleached beeswax candles Father Peter had mentioned in his talk that morning, not the white wax that spoke of purity and joy usually used, but rather, dull ochre candles in dark wooden candlesticks. No silver or gold gleamed anywhere, the golden altar cross having been replaced by a somber wooden crucifix.

But the most stunning symbol stood in the center of the aisle before the altar rail. A catafalque draped with a black pall and flanked with six massive candlesticks bearing again the unbleached orange candles. She knew the coffin was empty. Father Peter had told them about it earlier. Still, the imagery of death was overpowering, increasing the weight on Felicity's spirit.

The clergy entered, their black vestments matching the black altar cloths, and the introit began, "Rest eternal grant unto them, O Lord... Unto thee shall all flesh come..." The earthy scent of the incense added to the sense of solemnity and mystery and brought a sense of reverence for the dead. Felicity could almost see the souls of the departed ascending as the wisps of smoke floated upward as to heaven. She started to argue with the feeling of comfort the image brought but then the organ began the *Kyrie eleison*, Lord have mercy, and she was carried along by the familiar and yet strange liturgy.

She had just begun to relax with the reading of the comforting lesson from Romans, "Hope does not disappoint us..." When the organ began the urgent, driving rhythm of the *Dies Irae*. At first the melody was everything, then the vigor and intensity of the choir penetrated her consciousness and she found herself translating the Latin text as they sang: *Day of wrath, day of anger... the world dissolves in ashes... Sound of the trumpet summoning souls before the throne of God... Death astounding, nature quaking, all creation waking, to its Judge its answer making... All the wicked then confounded... All creation arise again.*

The sequence left her feeling weak, yet strangely invigorated. Almost as if she had truly experienced a day of wrath. A picture of violent horror, yet all ending in triumph. Enveloped in the paradox she moved through the familiar comfort of the communion to stand for the final prayer. Then she was jerked from her equanimity as the priest changed his chasuble for a flowing black cope and processed, followed by the servers, to the catafalque, to stand at the foot of the bier. "The sorrow of death compassed me."

Felicity found her place in her worship folder to join the response. "And the pains of hell came about me." Felicity shifted uneasily. She did not want to return to such thoughts.

The prayer that followed was one for mercy and forgiveness. Then the cantor repeated the plea, *"Libera me, Domine..."* As he sang, Father Peter moved around the catafalque, sprinkling it with holy water. "Deliver me O Lord, from death eternal, in that day tremendous when the earth must pass away..."

The priest completed his circuit, then took up the thurible and began another round, censing the casket. "Deliver me when thou shalt come to judge the world... Lord have mercy, Christ have mercy."

Felicity took her seat, feeling completely drained. But calm. The battering emotions of the past days had all come to a culmination in this powerful service and somehow, instead of exploding within her as they had threatened, she had been brought to a place of calm. As if she had faced the worst the universe could throw at her and found an answer.

The words of the concluding prayer reached her as if from a great distance. "...that at the day of the general resurrection, we, with all those who are of the mystical body of thy Son, may be set on his right hand, and hear those most joyful words; Come, ye blessed of my Father, inherit the kingdom prepared for you from the foundation of the world..."

Still in the grip of the experience, Felicity remained in her seat as the candles were extinguished and the congregation moved toward the door. Then, from the tower over her head, as if from heaven, the peal began. Not the stately, single tone of earlier, but a full change-ringing peal. Her thoughts seemed to swing with the bells: Uncle Edward, Mother Monica, Saint Frideswide...

The same subjects as before. But now the anger was gone. She had no answers. But who was she to demand answers? She was back again at the debate, hearing Antony's stories in reply to the challenge of evil—the answer of a good death. Of triumph at the end.

Still focusing on the bells, she went out into the darkness of the night, but now the golden light from the church followed her. Not wanting to leave the cover of the sound of the bells showering down on her, she once again took her seat at the base of the monument. Now not in anger or despair, but rather, observing, analytical. Willing to listen and to be taught. At first the sounds seemed to run together, but then she caught the pattern and began to notice, with a clarity that couldn't be distinguished when she was indoors, the sharp brightness of the handstroke and mellowness of the muffled backstroke. The deadened sound of the alternate strokes attenuating the strike while continuing the hum. It was a mesmerizing echo effect with blows loud then soft.

And it was so like life. The brightness and the dark. One following on another. And the thing was to endure until the dark was conquered and the bright triumphant.

Brian had said they would be ringing a quarter peal. Stedman Caters he had called it, if she remembered correctly. Certainly she remembered him saying that it would last 50 minutes. If only she had thought to wear a coat she might have stayed where she was the full time, but there was no way she could sit out in the open that long in her simple knit shirt. Still, she didn't want to leave the bells.

Moving to the stately rhythm surrounding her, she went along the street to a coffee bar. She couldn't hear as clearly in here, but the sound followed her, covering the muted conversations of those grouped around the small round tables. She started to take a chair at an empty table, then saw Clare sitting alone in a corner. "Okay if I join you?"

"Please. I told Brian I'd meet him after the peal, but it's a long wait."

"I'll get my coffee and be right back." Felicity moved toward the counter at the back of the room. A man moved his chair to let her pass. The movement made her look his direction. "Oh, Derrick. Hello." He acknowledged her greeting, then returned to his conversation with the man across the table from him, so she went on. She ordered coffee, then, realizing she had skipped dinner, chose a croissant to accompany it.

Back at the table she added a generous dollop of cream to her cup and smiled at Clare as she stirred, but Clare seemed as engrossed by the bells as she was, so they talked little. Felicity was on her third cup of coffee and second croissant when the peal came to an end. It seemed that the whole room, even those who hadn't evidenced that they were listening, looked up in wonder, as if to find something missing. The silence in the room held long enough for the vibrations to die, then conversation resumed around them.

"Come back with me?" Clare nodded her head toward the church. "Brian has to take the muffles off then we'll join the others at the pub—bell ringers' tradition, he said."

"Sure." Felicity started toward the door but Derrick stopped her.

"Sorry, didn't mean to be unfriendly earlier. Possible client." He indicated the man he had been talking to.

"No problem." Then thinking she should say something more, added. "I saw Gwena today, briefly. Her uncle is very ill."

"Yes, she mentioned he was poorly."

"Well, it was nice to see you. The bells were lovely, weren't they? We're meeting one of the ringers." She indicated Clare waiting by the door.

"Right. We must all get together again soon."

Felicity agreed, but doubted that it would happen.

A light showing in the high, narrow window of the tower told them Brian was still at work on the bells. Removing the muffles was probably as cumbersome an affair as putting them on. The church was empty and dimly lit when they entered, still filled with the warm scent of candles and incense. When Felicity opened the door to the tower the light seemed bright by comparison, beckoning them upward.

In the ringing chamber all was in order, the pulls left in tidy loops below their red, white and blue striped sallys. "Brian, we're here," Clare called. When there was no answer she shrugged. "Probably has his head in a bell." She moved to the stairs and called again with her foot on the bottom tread. "Brian?" Still no answer.

The silence made Felicity look around the room. Shouldn't they be able to hear movement overhead? Then she noticed one of the pulls hanging askew, its sally not on a level with the others. "Brian?" urgency in her voice. She chilled at the continued silence.

"Clare, wait." Felicity pulled her back.

"What? Why?"

"Just let me go first." She didn't know why, but the hairs on the back of her neck were tingling.

With each tread everything in Felicity protested at going into that chamber but if there had been an accident she couldn't let Clare face it alone. She took a deep breath and stepped onto the wooden platform. A light bulb burned high on each of the four walls making the metal of the bells gleam dully. "Brian!" Clare called from behind, but the only reply was her own voice echoing off the bells.

And then Felicity saw. Purple trainers and legs extending along the catwalk on the far side of the tower, upper torso engulfed in a bell. Nothing moving.

She took a step backward, forcing Clare down the stairs. "There's been an accident. Go for help," she ordered.

"Brian? Is he hurt?" Clare tried to push past her, but Felicity held her ground.

"Go!" She repeated. "Ambulance. Police. Get someone."

Clare stuck her hand in her pocket. "My phone. I forgot it."

"Mine's dead. Go get help." She refused to let herself yell. They needed action, not hysterics.

It was only as she heard Clare's steps descending the stone stairs that Felicity realized she was alone in the tower. But she couldn't leave Brian. Gripping the railing she went back into the bell chamber. "Brian, I'm here. Clare's gone for help." She prayed for a response—a groan, the slightest movement. But there was nothing.

She felt stiff with cold but she forced herself to inch forward along the platform to the far side of the tower. Gripping the beam supporting a bell she reached out and touched his leg. If he couldn't hear perhaps he could feel her touch, know he wasn't alone.

Clenching her teeth Felicity turned her head to view the bell encasing Brian's upper body. The bell hung at an angle, as if it had not been fully down when he reached in to remove the muffle. She looked back at his feet and saw the scuff marks in the dust along the plank, as if he had been pulled forward.

What could have happened here? If Brian had attempted to remove a muffle from a bell in the up position and it had swung down... No, he wouldn't have done that. Only a few hours ago he had explained how dangerous that would be.

But if he had pulled the bell toward him to get a better grip on the buckles and then slipped... Or if the bell had been left at a slight angle—was that even possible? Could a bell be booby-trapped? No, it was an accident, surely.

However it happened, it seemed clear that the massive weight of the bell had shifted with Brian under it, bringing its enormous force crashing into his body.

Twenty-Two

Felicity descended the ladder to the ringing chamber, trying not to think about the broken body lying just over her head, forcing herself not to look at the lopsided bell pull and keeping well away from the ominous rust-colored blotch on the grey carpeting below it. She wrapped her arms around herself, rubbing her upper arms to circulate some warmth.

She needn't stay in the tower. She could go down and wait in a pew. She could even get out a prayer book and say some of the prayers from the Service for the Dead. How ironic, that is what they had just had. That was what Brian was ringing the peal for. But he could have had no idea it was his own death he was knelling.

She started for the stairs, but somehow she couldn't leave. It would be like abandoning her friend. No, she would stay, even though she knew Brian was beyond all earthly help.

At last she heard the door open below and footsteps ascending the stairs. "We're coming," Clare's voice rang up the stairwell. "Has he come round yet?"

Felicity met her at the top of the stairs and took the younger woman in her arms. "Clare, you've got to be strong. He isn't going to—"

And then she saw the tall man who had followed Clare up. "Oh," she stepped back. "Mr. Luffington."

"I met him outside. He rang for an ambulance." Clare

walked past her into the chamber.

Allyn stepped forward. "When Brian didn't show up at the pub I decided maybe I should come help him. Thought he might be having trouble with the muffles. They can be tricky. Clare said there'd been an accident." He started toward the stairs to the bell chamber.

"No. Don't go up." Felicity put out a hand to stop him.

He brushed past her. "If he's hurt I blame myself. I shouldn't have left him to it on his own."

Moments later Felicity heard the approach of an emergency vehicle below and Allyn descended the wooden stairs, shaking his head. "It looks bad. I'll show them where to come."

Clare started to tremble and make little whimpering sounds. She needed strong sweet tea and a warm blanket. They both did. The best Felicity could do was wrap her arms around her friend and lead her to a chair.

"I don't think you should—" Felicity began, when the medics lumbered up the stairs carrying a stretcher between them, but nobody was listening to her. The scene would be disturbed, no matter how strongly her instincts told her it shouldn't be.

She turned to Allyn Luffington who had followed the ambulance team back up. He was now standing in the center of the room, looking at the bell pull hanging awry and shaking his head. "Allyn, is it possible—could someone have rigged that bell to fall on Brian?"

He looked startled but paused to think before answering. "I don't see how." He continued to consider. "I suppose it's possible—just... If the bell were somehow propped so it was mostly down..." He was muttering, more thinking out loud than speaking, "pulling the clapper over to reach the muffle could make it shift..." He shook his head. "Very unlikely. And anyway, why? Who could possibly want to hurt Brian?"

A sob from Clare made Felicity wish she could continue this in a more private place but before she could suggest anything a heavy tread on the wooden steps told her the medics were returning. Without the laden stretcher she had expected. Apparently Felicity wasn't the only one with heightened instincts.

A tall, blond medic wearing the name badge Bob on his green uniform explained they had rung for the police and kindly, but firmly ushered Felicity, Clare and Allyn down to the sanctuary and then produced the blankets and flask of hot tea Felicity had been longing for.

It seemed like hours later when the freckled face of PC Evans roused her from a near doze. She had tried to stay awake to be a comfort to Clare, but Clare had pulled her blanket around her and retreated into a small ball of misery at the end of the pew. "What can you tell me about this?" Evans asked.

Felicity shook herself out of her stupor and told him about going into the tower earlier in the day to watch Brian muffle the bells, then returning with Clare to wait for him.

"And you're the one who found him?"

"We called out and I was worried when he didn't respond. It seemed too quiet. So I went up first. If there was anything wrong I didn't want Clare..."

"Yes. And what did you see?"

Felicity shut her eyes, forcing herself to see the scene again. She described it as well as she could.

"And you didn't touch anything?"

"I touched him. Just his leg. It was all I could reach. I wanted him to know he wasn't alone."

PC Evans nodded. "Is there anything else you can tell us? Anything you noticed?"

"I've been trying to think. I keep remembering Brian telling us how heavy the bells are and that they should always be muffled in the down position for safety." Her throat closed.

PC Evans thanked her and started to close his notebook. "I'll type these up. If you could just stop by the station in the next day or two and sign them we shouldn't have to bother you again."

"Yes, that's fine. But—if you have a minute..." What a silly thing to say. The police were obviously stretched to the limit. But he waited patiently. "It's on another matter. Unless everything is somehow connected, although it's hard to see how—" Now he looked less patient. "Right, sorry. The St.

Frideswide manuscript—the charter Sister Gertrude and I were working on—"

He nodded. "Seems to have caused a lot of trouble: Fire, the Sister drugged, you attacked..."

She greatly appreciated his matter-of-fact approach. "Yes, that's it. And Mother Monica..."

Again he nodded. She went on, "There has to be a connection and we might have found something." She explained about Antony's research into the ancestry related to the charter. If PC Evans suppressed a yawn he was sufficiently tactful that she couldn't be certain. But when she got to the part about the current possible heirs his alert stillness told her she had his full attention.

Evans thanked her and called another officer over to escort the women home.

To her surprise Sheila was still up at Hursley House. Felicity told her as succinctly as she could what had happened and turned Clare over to the motherly ministrations of the former nurse, then dragged herself up to her tiny room at the top of the building.

She flopped down on her bed and tried to think. She wanted to make sense out of all that had happened. There had to be a pattern. Wasn't that what Morse had always looked for? At first all her mind produced was a tangle of swirling images: reliquaries with oozing red contents, a brown nun's habit floating on the Cherwell, a smudge of black smoke issuing from a convent. Memories of photographing St. Frideswide's well mixed with scenes from Frideswide's life— of the pursuing Algar being struck blind. And then she was back at Fairacres with Sister Gertrude in the crumbling summerhouse. A black spider in the corner morphed into a departing black-cassocked figure.

She sat up with a jerk, her crumpled pillow falling to the floor. Father Ben. She recalled now his turning up in the infirmary after the first attack on Gertrude and herself. And his escorting them to Binsey the day the camera was stolen and the card with photos of the charter removed. And the black-clad figure she had glimpsed running across the field away from the drugged Gertrude must have been Ben, too.

That was undoubtedly the same line of reasoning the police followed that led them to arrest him. Weighty evidence, indeed. But if Brian's death wasn't an accident, but was somehow part of the whole, horribly impossible scenario Father Ben couldn't have done that.

And that meant the killer was still out there.

Twenty-Three

No matter that dawn hadn't broken yet, Felicity had to talk to Antony. She still hadn't charged her mobile, but she knew there was a landline in the lounge downstairs she could use. Even after she pulled on a sweatshirt over her clothes, and stuck her feet back in her shoes, she still shivered. Once in the lounge, she wrapped herself in an afghan covering the back of a worn recliner, then settled into the corner of the sofa with the phone.

It rang five times. She could picture the insistent, grating sound echoing through the dark interior of the tall, narrow terrace house Antony had described. She could only hope the ringing wouldn't waken Aunt Beryl, and that Antony alone would hear it. After two more rings she was ready to hang up until a sleepy voice said, "Hullo?" She could hear the anxiety in his voice.

"Antony, it's me."

"Oh, thank God. I was sure it was the hospital."

"I know. It's awful when the phone rings in the middle of the night. Well, it's not exactly the middle now. But I know you're expecting a call to say Edward died and—Oh, Antony—" She had rung him thinking of her own comfort, not considering what her news would mean to him. "Antony, I'm so sorry. It's Brian." And now, for the first time in the whole, appalling nightmare, she broke down and sobbed.

"I'm sorry. I'm so sorry," she finally managed to say when she recovered her voice enough to form words. "I just wanted to talk to you so desperately and now I have to tell you this awful news and I feel so responsible because I'm not really in charge of anything but with you gone I should have been and..."

"Felicity!" His voice broke through her hysterical outpouring with a firm command. "Be quiet. Now, three deep breaths." She breathed. "All right. Calmly now. Take your time and tell me what happened."

She obeyed.

A long silence followed. She knew he was thinking. Carefully, as he always did. Finally his voice came out on a rush of held breath. "Brian. That doesn't seem possible. He was one of the brightest..." Another long pause, then, "How's Clare?"

"Shocked. Sheila's looking after her."

"Yes. Good. How are you?"

"I don't know. No, I'm shocked, but I'm all right. I just knew I had to talk to you." She could tell Antony was taking in little of what she said.

"Father Clement. He needs to know. And Father Anselm. I should ring Brian's parents, but I don't have their number."

"I'm sure the police will have taken care of all that."

"Yes. Still... Felicity, are you sure you're all right? Can you sleep?"

She was beginning to feel warmer. "Maybe. I think so."

"Right then." Felicity listened as he said a brief prayer for the repose of Brian's soul, for comfort for his family and friends, for guidance for the police.

"Amen." Felicity joined him on the last word.

"Now to bed with you. And Felicity—"

"Yes?"

"Lock your door."

She locked her door, then secured the door with a chair wedged under her doorknob. Still wearing her clothes she crawled into bed and pulled the duvet over her head.

She wasn't at all sure she could sleep, but she was warm and secure. Eventually she relaxed into unconsciousness. The deep, hollow knells of the great tom bell echoed through her dreams, pulling her forward down a long corridor. Shadows lurked in the recesses beyond the arches, and dust motes silvered the pale light—the images wavering with each reverberation...

Felicity opened her eyes to pitch darkness. *Not day yet?* Then she flung back her duvet. Lancets of afternoon sun pierced the gaps in her ill-fitting curtains. But the urgent sounds continued. Not a knelling tenor bell but insistent knocks on her door.

She lunged across the room, flung the chair aside and turned the key. Dreading the inevitable bad news awaiting her on the other side of the door, she pulled it open.

"Antony!" She fell into his arms.

Several minutes later, when she had restored her hair and clothes to a semblance of order, she joined him in the kitchen where he was preparing tea and toast for the both of them. "I hope I'm not still dreaming. How did you manage...?"

"Of course I would come. You needed me."

Felicity blinked at the lovely simplicity of his words. "But Beryl, Edward..."

He shook his head. "Edward's still in a coma. Beryl has help. I'm needed here. Brian's family will arrive later today. I have to do what I can for them." He shook his head. "I can't imagine what they must be going through."

"Have you spoken to the police?"

"It seems to have been an accident. I suppose the coroner will decide."

Felicity nodded. "I hope I don't have to testify. Or Clare. That would be awful for her." Then she thought—"What about the others? The seminar? What will you do?"

"Father Clement advised we give them the option of carrying on to the end of the octave or completing their essays back at Kirkthorpe. I spoke to everyone while you were sleeping. I think they'll all stay on, they're stuck into their research here."

"Clare, too?"

"Said she has an appointment to visit Hopkins' college tomorrow—Balliol, that is. Stout girl. She's determined to carry on." Antony set his mug down. "Well, I'd best get on with it. Brian's parents will be here soon. I need to have his things packed for them."

"I'll help you." She stood up.

Brian's room was on the second floor, almost directly under Felicity's garret perch. Brian, as most students did, had left his door unlocked. Felicity was first in. "He didn't waste much time on housekeeping, did he?" She stooped to pick up a pair of jeans and a sweatshirt from the middle of the floor.

"What happened? What's going on here?" Clare's voice made Felicity turn back toward the hallway.

"We're packing Brian's things for his parents," Antony answered, stepping aside to let her enter the room.

"This isn't right." Clare gazed around the room. "Brian would never have left his room like this. I tease him all the time because he's, er — was — so much tidier than I am." She bit her lip to stop it trembling.

"He was probably in a hurry to get to the bell ringing," Felicity suggested. "Didn't he say he only agreed to muffle the bells at the last minute?"

"Yes, the whole thing with the bell ringers just came up, but he said it was a touch he had rung a lot in the past. He was really excited to have been invited." She sank down onto the bed littered with papers, her hands tightly clasped between her knees. "And he was so cautious. I don't see how..." But she could say no more.

Felicity straightened the duffle bag lying on its side at the end of the bed and picked up a tee shirt, folded it and put it in the bag. Antony turned to the desk covered with books about Cardinal Newman and the Oxford Movement. He set aside the books that would need to be returned to the library and put Brian's personal belongings in his rucksack. He paused to scan a few pages of notes, then shook his head. "He was a really fine scholar. It's such a shame."

Felicity shook out the discarded jeans and started to fold them, then felt something hard in a pocket. "Oh, I'm surprised he didn't have this with him."

"His mobile!" Clare reached for it. Felicity gave it to her then continued her packing.

A sob from Clare made Felicity turn back to the bed. She sat down and put her arm around her friend. "This is too much for you, Clare. Let me take you back to your room."

"No." Clare shook her head. "No, it's good, really. Painful, but good. I wouldn't want to forget. It's our texts." She sniffed, but her voice was steady. "He was always so funny. And so interested in everything. He always wanted to know all the details. No one but my mother ever cared so much about who I was with and what we said. It was really sweet."

She held out the screen so Felicity could see a text. "See, at breakfast I told him all about our talk in the park that morning. Then later he was still thinking about it, so he sent me a question."

Felicity thought it rather odd, but she didn't say so. "Where was he when he sent this?"

"He didn't say. Meeting someone, I think. Probably just walking along and thinking about our conversation. It's so like him. He was so thoughtful."

Felicity returned to her packing without replying.

"That's odd," Antony said to the room in general as he pulled out the bottom desk drawer.

"What?" Felicity asked.

"I haven't found his laptop."

"He just used an iPad," Clare said. "Isn't it in his desk?"

It wasn't.

"Do you think he had it in the bell tower with him?" Felicity suggested.

"That's possible. He was studying something he called a method diagram on it. Said he needed to refresh his memory because he hadn't rung in a long time. Just a lot of numbers in rows and columns. Didn't make any sense to me."

"Well, if it *was* there the police probably have it. They'll give it to his parents. I'll mention it to them." Antony picked up both bags and looked around the empty room. "We haven't missed anything, have we?" He descended the stairs, banging the railing only twice.

Felicity considered waiting with Antony to meet Brian's parents, but Clare wanted to meet them as well, and Felicity felt that would be enough people for them to face. "I think I'll go to Fairacres," she said to Antony. "The sisters should be told what has happened."

Antony nodded and held out his hand. They stood for a moment in a firm handclasp. "I'll see you later."

"Thank you so much for coming." She brushed his cheek with her lips.

All the way on the bus Felicity kept thinking about Brian's text. Why was he so interested in her conversation with Clare? What had she said? Something about Antony's research about the barony being abeyant, but nothing highly sensitive, surely. It was all there in Debrett's or whatever he had been reading. Was Brain really that interested? Or was he passing on gossip to someone? The press?

Felicity paid very little attention to newspapers, but she glimpsed an occasional headline. Ever since they found out about the mutilated body parts the media had been having a heyday sensationalizing the Oxford Butcher. Could Brian have been selling tidbits to a reporter? But if so, they would have protected him, not arranged for his murder. Besides, Brian's death was an accident. It had to be.

She was still chasing uneasy, random thoughts around in her mind as she got off the bus and walked along Parker Street. A young man, apparently homeless, was waiting at the bottom of the lane. He spotted her and stepped forward. "Pardon me, miss. Do you have just a minute?"

Felicity shook her head. "Sorry, I only brought enough for my bus fare."

"How do the sisters feel about this latest development?"

In spite of herself she stopped and gaped at him. The press? It was as if her own thoughts had conjured him up. Did he mean Brian? Had the press connected the two deaths? How? She started to push past but he was insistent. "Does this mean the police got it wrong? Is the Oxford Butcher still at large?"

Felicity shook her head and pushed forward. "Has it shaken the nuns' faith? Is this a personal attack on the order? Were the relics desecrated as a slap in the face to them?"

Resisting putting her hands over her ears, Felicity rushed toward the door. "Wait, you're the one who found the nun in the burning building, aren't you?"

How on earth did he get hold of that? And a garbled version at that. She yanked the bell pull so hard she was amazed it didn't come off in her hand. Tall, angular Sister Hannah opened the door before the jangle ended. Felicity had to curb her impulse to lunge forward before the nun stepped out of her way.

"Felicity, come in. How lovely to see you." Hannah's greeting was as calm as if she were welcoming a visitor to a garden party, not to a house under siege.

"The press. Are they out there all the time?"

"I'm so sorry you were accosted." Hannah ushered her forward. "They don't bother us. Sister Anna stepped out once and offered to pray with them. They were amazed. I think they got the idea we'd taken a vow of silence. Except when it comes to giving interviews, of course."

Felicity smiled. She could picture the tiny, frail Sister Anna with her blue-veined hand raised in a blessing. How dare that puppy imply the nuns were in tumult? Grief, yes; confusion, no.

"I have some news," Felicity began. Hannah's eyes lit expectantly. How she wished she could tell her their long wait was over. "No, bad news, I'm afraid. Is it possible Sister Dorcas might be available?"

"Mother Dorcas now. We had chapter yesterday. The choice was unanimous. We are very fortunate." Then she looked at the floor and added, "I'm the new guest sister."

"An excellent choice." Felicity had admired Hannah's quiet efficiency before. She would fill the office perfectly. The new guest sister led the way to Mother Superior's office.

The door stood open. Dorcas looked up and immediately rose from her desk. "Felicity, do come in."

"Congratulations, Mother Dorcas."

Dorcas grimaced. "I think condolences might be more in order." She looked around the room with a shake of her veiled head. "I've been sorting, trying to make sense of everything. Of course Mother Monica's records are in perfect order but it's like being taken from the stockroom and made CEO of a company. I had no idea she did so much. She was always so serene, had time for everyone, all our small needs." She took a deep breath. "Do keep me in your prayers. I don't know how I shall even begin to do it all."

"Of course I'll pray. And you will be splendid. But I'm afraid I have to burden you with more bad news. One of our students, an ordinand—" She told her as succinctly as she could.

Dorcas crossed herself and indicated that they should both sit down. "Oh, that's terrible. The poor lad. And his family. We shall remember them all in our prayers."

Yes, the nuns had a structure for dealing with everything life could throw at them. Faith, certainly, but also a very practical method that told them what to do. And a liturgy that gave them the words. They were never at a loss. And they were never alone. They had community. Whatever came, they faced it together.

"And Father Antony," Dorcas continued. "A heavy care for him."

"Yes. He is with Brian's parents now. The police need them to identify...him." She couldn't bring herself to say 'the body'. This time yesterday Brian had been a vital, living person, excited to be taking part in something he loved.

Dorcas nodded. "That's the hardest part—helping the family. There's nothing that can be done and yet so much to do." She indicated an open box in the middle of her floor. "Lucille is coming this afternoon. I must have Mother Monica's personal things ready for her. Of course we keep very few personal possessions, but there may be things of sentimental value to her family."

Felicity couldn't imagine Lucille Knighton being in the same room with the word sentimental, but she merely smiled.

"I've been putting off clearing out her room." She stood up. "Perhaps you would have time to come with me?"

Felicity gulped. Twice in one day to go through a dead person's things. "Yes, of course, I'd be glad to help."

There was no question about the tidiness of this room's occupant. Her narrow wardrobe held two spare habits and a cloak for winter. Three pair of polished black shoes sat side-by-side on the bottom shelf. Felicity held up a pair, noting the deep creases across the top of the right shoe where her foot had bent as she genuflected numerous times each day. The toes of both shoes were scuffed where they had rubbed the wooden floors as their wearer knelt in prayer.

"The habits can be handed on to another sister. The shoes can go to Oxfam." Dorcas indicated the black plastic bag she had brought, then turned back to the stack of papers on the small study desk in the corner. "Very few people knew that Monica wrote poetry. Some of this is very lovely. Not much fashion for sonnets these days, but perhaps Sister Gertrude should take a look at them with an eye to publishing."

Felicity was amazed at what a room as spare as this one, could tell about its occupant. The crucifix over the bed and the religious pictures on the walls were as natural a part of the room as the air that filled it. A fine icon of the Virgin and Child hung above the *prie dieu,* the deep indentations on its cushion testifying to hours spent in prayer.

Felicity turned to the bedside table. "Oh, perhaps her sister will want this." She held up a rosary of carved black beads with an ivory corpus on the silver cross, then wrapped it in a tissue and gently laid it in the box of books that would go to Lucille.

Felicity opened the small drawer in the nightstand and took out Monica's Bible. Black leather binding. Revised Standard Version. Well worn. Favorite passages marked with ribbons. She turned to the first page and read the inscription:

> *Presented to Phyllis Beaumont*
> *By her father George, Lord Ansty*
> *On the occasion of her confirmation*
> *14th April 1962*

Felicity blinked as the words swam before her eyes. She had seen those names before, in a far more familiar handwriting. But this was Monica's Bible. Why did it have someone else's name in it? Surely it hadn't come from a used bookstore? A cousin or something had passed it on to her? "Mother Dorcas, Monica's Bible has the name Phyllis Beaumont in it. Is that a mistake?"

"Oh, no, that's correct. Monica was her religious name. She

took it when she joined the order. You know, for the mother of St. Augustine."

Felicity nodded. Yes, she understood about taking a new name with one's vows, but it didn't make sense. If she remembered the names in Antony's notes correctly, Phyllis's sister was named Margaret. Not Lucille. Yes, she was certain that Baron Ansty's daughters had been named Margaret and Phyllis. So who was this woman coming to collect Phyllis/Monica's belongings and claiming to be her sister?

She was still puzzling over the implications of her discovery when Sister Hannah knocked on the door. "Mother, there's a Lucille Knighton in the parlour. She said she has an appointment."

"Quite right. I'm just coming." Dorcas picked up the box and headed back through the convent.

Lucille came to her feet before they were even in the room. "Do you know there's an impudent fellow hanging around outside your gate? Had the nerve to question me about my sister's death. Didn't know she was my sister, of course. I gave him a flea in his ear. Why do you stand for it? Call the police. Coddling riffraff does no good to anyone."

"Hello, Mrs. Knighton," Dorcas greeted her. "I have your sister's things for you, but may I offer you some refreshment first?"

"No thank you. I'm meeting a friend at the Randolph," she said, her cheeks turning pink.

Felicity was amazed. She would never have suspected that Lucille Knighton could come close to blushing.

Felicity looked at the Bible she was still carrying. "And you'll want your sister's Bible. But I don't understand about the names."

"What?" Lucille glanced at the nameplate page Felicity held out. "Oh," she gave a dismissive snort. "That nonsense about taking a religious name. An ancient line like ours, and she throws it all over. Not that it mattered to me. I always called her Pooky anyway. Still, *Monica*. I ask you. We've never had a Monica in our family. Phyllis was our grandmother's name. Should have been good enough for anybody."

"Actually I was wondering about your name. Wasn't the

Baron Ansty's eldest daughter named Margaret?"

"Of course I was. Margaret Lucille and proud of it. Won't catch me calling myself Monica. Margaret was our mother's name, so I went by Lucille. Avoided confusion." And woe be it to anyone who tried calling her Lucy. Lucille all but snatched the Bible from Felicity, issued a general farewell to the room and departed.

Felicity didn't wait for the door to close. "Mother Dorcas, may I use your telephone?" She must remember to charge hers. Hopefully Antony would have his mobile with him.

He answered on the second ring. "Antony, I'm sorry to interrupt. I know you're probably with Brian's parents, but I just found out the most amazing thing... Remember those two daughters of Baron Ansty that made the barony go abeyant— well, the one named Phyllis was really Mother Monica. And, the oldest one—named Margaret, remember? That's Lucille Knighton. She was at Fairacres today." She lowered her voice, although there was no one around. "Do you realize what that means? Lucille must be the murderer. She killed her sister so she could inherit the barony. I knew the police were wrong about Ben."

She paused to catch her breath. "Antony, did you hear a word I said?"

"Felicity, I'm sorry. I'm at the police station—"

"Wonderful! You can tell the police now. She's at the Randolph. They can arrest her there."

"Look, Brian's parents just came in from identifying his body. They seem pretty shaken. I have to go."

"Tell the police!" She got it out before the line went dead.

Her first impulse was to get back into town as fast as she could, march into the Randolph and accost Lucille Knighton herself. Then a wave of second thoughts hit her. Monica hadn't only been murdered, she had been tortured as well. Would her sister have done that? Whoever did it, Felicity certainly didn't want to face them alone.

And what about the other things that had happened? She rubbed the spot on the back of her head where she had been hit the day the Press was ransacked. Drugging Gertrude, snatching her camera, Brian... Had Lucille snuck back from—

where did she say she lived? Loughborough? Where was that? Near Nottingham, maybe? Well, from wherever she was, to do those things? Easy enough to imagine her whacking someone over the head, but sneaking? Felicity shook her head. If Margaret Lucille Knighton had wanted Felicity's camera she would have marched in and demanded it.

So did she have an accomplice? Brian? Father Ben?

Better to wait and talk it over with Antony. Even if it did mean being patient for hours yet until he was free.

When Antony finally returned to Hursley House, dinner in hall was long over. He looked so drained Felicity offered to fix him a hearty plate of beans on toast, and, in spite of her impatience, refrained from bringing up the subject until he had consumed the final bite. At last he put his knife and fork down and pushed away his plate.

"Now, tell me. Did you tell the police? Did they listen to you? Have they arrested Lucille?"

"Yes. Yes. No."

"What? They listened but didn't arrest her? Why? It's an obvious answer."

Antony shook his head. "There's someone with a much stronger motive. You're forgetting. Monica—well, Phyllis—had a son."

"Lucille said he died."

"He's very much alive and in custody by the Thames Valley Police."

"What? Who?"

Antony looked unhappy. "Father Benjamin."

Felicity felt her mouth fall open. "Father Ben was Monica's son?"

He nodded. "That's why they arrested him. And I'm afraid the police believe our evidence proves the case against him. Of course they may be right, but I didn't want to believe it."

"But Monica's son's name was Leroy." She stopped. "Oh, it's that religious name business again, isn't it?"

"That's right. Actually the police have paid very close attention to what we've told them. They're the ones who chased down the fact that Ben was in line to inherit to the barony."

"So he killed his mother..." She closed her eyes to focus her thoughts. "No. That can't be right. If there was only one daughter, she would inherit, so killing his mother would be giving the inheritance away. Now, if it had been Lucille who was murdered..."

Antony put his head in his hands. "I think the theory was that Ben would now stand in his mother's place so it would be as if the baron had a male heir instead of just daughters. Or maybe I got it wrong. I'm so tired I can't think straight."

"Right." Felicity picked up his plate and headed to the sink. "To bed with you."

Antony was halfway across the room when his mobile rang. "Hullo?" It came out as more of a sigh. What little color he had drained from his face. "All right. I'll come as soon as I can."

He lowered his phone and sank back into his chair. "Uncle Edward died."

Twenty-Four

Antony woke the next morning with the weight of the world pressing so heavily on his chest he could hardly get his breath. How could there be so much death around him? *Take thy plague away from me; I am even consumed by means of thy heavy hand... In the midst of life we are in death... the grass withereth, the flower fadeth... man is grass...*

Tearing off his duvet he rushed to the sink and sluiced his face with cold water, more to wash away the jumbled words from the service of the dead than to clear the sleep from his eyes. Much as he might like to give into the temptation to brood, he must get on. He had already slept far later than he intended. Beryl. He must ring her first. Then he would have to face Gwen.

Correction. Morning prayers and shower first. He had to get himself together if he was going to be any good to anyone.

Half an hour later he gave his hair a final brush then snapped his collar into place. *Welcome to the world of the living,* he told his reflection in the mirror.

Beryl answered on his first ring. With a stab of guilt he thought it sounded as if she had been waiting for him. But her voice was calm. He could see her, dry-eyed and erect, dressed in black. He told her how sorry he was. "Are you all right?" Nothing but the most standard phrases would come to his mind.

She assured him she was quite all right. "In a way it's a relief." She spoke of Edward being in a better place. Antony wasn't the only one relying on clichés. But clichés could be comforting. Antony assured her he would ring her when he knew what time he would be there. "There's no rush. We aren't going anywhere."

After he hung up Antony wondered if Beryl had made a joke. He was still puzzling when his world brightened. With a brief knock that she didn't wait for him to answer Felicity came in carrying a breakfast tray. "Just Weetabix and toast, I'm afraid. That's all there was in the kitchen." She put the tray on his desk and poured him a cup of tea, fixing it exactly the way he liked it with two sugars and lots of milk. 'Nursery tea,' Gwena always mocked him.

"I've spoken to the others." She poured a second cup for herself and perched on the end of his bed. "Everyone says don't worry about them, they can get on with their reading. I think Marc is getting up a subscription for a funeral wreath. That's really sweet." She paused for a drink. "Oh, yes, and I rang Father Clement. He said the college and community would be praying."

"Thank you. I hadn't even thought of that. I'm not sure my mind is functioning very well. It's been too much."

"I know. But it's all over now. I mean, with Monica's murder solved we can put all that behind us." Her words made him scowl. "I know," she agreed. "I don't like the answer either."

"It leaves so much unanswered besides the tangled inheritance issues." He shook his head. "Ben seemed so gentle in an awkward sort of way. Can you see him torturing his own mother? And then why would he—a priest—desecrate the reliquaries? I find it hard to believe the inheritance even meant that much to him."

"Well, you never know what's in another person's mind. But he must be mad. I suppose they'll have him examined. Maybe he contracted some kind of a fever in Barbados that affected his mind. Maybe a witch doctor..." She took a swallow of tea.

After a moment she continued. "Never mind, I didn't

mean to get off on that. I need to tell you that Dorcas rang. The police said they can have Monica's body. Um, this is probably a bad time to be asking, but they would like you to take her funeral service. I told her about your uncle, so they'll understand if you can't do it."

"Did she say when the requiem will be?"

"They thought Monday, the eve of Saints and Martyrs of England."

He nodded. Of course he would do it for them. *But how much more, Lord?* "Thanks for breakfast." He stood up. "Must go see Gwen."

"Good, I'm ready."

"Felicity, you don't have to." No matter how much he would love her company he didn't want to expose her to another slanging match.

"Of course I don't. But I am."

Far from slanging, however, he had never seen his sister so subdued as she was when she opened the door to their knock. "Antony, come in." She took him in her arms and gave him a hug. "Nice to see you, too, Felicity, come on in."

Gwena returned to her parlour. "This must just be so awful for both of you." She gestured for them to sit down. "Derrick, bring two more mugs," she called toward her kitchen. A clatter of crockery told her the message was received. "Allyn just told us."

"Allyn? How did he know?"

Now Gwendolyn looked as confused as Antony felt. "He was there. With the police, he said."

Then Antony realized. Her comfort had been for the death of his student. "No, it's something else. Uncle Edward died."

Antony was amazed at the change that came over his sister. She looked so stricken he stood and guided her to a chair. "Oh—" she swore. "I should have gone with you when you said." Anger flushed her face. "Must you always be right? It's your fault. You should have insisted. You didn't tell me I'd never see him again."

"It isn't Antony's—" Felicity began but Antony gestured for her to be quiet.

He put a hand on Gwena's shaking shoulder. "It's all right,

Sis. It wouldn't have made any difference. He never regained consciousness. You couldn't have done anything."

"It would have made a difference to me! I could have held his hand like he did mine when I was afraid." Antony was amazed. He didn't know Gwendolyn had ever been afraid of anything.

"I would never have become an actress if he hadn't held my hand until that moment I walked on stage when I was ten years old." She gave Antony a fierce look. "Don't remember that, do you?" He shook his head.

"Of course you don't. You weren't there. You stayed home."

Now he remembered. "I was poorly."

She sneered. "You were always poorly. A good excuse to stay in bed and read. And, of course, Beryl stayed with you—your faithful nursemaid. But Edward went with me. He held my hand walking all the way to school and all the way backstage. And then I stepped out with the lights and the audience and it was magic and I knew I wanted to do it forever." Now she was calm, settled into her reminiscence. "Jack and the Beanstalk. I was Jack. I hated it when the teacher gave me the role. I wanted to be a fairy princess. But it was a wonderful role. And Uncle Edward told me how brilliant I was all the way home and made me a big mug of cocoa." And then she collapsed in tears.

"I wasn't there to hold his hand," she repeated when her sobs subsided.

The conversation became general when Derrick and Allyn entered from the kitchen with the tea but as soon as they emptied their mugs Derrick stood up. "Will you be all right if I go now, Gwen? I'm really hoping Allyn's client will be interested in this chest I've acquired. The ivory inlay is something quite special."

"Yes, of course. Off you go. Goodness, you only stopped by to give me a bit of news—Sorry about involving you in a family scene." She started to get up.

"No, don't bother. We'll see ourselves out."

When he heard the front door close Antony turned back to his sister. He hated to set her off again, but he needed to broach the subject. "Um, about the funeral..."

"Of course I'll go." She sounded insulted that he would question it. "Better late than never, huh? Our run ends Saturday night. It needn't be before then, does it?"

"No, not at all. I'll ring you." He stood up.

Felicity offered to stay with Gwen, but she declined. "No, I have to get my head together before I go to the theatre. I'm better alone."

She walked them to the door, then, to Antony's enormous surprise, she put her arms around him again. "Thank you for coming, Squib. I know it's not your fault."

Back out on the street Felicity slipped her hand in his. "You okay?"

"Yeah. It's just—so many things I'd do different if I had a chance."

Felicity nodded. "I know." After a few moments she asked, "When do we leave?"

"You're going with me?" He made no attempt to conceal the pleasure in his voice. "I had rather hoped, but—"

"Of course I am. I don't have anything to do here. And you need me."

"Always." He squeezed her hand.

Then she stopped. "Oh, I almost forgot, though. I told PC Evans I'd go to the station and sign my statement. I'd better do that before I leave town. And I was thinking—Father Benjamin—They'd let you visit him, wouldn't they? I mean, with the collar and all."

"Yes, probably. But why?"

"Well, isn't that part of your job? Visiting the imprisoned and all that? Like the Holy Club. And I've been thinking—if he's innocent he must be feeling pretty desperate. And if he's guilty he must be feeling pretty, well—desperate, too."

He narrowed his eyes. "Are you up to something? We're not investigating this, you know."

She spread her free hand. "Of course not. I just think it would be a good thing to do."

And a few minutes later when the duty officer led him into the dismal cell it was clear that Benjamin thought it was a good idea, too. But Antony wasn't so sure. Even walking down the hall behind the uniformed policeman he had felt the walls closing in. He hadn't realized he was claustrophobic, but now, with the door locked behind him...

Ben came to his feet from the narrow bed where he had been sitting. Antony gulped. Was he facing a wronged man or a cold-blooded murderer?

Antony gave himself a stern, priestly lecture. Either way he was facing a human being who was in need. And Ben was almost pathetically grateful to see him.

"Have you had many visitors?" Antony began. "I wasn't sure they'd let me in, although this is a pretty good pass to most places." He touched his collar.

Ben sat back down on his bunk and gestured for Antony to sit on the chair at the small table. "They've assigned me a lawyer. She's been in twice. Frankly, I don't think she has a very high opinion of my case. Mother Dorcas and Sister Bertholde came." He dropped his head in his hands. "They mentioned they're hoping you'll take her requiem." His voice thickened. "I won't be there. My own mother's..."

Antony was trying to think what to say when Ben coughed and sat up straighter. "In all my years of prison visiting... I never had any idea what it was like to be sitting on the other side of the table, so to speak." He shook his head. "I couldn't have imagined."

Again silence, the four bare walls echoing the hopelessness in his voice. "I didn't do it, you know."

"Why did you keep your identity a secret?"

"I didn't really. That is, I didn't lie or anything. No one asked about my background and I didn't volunteer. The irony is that one of the reasons I came back was because Mum had been thinking about granddad's title just sitting there. I don't think she had thought much about it for years but then Sister Gertrude brought a manuscript to her. Of course, Gertrude didn't have any idea it was connected to our family, she just wanted her superior's approval for undertaking the publication."

He looked up. "Sorry, long story and I'm rambling. Anyway, it was time for me to come back and I thought I could help. But when I got here it was already too late."

More to keep off the despair of silence than for the information Antony asked, "That day at Binsey — did you take the camera?"

"Of course not. Why would I do that? My fingerprints were on it because I held it for Felicity. It's as simple as that. I swear."

"Time." The guard who had been standing just outside knocked on the door of the cell. There was so much more Antony would have liked to ask and yet he was relieved to be free of the responsibility.

But he wasn't truly free. Even out in the crisp air the smell of the cells stayed with him. Too much antiseptic and yet not enough to mask the darker odors. All the time walking back to Hursley House Felicity chatted, but part of his mind was still with Ben. Little wonder if his counsel was having trouble mounting a defense. There was very little to establish an exact time or place anything had been done. Therefore Ben could produce no alibi. And no one else seemed to be connected to the case. Except Lucille, of course.

Antony didn't realize he had spoken out loud until Felicity answered. "Yes, I asked PC Evans about Lucille, she seems a much better suspect to me, but apparently they looked at her pretty closely and she hadn't been anywhere near Oxford for ages."

It all continued to circle in Antony's mind as he packed his small bag, the image of Ben's dark-shadowed eyes haunting him with an accusation that he had been of no help.

And it was even worse when he and Felicity arrived at the Oxford train station a few hours later. The tabloids screamed their headlines: "Oxford Butcher Hacks Own Mother," "Mum was a Superior Mother," and, inevitably, "I Dismember Mama." All accompanied by a grainy picture of a dark-haired man in a dog collar that might or might not have been Father

Benjamin. Antony couldn't begin to guess what sensational stories they would dig up or manufacture.

Hoping he might be able to clear his mind by talking through it Antony recounted his interview with Ben to Felicity as soon as they were settled on the train. Her response was immediate: "So, did you believe him? Does his story make sense? Did he keep his mother's letters—or emails or whatever they were? Or would that just make it worse for him? Prove he was thinking about the inheritance? Why didn't you ask him—?"

"Felicity," Antony held up his hand to stop the flow, but without the amusement her outbursts usually brought him. "I don't know. That's the answer to everything. I wish to God I could say I believed him. I want to, of course. But I don't know enough about anything to make a fair judgment. That's why we have to leave it to the police."

Except he couldn't.

"Antony, look at this nonsense. It's outrageous!" Felicity had picked up a discarded Daily Mail from the seat across the aisle. She held out a two page spread that purported to be an inside interview with a holy sister. The accompanying photo had to be an actress got up as a nun.

Antony shook his head. Besides trivializing a horrible tragedy and promoting what could well be a miscarriage of justice, it all made the Church look so bad.

Sometime later, when the taxi pulled up in front of the familiar Victorian terrace house in Blackpool, Antony made a determined effort to put Benjamin and his problems firmly out of his mind. He was in another world now, with another set of duties to perform. Aunt Beryl met them at the door. He hesitated for a moment, then took her in his arms. He almost pulled back in dismay. She had always been thin, but now she was emaciated. "Aunt Beryl, you must eat."

"I will. Now you're here."

Her words pierced him. He should have been here sooner. He should have come more often. He stood frozen with guilt.

"Hello, I'm Felicity." A blur of golden hair and a poppy red shirt squeezed past him in the narrow, dark hall, filling it with light and color. "And you're Aunt Beryl. I've been longing to meet you. Antony has told me such wonderful things about you."

He had? He hoped so. He should have.

In a shorter time than he could have imagined, Felicity had maneuvered them all into the parlour, turned up the bars on the heater, then produced the Brown Betty from the kitchen, filled with steaming tea twice the strength he ever remembered drinking in this house before. "And look what I saw in a bakery window in Oxford." She reached into her rucksack and pulled out a fruitcake that must have weighed several pounds. "I couldn't resist." She took the knife she had brought in on the tea tray and began slicing thick slabs. "Actually it was just plain so I waited while they put marzipan on it. I made them put it down the sides, too. I just hate it when they only put a thin little layer on the top, don't you? I want enough to sink my teeth into."

Had Beryl ever put marzipan on her fruitcakes? Antony couldn't remember. But she was obviously enjoying it now. When they had all consumed a second slice and emptied the large teapot, Felicity looked around. "What a cozy room." Antony was amazed. Of all the words in the English language that could describe the room: shabby, dim, outdated... Felicity chose the one word that was both accurate and complimentary.

She rose and lifted a black and white photo from the mantelpiece. "Oh, is this Edward? He looks like a lovely man. I'm so sorry I never got to meet him." Instead of returning to her chair she sat beside Beryl on the sofa. "Tell me about him."

The two heads, grey and gold, were bent together over the photo album Aunt Beryl produced when Antony slipped from the room sometime later. Warmed, fed and relaxed, with the knowledge that Beryl couldn't be in better hands, he turned to the cold, business side of death. Papers that needed sorting, forms that needed filling, arrangements that needed making. At last there was something useful he could do for the aunt who had seen to everything that needed doing throughout his childhood. Fortunately his accountant uncle had left everything in excellent order.

Antony leaned back in the old, oak desk chair and looked

up at the collection of small, wooden figures behind the glass doors of the tall case in the corner. He could see Edward sitting by the fire working on his delicate woodcarvings while Aunt Beryl and Gwen watched the telly. Sometimes Antony had joined them and sometimes he chose to go to his room to read. Most often, when he chose to stay, it was because of the warmth of the fire rather than the attraction of the television. Or of being with his family.

Chagrined, he turned back to the papers on the desk.

The next morning, after a far better night of sleep than he could have imagined, Antony savored the last bites of his second sausage then placed his knife and fork across his plate with a satisfied sigh. He grinned at Felicity across the table. "If we weren't already engaged I'd propose to you. How did an American learn to cook a perfect English breakfast?"

"Beginner's luck. And Aunt Beryl. She was out to the butcher's at the crack of dawn to get those proper sausages for you. And freshly-laid free range eggs. Then she gave me a lesson in what to do with it all."

He shook his head with amazement. "Fried bread, even. I hope you took notes." Had Beryl cooked like this for him when he was growing up? And he took it all so for granted that he didn't even remember? Had he even said thank you? Ever? "I hope I didn't eat you out of house and home when I was a youngster, Aunt Beryl."

"It's a pleasure to see you eat now. You were finicky as a child."

Oh, no. Was that it? Had she lovingly produced perfect brown sausages like those he had just consumed, and thoughtless brat that he was, had he turned his nose up at them? The accusations Gwena had flung at him must have been true. "I'm so sorry. I must have been impossible."

He had never seen his aunt's face take on such a soft look. "Never. You were always such a joy. So steady, reliable, never under foot, never complained. I told Father Lowe, just the other day, how lucky Ed and I had been to have you children given to us. Ed had his woodcarving, and his accountancy, of course, but I wouldn't have had anything if I hadn't had you."

She talked on, reminiscing about how proud they had been at the school prizes he had won and the plays Gwendolyn had starred in, but he couldn't take it in. *You were always such a joy.* He heard it over and over in his head. The simplicity. The sincerity. It transformed his whole childhood. Something deep within him relaxed, spreading warmth through his body. He had been loved.

"I told him I was certain that would be all right with you."

Antony startled as Beryl's implied question hung in the air. "Sorry. What was that?"

"Father Lowe. He'll drop by this afternoon about the arrangements."

"Yes, that's fine. I found Uncle Edward's instructions in the desk. All very straightforward."

"Yes, Ed didn't like a fuss."

Antony nodded. He had never seen less fussy funeral instructions than those left by Edward Sherwood.

A bit too simple for Father Lowe, it seemed, when Antony explained later that afternoon. The Vicar of St. Dunstan's frowned. "Of course we try to comply with the express wishes of the departed. And in these days, when so little tradition is adhered to any more... Still, cremation with only a committal service." He shook his head, but it was more of a shiver. "And on a Sunday." More shaking of the head.

"If I remember correctly, only Requiem Masses are proscribed for Sundays, Father." Antony tried to be gentle in reminding the vicar of the rubrics.

"It's done sometimes at home." Felicity handed the vicar the cup of tea Aunt Beryl had just poured. Antony smiled at her, but he could tell her endorsement of American ways didn't go down well.

The Reverend Lowe sniffed. "A true Christian should be buried from the church. Still, as I say, we try to comply. Perhaps, since the inurnment is to be on Sunday," a soft sigh bespoke his compliance, "if the family feels it appropriate we could include some of the readings and prayers at the end of Holy Communion and process directly to the churchyard."

"My sister's train doesn't get in until one o'clock, I'm afraid," Antony said.

Father Lowe looked pained. "Very well. Since Edward expressly requested you to officiate I'm sure you'll know best." Antony felt certain that if there had been a convenient basin of water Father Lowe would have washed his hands.

"Thank you, Father." Beryl looked relieved. "I just have one request. I don't think Ed would mind very much. I do think it would be nice to sing 'Amazing Grace'."

"As you wish. Father Antony will undoubtedly know best." The vicar set his teacup down and stood. Duty done. Any heresy that was to be committed would now be on Antony's head.

Antony handed his teacup over for a refill. That hurdle cleared. Could they really be set for a spot of smooth sailing now?

Twenty-Five

"In sure and certain hope of the resurrection to eternal life through our Lord Jesus Christ, we commend to Almighty God our brother Edward; and we commit his body to the ground; earth to earth, ashes to ashes, dust to dust. The Lord bless him and keep him, the Lord make his face to shine upon him and be gracious unto him, the Lord lift up his countenance upon him and give him peace."

Felicity joined in the "Amen" with the little group clustered in St. Dunstan's churchyard. To her surprise Gwendolyn's voice was the most fervent, although Derrick, standing stiffly on her left, barely muttered.

Chilled drops began falling from the grey clouds overhead as Beryl stepped forward, stooped to pick up a handful of earth from beside the small hole and sprinkled it on the urn. Gwen was next, removing her black glove to perform the ritual. Then Felicity. *'Ashes to ashes, dust to dust,'* indeed, she thought, as the small clod made a soft plunk.

Felicity stepped back and took Beryl's arm in an attempt to warm her as the prayers continued. And finally, Antony pronounced the words Felicity always found so comforting:

"Rest eternal grant to him, O Lord."

"And let light perpetual shine upon him," They were in the shadows, Edward was in the light, Felicity thought as she responded with the others.

"May his soul, and the souls of all the faithful departed, through the mercy of God, rest in peace."

"And rise in glory."

She thought even Derrick joined in the "Amen."

With the rain increasing they made rather quick work of singing Beryl's requested hymn then walked up the street for sherry and sandwiches at her house. The comfortable Mrs. Bolton, Beryl's longtime friend and neighbor had it all in hand, so Felicity was free to turn her attention to the guests. She had been surprised when Derrick showed up with Gwena, but she was glad he was there to support her. Standing by the graveside Felicity had observed them in their black wool coats, Derrick so tall with his dark, spiked hair glistening; Gwena, tiny with her smooth cap of yellow hair. In spite of her reservations about Derrick she had to admit they made a stunning couple.

Felicity had never before imagined the independent Gwendolyn would seem so reliant on anyone. She approached them as Derrick handed Gwen a glass of Sherry. "I'm so glad you could be here, Derrick."

"Happy to be here for Gwen. Nice short service. I approve. As much as I approve of anything of that sort, of course." He took a sip of his sherry and didn't even complain that it was too sweet.

Felicity turned to ask Gwen what her plans were now that "Misalliance" had closed. Gwen mentioned a couple of plays she was hoping to get parts in. "And, of course, I'd like to stay near Oxford." As she talked about the desirability of being near Derrick Felicity observed him on the other side of the room. At first she thought he was spending so long at the sideboard to make a careful selection of sandwiches for Gwena, then she realized he was scrutinizing the furniture.

Old and dark, rather heavy, Felicity would have said if anyone had asked her what Beryl's furniture was like. If she had even noticed that much about it. She was most aware of the worn red velvet on the couch. It was an unusually deep plush, and she loved to run her hand over it when she sat there. But there was no denying that Derrick surveyed every item with an antiques dealer's eye. She could almost see the pound signs in his eyes as he ran his foot over the intricate design of the Turkey carpet, rubbing the pile one way, then the other.

He returned with plates of sandwiches for both Gwen and Felicity. Felicity was happy to have them even if she felt they came with strings attached. "I don't suppose your aunt will be staying on here alone now, will she?" Derrick did a poor job of making his query sound casual.

"I have no idea—" Gwena began.

But Felicity cut her off. "I'm certain she will." Actually she had no idea, but she wasn't going to let this bird of prey think he could walk off with the spoils. "She has lived here for fifty years. She told me she came here as a bride. It was in Edward's family before that. All her friends live in the neighborhood. She can walk to church." She warmed to her subject. "She would be desolate anywhere else. Completely lost. Why would you think she'd want to move?" She ended with a challenge.

Derrick took half a step back from the spark in her eyes. "It's a big place for one person. Just the heating bill must be astronomical." He swept the room with a calculating glance. "And there may well be death duties. Value here could easily be over the threshold. I'll bet the old bird hasn't given that a thought. You need to have a chat about the facts of life with your aunt, Gwena."

Felicity was too outraged to reply. Gwen burst out laughing, then quickly stifled it when she realized her surroundings. "That's ridiculous. Beryl and Edward lived like church mice their whole life. School fees for Antony and me were the only extravagance they ever undertook."

"Exactly my point. She probably has a tidy sum socked away. She could sell up here and move into a really posh retirement home. Have every whim catered for for the rest of her days."

Felicity found her voice. "And just who do you suggest should be in charge of the estate sale?" She made it sound like an accusation.

"I would be more than happy to help in any way I could. I could certainly advise on the value of this furniture. That sideboard, for example. Authentic Jacobean, I'm certain." He named a staggering figure. "I recently appraised a similar one for a client. He expects to come into a whole houseful of it quite soon." She had the impression he was salivating. "I'll be handling the sale for him, of course."

"Well then, you won't need Aunt Beryl's will you?" Felicity turned so sharply a sandwich slid off her plate. Out of the corner of her eye she saw Derrick dive for it before anyone could tread shrimp paste into his Turkey carpet.

Felicity was shaking with anger. She didn't dare face any of the other guests so she took refuge upstairs in the room assigned to her. The trailing azure flowers on the wallpaper and faded blue drapes were calming. She had been there only a short time when there was a soft knock at the door. "Yes." She hoped it would be Antony.

Gwendolyn stuck only her head in. "Sorry if I'm disturbing you."

Felicity jumped to her feet. "Oh, come in. You shouldn't have to knock. This was your room, wasn't it?"

Gwena sat on the bed and ran her hand over the faded blue comforter, then looked at the wallpaper. "I always thought of this room when I played Laura in 'Glass Menagerie'. Her gentleman caller called her Blue Roses because she'd told him she had pleurisy and he misheard her. I never could get the southern accent right, but I loved the role."

"You must have so many memories tied up with this house."

"I do. That's what Derrick simply can't understand. To him it's all business. I'm afraid that's why I came up here—to get away from him. He was banging on about how if we sold this furniture with his other client's, we could double the price. I didn't want to argue in front of guests, so I invented a headache." She flopped back on the bed, her arms spread wide. "You know, I think I might stay on here for a few days with Aunt Beryl."

Felicity picked up a book she had left on the dressing table, which she now saw was a rather lovely Victorian vanity. "Why don't you take a rest? I'll just sit here and read if it won't disturb you."

And that's how Antony found them maybe an hour later. "Sorry to interrupt. You two look so peaceful. I just wanted to report that the vicar finally left with the Wainwright sisters, so that's the last of the lot."

"Aunt Beryl must be shattered." The bedsprings creaked when Gwena sat up.

"I'm sure she will be when she stops. That's why I thought we should have our little meeting now."

"Meeting?" Felicity asked.

"Nothing formal. Not like the family gathered around a long table with the dour solicitor droning on as one sees in films. But since Amanda is here I thought she could answer any questions anyone might have before she goes."

Gwen seemed to understand all that, but Felicity was completely in the dark. "Would you care to interpret?"

"Amanda Smith-Jordan. I think you met her downstairs. Long, straight black hair." Felicity nodded. "Her father was Edward's solicitor, but Amanda has taken over. I found Edward's will in his desk. I don't think it's very involved, but there might be questions, so I asked her to stay on a bit."

"Sure. Good idea." Felicity started to return to her book since a family meeting wouldn't involve her.

But Antony seemed to think otherwise. "You'll be family in just over two months." She hoped his broad view of family didn't extend to his sister's boyfriend. She was relieved that only Beryl sat by the fireplace chatting to the woman that Felicity had taken earlier for a schoolgirl. How could she possibly be a solicitor? The clatter of crockery in the kitchen suggested that Derrick had tactfully undertaken the washing up. Probably so he could count the silver spoons.

Antony handed Amanda a thick envelope. "Why don't you read it out to all of us?"

Amanda drew the document from the envelope and unfolded the sheets of heavy white paper. She opened her mouth to read, but Gwen got in the first word. "Oh, please!

Spare us the party of the first part and party of the second parts. Just tell us what's there. Surely no one here is going to be upset about anything." Antony and Beryl both nodded their agreement. "Whatever Edward wanted done with his stuff is fine by me. Although I would like to have one of his woodcarvings as a memento."

Amanda cleared her throat. "It's very simple for the most part. Edward Sherwood leaves to his wife Beryl Sherwood a life interest in the bulk of his estate, which is this house and a post office savings account, including a Christmas club. And, yes," she smiled at Gwen, "he requests that his wards, his nephew Antony and niece Gwendolyn, select any of his carvings they might like to have for themselves and that the remaining collection be donated to Save the Children."

"Oh, that's lovely. Thank you, Uncle Edward." Gwena spoke as if he were sitting across the table from her. "I dibs the collie dogs. I adored them as a child."

"There's just one unusual provision which, in the present circumstance, doesn't apply, but it's interesting that the dec..., er — Mr. Sherwood," Felicity was enormously grateful she refrained from referring to Edward as the deceased, "stipulates that if either of his wards should predecease him, leaving progeny, the child or children would not stand in their place." She placed the will on the table beside her chair. "As I say, this is most unusual, but as you are both alive it's nothing we need worry about. I only mention it because I think it shows how personal Edward felt his carvings were." She stood up. "Unless there are other questions I'll be going. I know it's been a long day for all of you." She handed a card to Gwen and to Antony and placed one on the table by Beryl. "If you have any questions about anything at all, don't hesitate to ring me. I know my father served Edward's father and I think the relationship went back a generation before that."

Antony saw Amanda to the door. Her departure was closely followed by Derrick's. He gave Gwena a peck on the cheek. "Ring me when you get back to Oxford." She agreed and closed the door behind him with a sigh.

The brother and sister were barely back in the room when Gwena turned to him. "Race you to the study." Felicity thought she caught a glimpse of the children they must have been as Gwen darted up the stairs and Antony followed at a more subdued pace.

Beryl rose. "I think I'll retire now."

"Can I bring you some supper on a tray? A scrambled egg or something?" Felicity offered.

"That's very thoughtful, my dear, but I won't be wanting any supper."

When she was gone Felicity began tidying the room, returning sherry glasses to the sideboard and throwing rumpled serviettes in the laundry bin. She slipped the will back into its envelope and placed it on the mantel, thinking about Uncle Edward's odd stipulation. Neither Antony nor Gwena had children, so it was a moot point, but what if there had been a grandniece or nephew? She smiled, perhaps Edward drew up the will when Antony was thinking of becoming a monk and Gwena's life was rather flagrantly irregular so the idea of any progeny seemed unlikely— undesirable, even.

Her smile faded to a frown. She picked up the tray of uneaten sandwiches and headed to the kitchen, thinking about the tangled inheritance law for the Ansty barony. If only it were spelled out in as simple a document as Edward's will, instead of being laid down by parliamentary law, then Father Ben might not be in custody at this moment. She wrapped the sandwiches and put them in the refrigerator, then returned to the parlour for the tray of glasses.

Amanda Smith-Jordan's card lay on the table where she'd left it. Felicity picked it up and looked at the number. "Well, she said if we had any questions at all," Felicity said, as she walked to the phone in the hall.

Amanda answered on the third ring, just when Felicity was beginning to wonder if she should ring off. She shouldn't be bothering Beryl's lawyer at this hour on a Sunday.

"No, no. It's no trouble at all," Amanda assured her when she answered a moment later.

But when Felicity explained her problem, there was a long silence at the other end. "I'm sorry. I know you meant any questions about Edward's will," Felicity rushed into the silence. "This is a matter for—um, a friend in Oxford." She explained the situation.

"No, that's absolutely fine. I don't mind your asking. It's just that, I'm a family lawyer, although I do wills and inheritance issues, this just isn't anything that has arisen in my practice. In these egalitarian days very few English people have any contact with this sort of thing. Or care about it as it doesn't impinge on their lives at all."

Felicity was thinking that it certainly impinged on Father Benjamin's life. She was about to say thank you and ring off when Amanda asked, "You said you'd researched it. I take it you don't understand what you found?"

"That's right."

"So what did you find?"

Felicity had spent so much time puzzling over the question she had Antony's notes memorized.

Amanda thought for a moment. "If it's as you say, that means that when one daughter dies her son would take his mother's place. The barony would then be in abeyance between the aunt and nephew."

"So there was no motive for Ben to kill his mother! I knew it!" Felicity almost shouted.

"What?" A puzzled voice rang in her ear. "I'm afraid I don't understand."

"Oh, sorry. I—Oh, never mind. Thank you so much. You've been a really big help! Thank you." She put the receiver down on her own babbling. She started to run up the stairs to tell Antony, then stopped. He needed this time with his sister. She could tell him later.

Besides, after the first flush of excitement she realized this was excellent news for Ben, but it left everything unexplained. If inheriting the barony wasn't the motive then what was? As much as she had disliked the earlier answer, it did seem to make sense. Now there were no answers to anything.

Twenty-Six

"I'm so glad Gwen is staying with Beryl for a while. I'm sure it will be good for both of them," Felicity said to Antony as the train sped southward on Monday morning.

Antony's mild agreement came as if from a long distance.

"Antony!" Felicity wanted to shake him. "Talk to me. You've been a hundred miles away all morning. You weren't even excited about my news from the lawyer." Felicity felt like she might as well have been traveling alone. At first she had been content just looking out the window as the wide white sands surrounding Morecombe Bay slipped past her window, then the autumnal English countryside, interspersed with industrial sites. Even when they changed trains in Manchester's busy Piccadilly Station he had hardly said more than to name the track their train would be on.

"Sorry. I think I'm rather in shock."

Felicity instantly regretted her hasty words. "Oh, I'm sorry. You're missing your uncle. Somehow one forgets that priests need time to grieve, too."

"Yes. Er—no. That is, yes, I do miss him and of course I am grieving. But that's to be expected. What I've been dwelling on—the most extraordinary thing… I think I've been completely reliving my childhood. When Gwen and I were looking at Uncle Edward's woodcarvings, the years just fell away. We started playing with them like we did as children. I set up the crèche and Gwen insisted on the shepherds bringing more dogs to the stable than sheep and we squabbled just like we always did—same words, even. And then we laughed until we both just lay down on the rug with all the little figures between us.

"I had forgotten the moments of closeness we had had as children. I think Gwen had, too. We wound up apologizing to each other. It was amazing." He sat in silence with a smile on his lips and a faraway look in his eyes.

"I wonder if that's what Edward had in mind when he made that odd provision in his will? He probably remembered watching you play with those together as children. That's why he wanted it to be just between you two. Or, if it came to it, left to one of you with your memories."

Antony nodded. "I'm thankful it didn't have to be that. We've lost enough time already. I don't know how much we'll see of each other in the future, but just knowing the door is open, the way cleared, is wonderful. I feel so light inside."

"Well, let's make plans for getting together. I'd love to ask Gwena to be one of my bridesmaids." She paused. "No, Maid of honour. What do you call them?"

"Chief bridesmaid." He smiled. "She'd love that. Not quite the starring role—that will be all yours—but a stellar supporting actress."

Felicity let Antony return to his thoughts of the past. She drew a notebook from her rucksack and began focusing on the future. She was still making notes for their wedding when the train pulled into Oxford.

They were crossing to the busses when Antony said, "I've been thinking about your news about Ben. Sorry, just couldn't seem to focus before. It really is splendid. I should visit him. His solicitor may have unearthed all that already, of course, but I need to be sure. Do you mind going on alone?"

"Of course I don't mind. But why don't I come with you? I don't mind waiting." She hadn't even started her list for catering arrangements. She could easily do that while Antony made a visit.

The Oxford Central station of Thames Valley Police was just down St. Aldate's from Christ Church College so, in spite of the grey clouds overhead, Felicity chose to wait on one of the benches along the entrance to the Broad Walk. That was where she had been waiting for Gwendolyn that morning they went running together. She shook her head. Had that really been less than three weeks ago? So much had happened in that time. She set her wedding planner aside and thought. It had been a lifetime ago for Monica, Brian and Edward. And life-changing for all who mourned them.

She was just starting the second page of her to-do list when Antony returned. "So soon? Didn't you get to see him?" Surely he wasn't refused admittance to the cell.

"No, I saw him. We had a remarkable visit actually. Cut short when his solicitor arrived."

"But you told him what we learned?"

"I did. The solicitor acted like she already knew, but I'm not sure she did. Ben was pleased, of course, but I could tell the inheritance itself was of little importance to him. He was much more concerned about missing his mother's requiem."

"How is he holding up?"

"It's strange—I've encountered this before when I set out trying to comfort someone, I often find I'm the one who's comforted. Perhaps because he's a priest Ben was concerned about Edward's death. We were talking about childhood memories when his solicitor arrived. It seems the time he's had alone in the cell has brought a lot to the forefront for him—just like being at Aunt Beryl's did for me."

"Probably part of his grieving for his mother. What did he say?" They were just starting up Cornmarket when the rain began. Antony opened his umbrella and they bent their heads together, as much so Felicity could hear his words, as to shelter from the rain.

"He told me about visiting his Aunt Lucille. Apparently he and his mother lived in rather reduced circumstances after his father died, but Lucille maintained the family home. He said the old Baron was awfully medieval and Lucille loved to relive the glory days."

Felicity laughed. "Yes, I can just imagine that. Can't you see Lucille dining at one end of an enormous, highly-polished mahogany table with one aging retainer to wait on her?" She actually had no idea if it had been anything like that, but Felicity saw no reason to bind her imagination to the merely factual.

"Ben didn't mention their dining arrangements. Apparently what stayed with him most were the stories his aunt told him and the things she would show him—pictures, mementos. He said nothing had changed since the Civil War."

Felicity's first thought was of a *Gone With The Wind* antebellum house with ladies in hooped skirts on the lawn, and Benjamin's grandfather sitting on the verandah sipping a mint julep. Then she realized what was wrong with that picture. "Oh, the English Civil War." She adjusted the pictures in her mind. Puritans and Roundheads. Cromwellian vandals stabling their horses in churches and smashing stained glass windows and—"Jacobean furniture. Like Aunt Beryl's. And like Derrick's client's."

She grabbed Antony's arm. "Antony, Derrick said his client would soon be 'coming into' this valuable furniture. That could mean inheriting. If he was referring to the Baron Ansty's Jacobean furniture, then he couldn't mean Ben. If Ben is convicted of murder he won't inherit, surely."

"Felicity, do you have any idea how many houses there still are in England stuffed with crumbling old furniture? Why should Derrick be referring to Lucille's furniture?"

"But it's not crumbling old furniture he's talking about, is it? It's exceptionally fine seventeenth century antiques that have been well cared for." She held up her hand. "Yes, I know. There's probably a lot of that still around, too, but what if it is Lucille's? Indulge me."

She drew a breath and plunged. "What if Lucille, thinking her nephew was dead, killed her sister to get clear title to the furniture?"

"But even if she did such a thing, would she sell it? She sounds fanatical about preserving it all."

"Well, maybe she's really in debt. Doesn't feel she has any choice." Felicity thought again. "Or maybe Derrick killed Monica to clear the way for Lucille, so that he could handle the sale of a lifetime. He could be thinking it would make his reputation in the antiques world—get his shop up there with

Sotheby's."

Antony shook his head. "Even supposing Derrick knew about the furniture, which is a huge leap, and supposing he knew the heir wanted to sell, he couldn't have been sure they would ask him to be the dealer."

"Well, yes, but..." Felicity could think of no more buts.

Twenty-Seven

Saints and Martyrs of England

Felicity could sense Antony's nervous strain the next morning when they arrived at Fairacres laden with the black chasuble and pall Antony had arranged to borrow from Pusey House. It was only midmorning, well ahead of the hour set for Mother Monica's requiem mass, but it had taken longer to collect the paraments than they had expected, and Antony always liked to have everything well in order whenever he was going to celebrate.

Sister Thérèse, the sacristan, led the way rapidly toward the church. Just inside the narthex their progress was halted by an imperious female voice. "Here at last, are you? I trust we aren't inconveniencing you, Father Antony."

Felicity saw Antony's features tighten, but his voice was soothing as he treated the sarcasm as a sincere comment. "Not at all, Mrs. Knighton. It's an honour to be asked to carry out your sister's obsequies."

Lucille Knighton strode into view clad in severest black from head to toe. "Yes, well, I'm glad to hear you realize that. Not every day you get to send off the daughter of a baron, what? I want to ensure everything is in order. Pooky had her eccentricities but she was still The Honourable and I won't have it forgotten—"

Antony squared his shoulders and drew himself up a full inch. "Mrs. Knighton, I can assure you—"

Felicity almost laughed, no one in the world was more of a stickler for the proprieties than Antony. But Lucille was in no mood to be reassured. "And I'll not have any of this modern, maudlin palaver. See that you stick to the Prayer Book. And keep it short. I can't be hanging about." She looked at her watch as if she had a plane to catch. Perhaps she did. Felicity glimpsed two small suitcases near the door of the narthex. That must be exactly the situation.

"Now, about the bell." Lucille continued. "Such a pity they only have one, but it will have to do, I suppose. I want a full muffled toll. Fifty two years, you know." The 'And I'll be counting,' was understood.

"It is the custom that bells are full muffled only on the death of the sovereign." Antony's voice remained level.

"Don't quote rules to me, young man. I checked with the Oxford University Society of Change Ringers. I was assured that a full muffle *can* be used on the death of the incumbent of a parish or the Bishop of the dioceses. Surely the Superior of a religious house would qualify."

Antony opened his mouth to reply but was cut off by a tall man stepping forward from the shadowed arch. "In medieval times abbots held the same rank as bishops. I believe the tradition endures."

Felicity blinked. Allyn Luffington? What was he doing here?

Lucille looked smug. "I don't suppose you've met." She made the introductions. "Mr. Luffington is a life member of the change ringers and he has kindly agreed to come along to see to the matter for me. Sister, if you will be so good as to show him the way."

Sister Thérèse looked at Antony. He nodded his surrender. She led Luffington, carrying two brown leather muffles, to a small door just between the sanctuary entrance and the bell pull, which extended through a hole in the ceiling from the small tower above. A great convenience for the sacristan not to have to ascend the stairs to ring the bell for each service.

"Now, Father. As the chief mourner, I shall, of course,

walk behind the casket." Lucille Knighton called them back to the task at hand. "'Lead, Kindly Light' will be a most acceptable hymn."

The others moved on to the sacristy, but Felicity held back. She had one farewell she wanted to say and since they would be returning to Hursley House shortly after the funeral, she didn't want to wait till later. She was certain she would find Sister Gertrude in the Press, and she did.

She hugged the plump nun. "Thank you so much for everything—for trusting me with the translation. It was an amazing experience."

"Oh, no, we thank you. And I'll see that you get the first copy off the press."

"How is it coming along?"

"Almost finished. I plan to proofread the galleys this afternoon. I just now sent the manuscript on its way back to the Whitby sisters. I'm so glad to have it gone after everything that's happened. I didn't want to take any chances so I hired a courier."

A muted gong, sounding as if it came from a long distance, made Felicity look around. Then she realized. The muffled bell. Calling them to mass.

A short time later Felicity took a seat in the back row of the choir stalls just inside the door, her first time to worship in the sisters' sanctuary rather than in the side chapel. The organ began "Lead, Kindly Light" and the procession entered. Somber in his black chasuble, Antony proceeded down the aisle to stand before the rose onyx altar flanked by unbleached beeswax candles.

Their steps marking time on the wooden floor, six black-cassocked priests bore the casket, covered by a black pall. Felicity looked, then blinked and looked again to be sure. Yes. There was no mistake. The sturdy, black-haired priest holding the front right corner was Father Benjamin. He had been released in time to attend his mother's service. His solicitor must have used her information about the inheritance to good effect.

Then she saw the two policemen standing guard in the shadows. Ah, compassionate reprieve, not a full release. She was grateful that at least Benjamin was allowed this favor.

She turned her attention back to the procession as Lucille Knighton, behind the heavy veil of her broad-brimmed black hat, walked in splendid, solitary state behind. Hands folded, veiled heads bowed, the Sisters of the Love of God followed a respectful distance behind, then filed into their seats in the choir facing each other in two rows on either side of the aisle.

Antony stepped forward to sprinkle the casket with holy water, recalling the waters of baptism. "We who are baptized are baptized into the death and resurrection of Christ. Likewise, we who have died with Christ in baptism will rise with him."

The familiar, comforting words of the service rolled over Felicity like the sweet scent of the incense. "Now is Christ risen from the dead, and become the first-fruits of them that slept. For since by man came death, by man came also the resurrection of the dead. For as in Adam all die, even so in Christ shall all be made alive..."

Of course, 'by man came death' was a reference to the death of sin brought into the world by Adam's fall, but to Felicity it spoke of the death of a much-loved woman to whom death came not as a natural course of human life, but violently by human hand. Antony moved on to the homily. "This last day of the octave of the feast of All Saints' is set aside as the commemoration of the 'Saints and Martyrs of England'. There could be no more appropriate day to celebrate the life of our sister than on the day we remember those who have been called on to give special witness to their faith in this land. Monica Simmeon, ne Beaumont, joins a long line of those wearing the white robes of martyrs. It reads like a litany of saints: Thomas a Becket, Margaret Clitherow, Thomas More, John Fisher, Thomas Cranmer, Nicholas Ridley, Hugh Latimer..."

The list continued and Antony went on to remind his hearers of the staunch witness of some of those he named, emphasizing, "Those from each side of the ecclesiastical divide in the Reformation era who, when the church was torn apart by the ravages of sin, witnessed to their faith with courage and constancy."

He went on to give special attention to Margaret Clitherow in whose reliquary Monica's hand had been placed. "Monica's torturer undoubtedly meant it as a desecration and humiliation to both women, but as is so often the case in the spiritual realm, it serves to emphasize the faith of both women."

Yes, it was a comforting thought. Felicity didn't doubt that ultimately God could bring good from all things, even from murder, but she, for one, was unwilling to leave it to the hereafter. Justice was, whenever possible, most satisfying in the here and now. Although what she could do to see it done in Monica's case, she couldn't imagine.

She was still thinking along those lines when she turned from the altar after receiving communion. At first it was the shock of seeing Allyn Luffington, the crusading atheist, sitting by Lucille. It was all very well his seeing to the bells, but why would he attend the funeral service? And then she saw the look that Allyn and Lucille exchanged. The rail in front of their choir stall prevented a clear view, but Felicity would have sworn they were holding hands.

The pieces slotted into place: Luffington who had access to both of the desecrated reliquaries through his connection with the Ashmolean. Luffington who despised Christianity. Luffington who had rung bells with Brian... And he was courting Lucille? That would give him a motive to see the barony reinstated. Surely Lucille was considerably older than he was? But maybe he was willing to overlook such a detail to become Baron Ansty. No, he wouldn't become baron, but maybe consort to a baroness—and access to her historic estate—close enough, surely, to satisfy his ambition.

Lucille's sister dead, Lucille's nephew accused of the crime, Lucille in sole possession of valuable property...

They stood for the closing prayers. "God, whom the glorious company of the redeemed adore, assembled from all times and places of your dominion: we praise you for the saints of our own land and for the many lamps their holiness has lit..."

On the other side of the choir Felicity saw a movement and knew that Allyn would be moving to the narthex to begin the tolling. Felicity slipped from her seat as the first solemn knell sounded. Every head in the sanctuary was bowed, no eyes on her. She stepped softly so as not to interrupt the fading echo of the toll before the second one started.

Keeping to the shadows, Felicity looked across the narthex to watch Allyn Luffington, his back to her, both hands gripping the sally. He bent forward with the downward swing, then stretched upward, arms extended fully on the backstroke. A full minute pause. Then downward again. Fifty-two years. A minute for each toll. This would take nearly an hour.

On the next pull Felicity followed the downward swoop and saw what she hadn't noticed before. The briefcase at Allyn's feet. Not just near his feet, but held tightly between his feet as if he feared someone snatching it and making off while he was occupied.

And Felicity knew what that briefcase held. The Frideswide manuscript. Ironically, Luffington was Sister Gertrude's courier. And now he would sell it for thousands of pounds to a collector? Or perhaps present it to his prospective bride, restoring her family heritage? Or when he was married to the Baroness sue to have the lands restored to the barony? Felicity's mind boggled at the thought, yet there was no doubting the meaning of the adoring look she had seen pass between them. No doubting the look, but she put little credence in the sincerity of the prospective groom.

What a win-win situation. When he tired of his titled bride, which wouldn't take long, he could see her off quietly and profit on her antique furniture—which Derrick had already valued. Even the manuscript would still be in Luffington's possession.

And Lucille said she was leaving immediately after the service. A flight to a romantic honeymoon location? From which the bride might never return? Felicity had to stop him.

She looked around for Father Ben's police escort. They must be in the visitors' chapel where they could keep careful watch without being seen. How much time did she have left? She had lost count of the tolls. Had there been ten? She had maybe forty minutes. She could run around outside to the chapel door.

Except that Luffington was between her and her only exit. Could she slip past? He seemed totally intent on his tolling, keeping count and judging the length of each pause. Should she try to sneak by him and hope not to be noticed? Or make a dash and hope to outrun him if he followed?

Or should she turn back into the sanctuary? Alert Antony, perhaps Mother Dorcas? For a moment her mind filled with an image of herself standing in the center of the choir and rallying the whole community. The idea of the brown-robed sisters swooping like avenging angels, ancient Sister Anna beating Luffington over the head with her walking stick was most pleasant, if impractical.

She looked back into the church, weighing her options. But when she looked at the room full of bowed heads, only one face was clear to her. There was only one person she wanted by her side whatever she faced. Antony.

She took one step inside the door but got no further. She felt herself jerked backwards with a vice-like grip on her arm. "You weren't planning on disturbing the good sisters, were you?"

Lucille pushed Felicity against the wall in the narthex and growled into her ear. "I won't have my sister's service interrupted."

Felicity struggled to free herself. "It's Allyn. Don't you see?" She wanted to shout, but was constrained to speak in a harsh, urgent whisper. "Don't marry him, Lucille. He'll kill you. Like he did Monica."

"He didn't kill Monica. Ben did."

"No, Ben's innocent. I found evidence. It's Allyn. He wants your fortune."

Lucille's tone switched from commanding to menacing. "You silly girl. I don't have a fortune, but if I did Allyn would be quite welcome to it. And I have no intention of allowing you to interfere."

She jerked Felicity from the wall and propelled her forward before Felicity could react. With a single movement Lucille pulled open the door of the stairway to the bell chamber and shoved Felicity inside.

Felicity heard the click of the iron key in the lock as another toll sounded.

"Let me out!" Felicity beat her fists on the heavy planks of the door but even in the long pause between tolls she knew the sound would carry to no ears. Probably not even to those of her captor only a few feet away. The convent was built to provide a haven of silence. Thickly insulated walls kept sounds from travelling.

Even before she twisted at the latch, she knew it wouldn't move. There was no going out. She must go up. It wasn't really a tower, more just an attic room. Not even a room. Just a space to hang a single bell. As she looked up at it the bell swung again. Even with the muffles the sound made Felicity stagger backward.

She turned to the tiny porthole window looking out over the wide green lawn to the gardens beyond. But Felicity wasn't interested in the view. The window tilted open. Surely there would be someone she could attract below. Frank in the garden digging potatoes? A workman? She could see no one, but they might be hidden by the bushes.

She drew breath. "Help!" But her cry was shrouded by the next toll.

She tried again in the reverberating silence, but realized how puny her voice was. Even the echo covered it.

Hands over ears to help her think, Felicity backed into a corner and sat. She could do nothing until the insistent clamor stopped. She closed her eyes to keep herself from watching the swaying bell. How much longer? She must make a plan, but she couldn't think. It was as if the clapper were inside her head. She put her head between her knees and counted.

Twenty-five, twenty-six, twenty-seven. She had endured almost half an hour of the insistent clanging in the chamber. Twenty-eight. It took her some time to realize the fading echo would not be followed by another clash. Felicity shook her head to ward off the deafening silence.

She sprang to her feet and rushed at the bell. She knew what she must do. The bell was her only weapon. She must remove the muffles and raise the alarm. And she must hurry. Even at this moment Lucille and Allyn might be snatching up their cases and making for the door.

Haste made her fingers fumble. The first strap was stiff and the buckle scratched her forefinger. The second came more easily. She moved on to the other side, praying Allyn wasn't still standing by the rope hanging through the hole just beyond her feet. If he saw it moving he would guess what she was doing. All he would need to do was to give the pull a sharp yank and she, gripping the clapper, would be pulled forward to be smashed by the bell.

And that, she realized, was exactly what Allyn had done to Brian. The thought made her drop the clapper and pull back, dropping the muffles on the floor.

At that moment she heard the door below open and steps ascend the stairs.

"Antony!" She turned toward the stairs.

"Sorry to disappoint, my dear, but your knight in shining armor is attending to the bereaved. It seems poor Lucille was overcome with her grief and needed the good father's attentions. I know you wouldn't want to keep him from his Christian duty."

Felicity backed against the wall. "Why aren't you running? I thought you had a plane to catch."

"How thoughtful of you to be concerned about my little plans. But I'm afraid I wouldn't be able to enjoy my honeymoon fully knowing I had left a loose end behind."

"You think you're going to get your hands on the barony property when you marry Lucille, but she won't inherit. Ben will."

"Yes, apparently another detail I'll have to clear up. But don't worry, I'll see to it. In the end it will all be Lucille's — and mine — free and clear. I assure you."

Felicity knew her only hope was to keep him talking and pray that Antony would find her in time. "Okay, you worked it all out to get your hands on the property. But Monica wasn't just murdered. She was tortured. You didn't have to do that."

"It was her own fault. I would have stopped. I gave her the chance. All she had to do was admit it was all nonsense. Cranmer recanted. Why couldn't she?"

"You tortured her to make her renounce her faith?"

"I gave her the opportunity. She was like those martyrs in the coliseum one hears of in storybooks—singing when they set the lions on them."

"Monica sang?"

"It was more of a chant. *Kyrie eleison, Christe eleison*. Over and over." He put his hands over his ears just as Felicity had done earlier to muffle the sound of the bell. "And the funny thing was that I had the feeling she was asking mercy for me, not for herself."

"And the reliquaries? Why all that?"

"To show what nonsense it all was, of course."

"And were they? Nonsense?" Felicity asked.

He was silent and for a moment she thought she had won a point. Then he moved toward her with a steely look. "Enough of this. As you say, I have a plane to catch." He grabbed her arm and pulled her toward the bell.

"They'll never believe another accident. Not after what you did to Brian."

"Pity about poor Brian. And he such a helpful, chatty lad telling me all about things I needed to know. Until he started wondering why I wanted to know." With his free hand Allyn gave the bell a mighty swing that left it balanced in the up position. "Very wise of you not to remove the muffles with it up. Such an unstable position. The slightest tug could bring it down." He pulled a loop of the bell pull toward her.

He held Felicity's wrists and wrapped them with the rope. Then she realized, it wasn't just her wrists he intended to bind. It was her neck.

"But, of course, yours wasn't an accident, was it? It was suicide. Such a shame for such a lovely young girl. She had so much to live for. But it was remorse, you see. Who would have thought she could have done such an awful thing to a nun? But, when you look at the facts, she was there all along, wasn't she? Every time. And, of course, she knew the value of the document."

"And why did I do that?" Felicity's mind raced. She hardly dared breathe, let alone make a sudden move. How much would it take to make that bell swing down and then carry her upwards on the next stroke? Could she possibly land a disabling kick at her captor? Not without dislodging the bell and precipitating her own hanging.

He moved aside to pick up the briefcase he had dropped at the top of the stairs. "Why, for the manuscript, of course. Very valuable and a fanatical collector wouldn't be fussy about its venue." Allyn grabbed her bound hands again and placed them on the leather case, stamping it with her fingerprints.

"Shame to leave it behind after all I did to obtain it, but of course the police will return it to the grateful Baroness. And I wouldn't want to deprive you of your motive." He dropped the case at her feet and wiped his prints from the handle.

Felicity cringed as he gave the noose a final check. "I suggest you say your prayers, my dear." He picked up the muffles she had dropped. "Convenient. These will explain what I've been doing up here. And I'll be able to swear you weren't here when I was. Must have slipped up after I left." He descended the stairs.

She heard him call a hallo to someone before the door slammed shut. In her mind she saw him greeting those in the narthex. Even Antony? Turning on his suave charm, 'Lovely service, Father. Sorry I have to rush. Such an honour to do the tolling. Just one parting knell to help wing the good Mother's soul upward and all that, eh?'

How long would it be until the air rushed over her head in a swoop of iron, the noose slackened, then bit with the fatal tug as she was lifted upward? She looked up at the iron hangman balanced above her head. Would the first swing be sufficient, or would the momentum of her flailing body send her back and forth?

Please, Lord, a quick break. Not a slow strangle.

And then she thought of the rope hanging down through the hole in the floor. Surely wrapping it around her wrists and neck had shortened it considerably. If she could raise it a bit more so Allyn couldn't reach it…

Not daring to look down for fear of pulling at the bell, she extended one leg in an exploratory gesture. She was glad she had worn a skirt today. She could feel the rope better than she would have been able to through trousers. Yes. There. She just brushed it.

Every nerve in her body focused. Balance on her left leg. Right leg *allonge*, extend in a *tendu*. Even as she stretched she could hear her ballet teacher calling directions. *En denhors*, outward, to the front of the rope. Hook it with her heel. Then *en dedans*, inward. Ever so gently, pulling the rope upward...

With the fullest extension of her long leg she moved the rope backward as far as she could. She calculated that should have raised the rope maybe three feet. And it was already shortened by binding her. Would it be enough? Allyn was tall. His long arms could reach high.

Could she hope that someone would notice the sally hanging above their heads and realize something was wrong? Someone other than Allyn, that is. Could she shift her weight and raise it more with her other foot?

She was concentrating so hard on her calculations she didn't hear the steps on the stairs until they were almost to the top. Of course. She closed her eyes against the inevitable. If Luffington couldn't reach the pull from the narthex he had only to make an excuse for coming back up. The dislodged rope was probably his excuse. She had played perfectly into his hands.

"Felicity!" She couldn't believe she was hearing Antony's voice.

Twenty-Eight

"Am I in Paradise?" Felicity asked when she emerged from Antony's kiss.

"If you are, so am I."

She looked at the rope he had ever-so-carefully unwound from around her neck and wrists before supporting her to the far wall of the chamber. "How did you find me?"

"I saw Allyn make a flying leap at the sally and knew something was wrong. "Well, I knew something was wrong when I couldn't find you. And then Father Ben's police guard took over."

"Oh, I'm so glad you found them."

"Not me. Lucille."

"Lucille summoned the police?"

"Her story was a bit garbled, but it seems to have been something you said to her."

Felicity's mouth fell open in amazement, but she took a moment to rub her neck, blessedly free of the rope, before she answered. "I told her what Luffington was about. He killed Monica, you know. I realized that when I saw him and Lucille together. It suddenly all made sense. But I'm amazed she believed me. She certainly didn't act like she did. I thought she must be in on the whole thing or hopelessly gullible."

Antony smiled. "Fortunately, our Lucille isn't anybody's fool."

Gripping Felicity's hand as if he would never let go, Antony led back down the narrow stairs. They arrived just in time to see the police escorting Allyn Luffington from the narthex in handcuffs.

The even more amazing sight, though, was Lucille Knighton striding across the narthex toward Father Benjamin. "Little LeRoy! So you aren't dead!" She engulfed him in a hug.

Just then Sister Gertrude spotted Felicity and rushed forward, wringing her hands. "I'm afraid I've made the most awful mistake. That man—whoever he is—" She nodded toward the door Luffington had just been ushered through. "I gave him the Frideswide document. He said he was from the Ashmolean. He had identification."

"Indeed, he was," Felicity agreed. "Don't worry. The document is quite safe." She gestured toward the bell chamber where she suddenly realized Luffington's briefcase still lay on the floor. "But be careful. The bell is in the up position. Don't touch the rope."

Gertrude looked surprised. "I wouldn't think of it." She hurried up the stairs.

Felicity and Antony exchanged smiles. "Nor would I," Felicity said.

Mother Dorcas approached them. "What a day this has been. So wonderful to have Father Ben restored to us. And who would have imagined that lovely gentleman...." She looked toward the door where the police had just exited with their charge and shook her head. "Would you two care to join us in the refectory for a small glass of sherry?"

"Thank you, Mother, but I think we'd prefer to get back." Antony's arm tightened around Felicity. "As you say, it's been quite a day."

"Well, in that case, I'll have Frank drive you. Much better than taking the bus."

A few moments later Felicity was settled in the back of the well-used estate car that had carried her into Oxford on the night that had catapulted her into this whole perilous experience, She thought of holding the reliquary she had believed to hold the hand of Margaret Clitherow on her lap, but any impulse to shudder was cut off by Antony taking her hand in a warm grasp.

Back in the parlor of Hursley House Clare, Sheila, Gareth and Marc took in Antony and Felicity's account with varying degrees of amazement. Clare was the first to speak. "Oh, if only Brian could be here." She bit her lip. "But I'm so thankful they have the real culprit. Why do you think—?"

"Apparently Allyn latched on to Brian as an old mate so he could pump him for information about what was going on," Felicity explained.

Clare nodded. "Yes, that was so like Brian. So friendly and wanting to help everybody. And I played right along with the scheme. I told him everything you said. But Brian didn't—"

"No," Antony assured her. "Brian had no idea."

"Until the last, when he started wondering and asked Luffington too many questions," Felicity added. "Then Luffington got rid of him."

"But what was that business with the camera?" Marc asked.

"Luffington was desperate to get his hands on the original charter—that's why he ransacked the Press, and smoked Sister Gertrude out to interrogate her. That must have been when he learned about the photos on the camera. I guess he figured facsimiles of the original were better than nothing at all."

"Luffington mugged you?" Gareth looked at Felicity.

She shook her head. "It's hard to picture him doing his own dirty work. The police will have to sort that out—if they ever do. But my guess is he was using Derrick, too. I'm sure Luffington was the client soon to have an old castle full of Jacobean furniture Derrick wanted to get his hands on."

"You don't think Derrick was in on the murder, do you?" Antony turned to Felicity.

"I don't know, but if he wasn't, I hope he has good alibis. I'll bet Luffington will try to shift the blame." She squeezed Antony's hand. "I'm sorry. I know that will be hard on Gwen."

Antony shook his head. "I'm not sure. I think she was beginning to see the light."

Sheila was the first to yawn and excuse herself. The soft tap of her cane on the stairs had hardly faded when Clare,

Marc and Gareth followed suit, leaving Antony and Felicity sitting alone together on the old grey sofa.

Felicity snuggled closer to him with a sigh. "So much death. Monica, Brian, Edward..."

"Yes, but also so much renewal. That's the real message of All Saints' and All Souls'. It isn't about death. It's about life."

"Do you think Ben and Lucille will be able to work it out? The inheritance and all that?" She asked.

"I think there's hope."

Felicity thought for a moment, then smiled. "Yes, a hopeful tomorrow. That's fair enough to be getting on with."

About the Author

Donna Fletcher Crow is the author of 43 books, mostly novels of British history. The award-winning *Glastonbury, The Novel of Christian England,* an epic covering 15 centuries of English history, is her best-known work. She also authors The Lord Danvers Mysteries. *A Tincture of Murder* is her latest in this Victorian true-crime series. The Elizabeth & Richard Mysteries are a literary suspense series of which *A Jane Austen Encounter* is the latest. *A Newly Crimsoned Reliquary* is the fourth of Felicity and Antony's adventures in the Monastery Murders.

Donna and her husband of 50 years live in Boise, Idaho. They have 4 adult children and 13 grandchildren. She is an enthusiastic gardener.

To read more about all of Donna's books and see pictures from her garden and research trips go to:

http://www.donnafletchercrow.com/

You can follow her on Facebook at:

http://ning.it/OHi0MY

Made in the USA
San Bernardino, CA
01 July 2015